For Pam

Characters

Rocco DeAngelis: paroled career criminal
Peter "Big Pete" Ruggerio: Gambino crime family capo
Thomas Ruggerio: Big Pete's eldest son
Vincent Ruggerio: Big Pete's youngest son, owner of Club Inferno
Louis "Spanish Lou" Roque: Tommy's right hand
John "Johnny O." Oterio: mobster
Frederico "Fuck Me" Boaise: Gambino crime family underboss
Edward "Veal" Marsala: Columbo crime family capo
Gaetano Paladino: mobster
David Berkowitz: mob lawyer (not Son of Sam murderer)
Joe Lava: accountant / financial advisor

RUSSIAN MOB
Sergei "the Duke" Rudukas: boss of Russian mob in Brooklyn
Yuri Smolinski: Russian mobster
Ivan Blatnikov: Russian mobster
Dmitri Levishenko: Russian mobster

DRAKE HOTEL HEIST CREW, 1993
Bobby Bruno: made member of Gambino crime family
Frank Ferrerra: mobster
Al Rende: mobster
Ambrose "Sammy Dee" DeCrezenzo: mobster
Danny Carbone: mobster
John Cappolino: mobster
Jerry Falana: mobster
Jerome "Jingo" Walker: mobster
Frank Alonzo: Big Pete's consigliere
Abel Franks: fence
Bruce Goldstein: mob attorney

NYPD, DRAKE HOTEL ROBBERY 1993–1994
Lt. Diomede "Dio" Bosso: executive officer, Major Case Squad
Ann Thompson: his administrative assistant
Det. Joseph "Joe P." Pollicino: detective, Major Case Squad
Det. Dot Bracey: detective, Major Case Squad
Sgt. Tom Daley: patrol sergeant
Det. Lt. Jay Stendrini: Organized Crime Control Bureau (OCCB)
Det. Al Andreason: Personnel Division
Matthew Damico: trial judge
Jill Ruane: assistant district attorney, New York County
Mary Jane "MJ" Signorelli: hostage at Drake hotel robbery

CLUB INFERNO, PALM BEACH GARDENS, FLORIDA
Janelle Fishman: assistant manager / bookkeeper
Darla Cummings: assistant manager
Kris Keefer: chef
Stu Rogers: head bouncer

OLD TRAIL VILLAGE, PRESTIGIOUS GATED COMMUNITY, PALM BEACH GARDENS
Paul Stockwell: former ambassador to France and Austria
Teresa "Tippy" Stockwell: his wife
John Pettway: director of security
Norm Penny: alarm system specialist / security officer

PALM BEACH GARDENS POLICE DEPARTMENT
Tom Pellitiere: chief
Jack Harkness, captain: chief of detectives
Det. Sam Daniels: robbery/burglary detective

PALM BEACH COUNTY SHERIFF'S OFFICE
Rick Romaine: sheriff

Lt. Frank Pooley: commanding officer, Homicide
Sgt. Bobby Dixon Executive Officer: Homicide
Det. Lydia Martinez: Homicide
Det. Jerry "Franks" Nathan: Homicide
Det. Lee "Beans" Bush: Homicide, Nathan's partner
Sgt. Chris Clarkson: Homicide

POLK COUNTY SHERIFF'S OFFICE
Det. Thomas Redstone: Homicide
Det. Mike Danton: his partner
Det. Sgt. Don Bronte: patrol deputy
TEQUESTA POLICE DEPARTMENT
Det. Gabe Manna

NYPD, 2010–2015
Michael Widman: police commissioner
Dennis Ryan: chief of detectives
Det. Steve Alison
Det. Len DeAngelo
Det. Sgt. Jed Donohue
Det. Adam Gregory
Det. Colleen O'Brien
Det. Marty Stacy
Det. Dino Borisovitch
Det. Rich Nicholson
Det. Dave Price
Michael Gray: probationary police officer
Diana Budion: patrol officer
Javier Lopez: career criminal

AAA LIMO SERVICE
Mal Thomas: owner
Heather Winters: dispatcher / office manager

David W "Billy B." Barth: driver
Ted Glenn: driver

OTHERS
Thelma "Tanya" Jackson: escort
Shaun Gillings: her pimp/bodyguard
Desiree Witherspoon: parole officer, Palm Beach County
Leon Townes: street thug
Lionel Spreewell: street thug
Carlton B. Crawford: director of security, Christie's Auction House
Robert McGuire: police commissioner, NYPD, 1973–1977

PART ONE

Rocco

CHAPTER ONE

Clinton Correction Facility was located in upstate New York in the village of Danamora. It was a cold and dreary place, and for Rocco DeAngelis, it had been his home for the last nineteen and a half years. Rocco had been convicted in 1994 of the New Year's Eve robbery of New York City's Drake hotel, a crime that had rocked the city and the NYPD, as the victims were some of New York's wealthiest residents. The case went nowhere for several months until one of the participants was arrested by the DEA on a major drug case and turned state's evidence against Rocco and the other members of the crew. Rocco refused to talk, and as a result, he was given the maximum sentence of twenty years.

Rocco was informed that he would be going before the parole board when it next convened. It would be his third time before them, but as he had completed almost his entire sentence and had a good prison record, he was confident he would be released. Although he was anxious to get out, he had some doubts about his future. His capo in his crew, Peter "Big Pete" Ruggerio, had died, and Pete's son Tommy now ran the crew. Sure, he knew Rocco, but he'd been a teenager when Rocco "went away." What would Tommy do? Could he still plan and execute a heist like the Drake? Rocco thought about this all the time, but now, as he was getting out, the reality of his future was not looking too promising.

Rocco DeAngelis was born in Brooklyn on February 7, 1955, to Italian immigrants Alphonso and Seraphina DeAngelis. Rocco had two sisters. Josephine, who was a Carmelite nun, was three years older; his sister Susanne was four years younger than Rocco. The family lived in the Sunset Park section of Brooklyn. Alphonse DeAngelis was a dock worker on the Brooklyn piers, while Maria worked as a seamstress in New York's garment district. Rocco had been small at birth, weighing only five pounds, and was slow to grow. He didn't reach five feet until he was almost thirteen. He had straight, dark hair and a funny-shaped nose that would grow too big for his small face. His light-blue eyes were his one attractive feature. The family lived in modest comfort, but at an early age, Rocco knew he would have to find his own way of making a living. Although he loved and respected his parents, he saw them as hard-working people who had little to show for their efforts. Rocco could not see himself working his ass off on the docks like his father. Because Rocco was a small kid, he was picked on and bullied by the other boys in his class at St. Michael School. He was also pigeon toed and could not run very well, and as a result, he took many a beating a faster kid could have avoided. He was also very quiet and kept to himself, not making many friends.

When Rocco was about ten years old, he started to break into the Topps baseball card factory, which was located in the Bush Terminal section of Brooklyn, not too far from where he lived. Being small, he was able sneak under the fence without any difficulty and steal hundreds of baseball cards. In the candy store, a kid could buy a packet of baseball cards that included five assorted player cards, plus a stick of bubble gum, for twenty-five cents. Each card featured a player's photo on the front and his stats on the back. Rocco sold ten cards for twenty-five cents—but of course without the bubble gum.

One day, after a successful job at Topps, Rocco was set upon by the neighborhood bully, a kid named Mickey Thorgelsen. Mickey smacked Rocco around and took about two hundred of the stolen cards. This was witnessed by a local mobster and dock boss named Big Pete Ruggerio. Ruggerio knew the kid and his old man and had heard that Rocco was stealing shit from Topps.

After Rocco was walking away from getting pounced, Pete called him over. "Hey, kid, come here."

Rocco, knowing who he was, walked over to him, not knowing if he was going to get another ass kicking or not.

"You like baseball, kid?" said Pete.

"Yeah," was all Rocco said.

"Here. Take this baseball bat, and tomorrow, when you see that kid, whack him with it." He handed Rocco the bat and walked away.

The next day Rocco saw Mickey walking by himself. Rocco calmly walked up to him and said, "You want this bat?" Before Mickey could answer, Rocco swung the Louisville Slugger right across the kid's right knee. The kid went down, and Rocco just walked away.

Mickey's parents filed a complaint with the police, and Rocco got picked up at his home. Big Pete, who had a couple of detectives on his payroll, interceded, and Rocco got off with a juvenile delinquent (JD) card. From that time on, one could say Rocco DeAngelis was an associate member of Big Pete Ruggerio's crew. For the next five or six years, Rocco continued to commit numerous burglaries in Bush Terminal. He mostly worked alone, but once in a while, he would take along Big Pete's son Tommy, who was a few years younger. Big Pete introduced Rocco to the neighborhood fence, Georgie Keys, who would take whatever swag Rocco brought him, take a cut for himself and Big Pete, and give Rocco the rest. Rocco never grew much more. He stayed around five two for several years, and then around age sixteen, he topped out at five five and 140 pounds.

CHAPTER TWO

Big Pete was a member of the Columbo crime family, smallest of the five New York families and one of two operating in Brooklyn. From 1979–1980 a turf war broke out between the Columbos and the much larger Gambinos. Big Pete's wife, Annamarie, was the sister of Gambino underboss Frederico "Fuck Me" Boaise. Boaise had earned his moniker because "fuck me" was his response to any comment not to his liking. Freddie told his brother-in-law that shit was going down between the two crews, and he offered Big Pete a chance to defect and join the larger Gambinos on the condition that Pete take out some of the Columbo leaders, with the exception of Joe Columbo, the head of the family. That hit would be done by a Gambino. Pete agreed and gave Rocco the contract on Edward "Veal" Marsala, a Columbo capo. Rocco, now in his midtwenties, knew this was his opportunity to get his bump and become a made member of La Cosa Nostra.

Like every job he pulled, Rocco planned everything down to the smallest detail. He followed Marsala for about two weeks and learned his every move. Most mobsters followed very detailed patterns of everyday life. Marsala, who operated a large bookmaking operation, met every day at the same time and place to pick up "the work" from the several bookmakers who worked for him. He would then take the work, which consisted of the betting slips and the money, to "the bank," which was located in the back of a candy store Marsala owned on Eighteenth Avenue in the Bensonhurst section of Brooklyn. On the day Rocco planned to take Marsala out, he dressed like a homeless person and waited near the front door of the candy store, pushing a shopping cart filled with the usual junk a homeless guy would lug around all day and begging for loose change. When Marsala stepped out of his car, along with his driver and bodyguard, Gaetano Paladino, Rocco walked up with his left hand out.

"Can you spare some loose change, mister?" Rocco asked.

Before Marsala could say "Get the fuck away from me," which is what he would have said, Rocco removed a double-barreled sawed-off shotgun from the shopping cart and put two blasts into Marsala's torso. Paladino, who was coming around the front of the car, reached under his coat for his gun, but it was too late. Rocco took a .45 automatic from his overcoat pocket and put four shots into Paladino before he got to the curb. Rocco walked up to Marsala and put two more rounds in his head and the remaining rounds in Paladino. He then calmly picked up all the shell casings and got into an awaiting car. The police arrived within minutes, but unfortunately for them, no one had seen anything or could describe the shooter.

The gang war continued for another six months, with casualties on both sides. When Gambino hit men finally took out Joe Columbo and his son Joe Junior, the war came to an end. The remaining Columbo soldiers called it quits, and after a sit-down with Fuck Me and Big Pete, territories and spoils were divided up. Big Pete was named a capo in the Gambino crime family and got all of the Columbos' former loan-sharking, bookmaking, and union operations. Of course, every crew had to kick up tribute to the head of the Gambinos, Don Carlo, who was now the boss of bosses.

Rocco got his bump and got made. However, he continued to keep a very low profile and only talked to Big Pete or Tommy, who was also taking a larger role in the family business.

After the takeover Big Pete wanted Rocco to take a more active role in running his gambling and loan-sharking operation. Rocco was reluctant, as this would require him to become more visible than he was comfortable with. However, he really had no choice but to comply. Unlike most of the guys in the Ruggerio crew, Rocco did not enjoy the night life, unless of course it involved some criminal activity. Rocco wasn't shy or socially challenged; he just had no interest in social activity.

In the mid-1980s, disco was all the rage, especially with young kids living in South Brooklyn. Big Pete had some interest in a popular disco called SuperStar in the Bay Ridge section of Brooklyn. Big Pete wanted Rocco to go there and see what he thought. Rocco had no idea what that meant or what Pete expected of him, but being Rocco, he did what he was told. When he got to the club, he met up with two other guys from the crew, Sammy "Dee" DeCrezenzo and Al "the Catcher" Rende. Both Al and Sammy were smooth-talking, good-looking guys who often picked up sisters or two girls together and tried to have sex with both of them. As other guys in the crew would say, "Their record is pretty good, for you sports fans keeping score at home." Rende had been an outstanding baseball player, a switch-hitting catcher who was recruited by the Boston Red Sox while still in high school and considered a prospect until he suffered a severe injury. While Rende was changing a flat tire on his mother's car, the jack had given way, and the car had fallen on him, smashing his left leg and ending his baseball career. Rende's dad, who was a distant relative of Big Pete, got him a job in the dockworkers' union, and from there Rende made his way up the ladder to his present status of an associate member of Big Pete's crew.

Also at the club the night Rocco stopped by were a couple of Russian hoods. The Russkies, as Rocco called them, were soldiers in the Russian mob headed by Sergei "the Duke" Rudukas. While most of the Italian guys at the club acted like John Travolta in *Saturday Night Fever*, the Russkies acted like the two "Wild and Crazy Guys" portrayed by Dan Aykroyd and Steve Martin on *Saturday Night Live*.

Rocco, Sammy, and Al sat in a booth and ordered drinks from a cute waitress named Mel. When she brought the drinks back to the table, she put down Rocco's club soda and said, "You must be the designated driver."

Rocco had no idea what she was talking about. "How much do I owe you?" he asked.

"Oh, the drinks are on the house." She pointed to Tommy, who was standing at the bar. Rocco gave her a twenty. She smiled and walked away. When she came back to the table, Rocco asked her to sit down, but she said she couldn't while she was working. Rocco handed her another twenty, and she smiled and walked away again.

Tommy came over to Rocco's table and said hello.

"Hey, Tommy, how ya doin'?"

"Good, Roc. Is Mel here treating you OK?"

"Yeah, but I asked her to join me, and she said she can't while she's working. Sammy and Al haven't stopped dancing, and I'm sitting here all alone."

"No problem." Tommy turned around and waved Mel over to the table. "Hey, babe, this here is Rocco. He's a good friend of the family. Why don't you keep him company for a while, OK, Mel?"

"Sure, Tommy, be happy to."

Tommy walked back toward the bar, and then Rocco saw him leave the club.

Mel sat down and started to tell Rocco her life story, how she worked in a law firm during the day and waitressed at SuperStar on weekends. She said her name was Maryellen Lenihan, but everybody called her Mel because "those are my initials." Rocco got that but didn't say anything. Mel was about five two or so, shorter than Rocco, and had a good body. She wore her hair short, like Dorothy Hamill, which a lot of girls in the disco scene did. Rocco was close to thirty years old, and for the first time in his life, he felt an attraction toward a girl. He thought he could sit and listen to her talk all night long. Of course, he didn't say much, and Mel didn't ask him any questions, as she figured he was "connected." Before she got up to go back to work, Rocco asked her for her phone number and mustered the courage to ask her if she would like to go out with him.

"Sure," was all she said as she handed him her phone number. "I've got to get back to work, but I'm off Sunday, if you want to go out."

"OK," he said. He noticed as she walked away that she was pigeon toed, just like him. Well, he thought, we have that in common. Maybe I'll give her a call. But he never did.

About two in the morning, one of the Russian mobsters, Dmitri Levishenko, asked some babe to dance. She gave him a look like "you gotta be kidding me" and just turned and walked away. Dmitri was pissed, but he seemed to let it go until he saw the same girl dancing with someone else. He then walked out to the dance floor, hauled off and punched the dude in the face, and smacked the chick so hard people thought someone had fired a gun.

Sammy Dee was about four feet away and turned toward the ruckus when he saw Dmitri let loose. Without thinking, Sammy spun Dmitri around and caught him with a right to the jaw that nine out of ten times would have ended it. Not this time. Dmitri took the blow like a soft kiss, reached inside his suit jacket, and within three seconds had pulled out an eight-inch gravity knife and slashed at Sammy's face. Sammy was able to avoid a direct hit, but the shiv caught the top of his head about an inch above his right eye and went into the left side of his forehead.

All hell broke loose, but the bouncers, all of them huge football types, were on Dmitri and the other Russians within seconds of the fight. The club manager and bouncers knew most of the wise guys who hung out and gave them free rein, but the wise guys rarely got into fights. Big Pete's crew was under strict orders to avoid getting into trouble over bullshit. Most times they complied, but tonight was an exception. After the fight ended, Sammy took Al to the hospital to get his face checked out. Rocco left at the same time Dmitri and the other Russkies were tossed from the club. Rocco saw Dmitri and two others get into a late-model Cadillac and head toward the Belt Parkway toward the Brighton Beach neighborhood, known to the locals as Little Odessa. Rocco hopped into a waiting car service vehicle and told the driver to follow the Caddy. About fifteen minutes later, the Caddy pulled off the parkway and stopped in front of a club named Bely Mishka, which is Russian for "polar bear." Rocco knew it was owned by the Duke and served as a hangout for his crew. Rocco had the driver drop him off at a gas station about two blocks from the club, gave him fifty dollars, and told him to drive around for a half hour and then meet him back at the station. Rocco then went into the gas station, told the attendant that his car had run out of gas, and asked if he could borrow a gas can. The attendant, a foreigner Rocco could only think of as some kind of dot head, was reluctant until Rocco offered him a twenty. Rocco filled the plastic container and walked back to where Dmitri had parked his Caddy. He waited about twenty minutes and then took a brick he found lying in the street, smashed the front passenger-side window, opened the door, and poured the gasoline on the front seats. As the car's alarm blared, Rocco lit a match, tossed it into the Caddy, and walked away. The car went up in flames like a dried-out Christmas tree. By the time Rocco got back to the gas station, he heard the explosion as the Caddy's gas tank ignited. The car service vehicle pulled up. Rocco got in and had the driver take him home. Typical of Rocco, he never mentioned to anyone what he had done that night. Fuck those Russians pricks, he thought.

CHAPTER THREE

In the summer of 1985, Rocco's mom suffered a severe stoke. As a lifelong smoker and, like most of her generation, someone who never exercised, she had a future that looked pretty grim at best. Rocco's sister Susanne was married and had a kid. Her husband, Dennis Quigley, was a New York City fireman. Rocco thought he was an OK enough guy for his sister, but, as with everything else in life, Rocco either had no opinion or didn't share it. Rocco had some cash stashed away, and he decided to buy his mother's house and give it to his sister, with the condition that she live there, take care of Mom, and convert the basement into an apartment for Rocco. The money for the sale had been laundered through a neighborhood guy who was a semilegit investor named Joe Lava. Lava was an investment advisor with all the required SAC and NASD licenses, and he had a niche business catering to the wise guys in the neighborhood. He'd open a retirement account for people like Rocco with a small amount of money—say, $500. Each week Rocco would deposit his paycheck from his "job" at the *New York Daily News*, where several of the crew members held no-show jobs, thanks to Big Pete controlling the printers' union. The crew members were paid minimally for these jobs so as not to bring attention to themselves or the union. Lava would then invest the money in CDs, MMAs, and other conservative investments—again, not a lot of money. Rocco only had about $75K, but it was enough to give his sister the down payment for their mom's house.

Rocco was basically small time. None of his "jobs" earned him huge paydays, but he preferred it that way, as he could work alone or with one or two trusted guys. On the upside, no one bothered him. Big Pete got his tribute, and the cops viewed Rocco's burglaries as small-time break-ins probably done by some junkie. Like many successful businesses, Rocco's operation made its money on the volume of goods he stole for reliable fences, like Georgie Keys, who took their 15 percent cut. On average Rocco netted no more than five or six grand on a job.

PART TWO

The Drake Hotel Caper

CHAPTER ONE

In the summer of 1993, Big Pete told Rocco that a couple of guys in his crew were talking about a possible job at the Drake, a luxury hotel on Manhattan's Upper East Side. Every year the Drake would host the city's biggest New Year's Eve party. The crème de la crème of New York society attended the event. The hotel closed to the public, so most of the guests stayed overnight and attended a brunch on New Year's Day. After the party the guests were encouraged to secure their valuables in the hotel's safe-deposit boxes, located in the hotel vault, free of charge. Big Pete wanted Rocco to take over the job, to create and execute the plans for what could be a major heist. With the exception of Bobby Bruno, who'd approached Big Pete with the idea, Rocco could pick his crew. Rocco had worked with or knew all of the guys who were going to work the job—nine in all. Initially he was reluctant about so many guys being involved, but the job as it was laid out would need that many men.

The job was planned for December 31, 1993. Danny Carbone, who had worked at the hotel as an electrician and provided Rocco with the hotel's layout, would approach the doorman on duty and take him out. Frank Ferrerra would then don the doorman's jacket and hat and keep an eyeball on any traffic coming to the hotel. Jerry Falana and John Cappolino were assigned to securing hotel staff and guests or others, such as the doorman, night security guard, and cleaning personnel. The hostages would be secured in the main ballroom, where the party had taken place. Although each gang member carried weapons, they were used only to intimidate. No one was to be assaulted or mistreated unless absolutely necessary. In addition to carrying weapons, each gang member wore a disguise, such as glasses, facial hair, or a wig. Rocco also told the crew if they had to speak to do so with an accent. The crew practiced using a Russian accent and joked about it during planning meetings. Each had several pairs of plastic strip ties to secure the hostages, and each was equipped with a two-way radio. Rocco and Bobby Bruno, who were the only made guys in the crew, oversaw the operation from inside the hotel and, along with Jingo Walker, rounded up any people walking around the hotel and brought them to the ballroom, where they were secured. Sammy Dee and Al Rendi were assigned to the vault.

Once the doorman was secured, Rocco and Bobby Bruno drove a panel truck rented by Rocco using a bogus driver's license. Inside the truck were the power tools, sledgehammers, and acetylene torches that would be used to access the safe-deposit boxes. Prior to attacking the boxes, Al and Sammy placed heavy mover's mats over and on the vault's doors and walls to muffle the sound of the equipment that would be used to break open the boxes.

By 1:30 a.m. all hostages were secure, and Sammy and Al, along with Rocco and Bobby Bruno, started to hammer into the boxes. By 3:30 a.m. they had opened all two hundred boxes and started to exit the hotel. Jingo Walker pulled into the loading dock, and Sammy, Al, and Bobby loaded the canvas bags of loot and all the tools into the back of the van. Rocco remained in the vault to conduct a final sweep to ensure no evidence was left behind. Once they were all clear of the hotel, they alerted Carbone, Fleming, and Cappolino to leave the hostages secured and then to depart the hotel. They told the hostages not to attempt to get help for thirty minutes, further stating that one hostage was part of their crew and would kill anyone who started to move before the thirty minutes were up. The last three crew members were driven away in a car Ferrerra had rented under a fictitious name.

The plan was for all crew members to meet at the same vacant warehouse where the heist had been planned. Rocco had rented this place in Queens, again under an assumed name. Once all the crew members reached the warehouse, Big Pete's consigliere, Frank Alonzo, met them, along with a jeweler, a Hasidic Jew named Abel Franks. It took Abel the better part of the morning to assess the value of the loot, but finally he estimated the haul to be worth around $3–4 million, plus about $70K in cash. Alonzo then paid each crew member, with the exception of Rocco, $100K as agreed. The crew then dispersed one or two at a time over the next hour, with repeated instructions from Alonzo to keep their mouths shut and not to act "nigger rich," bringing unwanted attention to themselves. Rocco knew that was going to be difficult for this bunch to do.

Meanwhile, back at the Drake, security guard Ben Holder was able to free himself enough to call 911. Holder assumed the warning about a crew member being part of the hostages was bullshit. Within ten minutes the place was crawling with cops, detectives, and crime scene investigators, as well as TV and other media personnel. Ed Wagner, the mayor, and Police Commissioner Patrick Murphy were also at the scene. The media went wild with the story, calling it the crime of the century, like the Great Train Robbery of 1940 or Boston's Great Brinks Robbery. The papers interviewed several hostages, who stated that, aside from being handcuffed and robbed of their valuables, they had been treated well. They also mentioned that the two men who'd guarded them had sounded Russian or Eastern European.

Big Pete was greatly pleased with the outcome. It seemed the cops had little if anything to go on. The papers reported that the heist had been committed by as many as a dozen well-disguised armed men, probably from the Russian mafia or an Eastern European gang.

All this misinformation made Big Pete appreciative of the job Rocco had done and made him glad that he'd overruled several of his men, including Tommy, who hadn't wanted Pete to give this job to Rocco. Most of them thought Rocco was a small-time small man with the personality of a dead fish. For his part in the heist, Rocco was given $250K after expenses. He'd laid out about $5K in costs: rental of the warehouse where the crew met several times to go over in detail each member's assignment: procuring untraceable vehicles; purchasing duct tape or plastic ties, bought by Falana and Cappolino at several different hardware stores, to secure hostages' hands rather than using handcuffs; and purchasing tools and torches to access the safe-deposit boxes, bought secondhand by an old black guy named Horace Smith from a Puerto Rican auto-repair shop in the south Bronx. After the job Rocco had personally dumped the tools into the East River. To say his planning was meticulous would have been an understatement, and as a result, the job was well planned, well rehearsed, and well executed. The only issue Rocco was unsure about was whether he could rely on the crew to keep low profiles.

CHAPTER TWO

After several weeks, talk of the Drake hotel robbery was moved to the back pages of the local papers, and TV stations stopped talking about it altogether. Old news. While the NYPD continued their investigation diligently, there was little to go on. No prints, no tips, and most of the victims had insurance to cover their losses. The investigation was headed up by Det. Lt. Diomede (Dio) Bosso. Not yet forty, he was considered a rising star in the NYPD. He'd joined the force in 1976 after a four-year stint in the air force, where he'd been an MP stationed in Saigon at the end of the Vietnam War. He'd been wounded when the Viet Cong had attacked the American embassy and had been airlifted out just before the fall of Saigon. After Bosso joined the police force, he'd risen through the ranks rather quickly by scoring in the top 10 percent on each of his civil service tests. He was now the executive officer of the Major Case Squad, and he was soon to be promoted to captain.

Law enforcement was in his blood, Dio would say. Growing up in South Brooklyn, he'd been exposed to the ways of the streets, but strict parenting by his mother and father, both of whom had come to America as teens prior to the start of WWII, had made sure Dio and his older brothers, Ralph and Nunzio, toed the line. Both of Dio's brothers had died young. Ralph had been killed in a work-related accident while working as a sandhog building a section of the BMT subway line, and Nunzio, two years older, had been shot dead during a robbery while working as a bartender on the Upper West Side of Manhattan. Dio's mom had been devastated by the loss of her two older boys and had feared for Dio while he was at war overseas. Dio's dad had never recovered from the loss of his two oldest boys. He'd taken to the bottle and died in 1977 at the age of fifty-four.

Lieutenant Bosso had about twenty detectives working the Drake case for about the first two months. After the third month, with no tangible results, the chief of detectives, Bill Patton pulled half of Bosso's detail and reassigned them to their original commands to assist in the rising street-crime rate in the city. In February of 1993, terrorists bombed the World Trade Center, killing six people. Although the FBI had jurisdiction in this crime and quickly arrested the perpetrators, the NYPD refocused its attention on the new threat—terrorism—further depleting the number of detectives under Bosso's command. Undeterred, Bosso kept at it, sometimes going out on leads with one of his detectives rather than just sitting around pushing papers as other squad commanders did. Oh, there was plenty of paperwork, but Dio had been a detective for almost his entire career, so that was what he liked, and that was what he did.

Dio was married to the love of his life, Celia, whom he'd met at a Rolling Stones concert back in 1970. Dio had been working off-duty security, and Celia and her girlfriend had lost their tickets. Dio was able to get them into the stadium on the condition that Celia give him her phone number and go on a date with him. She did. They fell in love and married in 1972, the same year Dio got his gold detective shield.

Back then a young cop got promoted to detective one of two ways: either you had a hook or rabbi (someone in your family who was somebody or knew somebody), or you got involved in a high-profile arrest or shooting. Dio's path was the latter. One night while in uniform and on foot patrol on the Upper East Side, Dio spotted two black guys wearing long trench coats and looking in and out of the tonier high-end shops on Madison Avenue. They were on the west side of Madison Avenue, walking north from East Eighty-Third Street. Dio was on the east side walking south when they first caught his eye. Suspicious by nature, he ducked behind a parked car and watched as the two removed shotguns from under their coats and entered a Mikimoto jewelry store.

Back in those days, cops on foot patrol did not carry portable radios, and when they did, the radios were cumbersome and did not work very well. Dio went back to the diner he had just left and told the cashier to call the precinct and have them send backup. He then drew his revolver and crossed Madison Avenue. There were pedestrians on the street, and Dio did his best to wave them away. As he approached the store, one of the robbers glanced over his shoulder and saw Dio approaching. The robber exited the store, raised his double-barreled shotgun, racked the slide, and fired two shots at Dio. Dio dove behind a parked car as its rear window exploded from the shotgun blast. The robber then turned his attention to his accomplice, who was still inside the jewelry store, smashing cases and grabbing loot. In the few seconds while Robber #1 looked away, Dio came up from behind the parked car and fired two rounds. The first round caught the perp in his right shoulder, causing him to drop the sawed-off shotgun. The second round caught him center mass in his chest. He staggered back a few feet and fell to the sidewalk, mortally wounded.

The second robber now exited the store, pulling the screaming clerk along and trying to get his arm around her neck while keeping his shotgun at the ready. Dio knew he still had four rounds in his .38 standard police-issue Smith & Wesson, but people were running and screaming in his line of fire. He knew he had but a few seconds to react before Robber #2 would be in a position to take a clear shot at him. Without thinking, he charged Robber #2, and from about two feet away, he leaped at him, gun hand cocked. As he landed on the second perp, his gun hand and gun came down on the side of the perp's head, knocking him backward into the jewelry-store window. Dio, now on top of the perp, smashed his gun on the perp's head a second time, opening up a gash that started to bleed. The perp was screaming at Dio, calling him all kinds of motherfuckers. Dio then realized that the perp was much smaller than he, so he rolled him over on his back, holstered his gun, and rear cuffed Robber #2. Just about that time, Dio heard the sirens coming up Madison Avenue. Here comes the cavalry, he thought.

Back at the station house, the dead robber was identified as Leon Townsend, and his accomplice was Lionel Spreewell. Both had extensive criminal records and had been pulling off armed robberies of high-end jewelry and clothing stores on both the upper east and west side of Manhattan. Townsend was wanted for a homicide in North Carolina. Moot point, thought Dio. The department and the media had a field day with the shooting, and the next day, after going to court, Dio was told to report to police HQ, where the commissioner, Robert McGuire, pinned a detective's gold shield on his chest. Upon returning to the station house, Dio was informed that the second robber, Lionel Spreewell, had filed a civilian complaint against Dio for using excessive force during the arrest.

CHAPTER THREE

John Cappolino, one of the members of the Drake hotel crew, fancied himself a ladies' man, and in fact he was. Though married with a couple of kids, he always had a girlfriend on the side, as did most wise guys. John was hoping, like the other guys involved in the Drake caper, that they would curry enough favor with Big Pete to get made. Of the nine guys involved in the Drake, only Rocco and Bobby Bruno were made guys. Danny Carbone was rumored to be getting his bump next time an opening came up, as he had married Fuck Me Boaise's niece Peggy.

During the Drake robbery, Cappolino had been assigned to secure and guard hotel staff and guests. While he watched, he'd kept looking at a hostage who had caught his eye. She had not attended the New Year's Eve party but had been walking past the Drake on her way home from another party when she had to pee. She'd asked the doorman if she could use the ladies' room. Unfortunately for her, this happened just before Carbone took the doorman out. She was rounded up and ushered into the ballroom with the other partygoers. She'd caught Cappolino's eye, and he'd gone through her purse. From her license he'd learned her name was Mary Jane Signorelli, and she lived in the Bronx, about two blocks from where Cappolino had grown up.

A week or so after the robbery, he started to drive by her house several times a week, hoping to catch her coming home. Finally, on one occasion, he saw her leave her house, dressed to go out. He followed her as she made her way to another house, where she was joined by another pretty girl. They were picked up by a third girl in a late-model Pontiac Firebird. He followed them into the city, where they parked the car and went into a club called Xenon, a popular disco in the West Forties. Cappolino knew the place, and the bouncer at the door knew him to be a connected guy, so he let Cappolino in without making him pay the twenty-dollar cover. When he saw Mary Jane and her friends at the bar, he made his move, standing next to them and offering to buy a round of drinks. The three girls gladly accepted the drinks from Cappolino, who, at six feet tall and with dark curly hair, was an attractive man, even if he appeared a little older than other guys in the club. John was forty-two; Mary Jane was twenty-four and the other girls about the same. He introduced himself as John Saverese and told the girls he was a detective who worked in midtown. Girls always felt safe meeting a cop, so this guy could be trusted—or so they thought. John also had a fake detective badge he showed them when they questioned his story.

It was obvious to the others that John liked Mary Jane, so they went to dance, leaving John and Mary Jane alone. After about an hour of small talk, John asked MJ, as she liked to be called, if she wanted to get out of there and go somewhere less noisy.

"Well, I came with Debbie and Pattie, and I really can't leave them," MJ said. "They're my ride home."

"Don't worry, I got a car," Cappolino said. When he asked her where she lived, he pretended to be surprised by her answer. "The Bronx? That's where I grew up! What part?"

"E224 and Howard Ave."

"You're kidding! I grew up on E225 and Broadway." It was about four blocks away from her.

MJ was immediately smitten by John "Saverese's" good looks and smooth talk.

MJ told her friends not to wait, as John would take her home. Then she and John went out to a smaller nightclub on the Upper East Side called Parisi's, a known wise-guy hangout. Cappolino knew a few guys at the bar, and they all acknowledged him with the usual nod. They had a couple of drinks. Driving her home, Cappolino told MJ that she looked familiar. She told him about being held hostage during the Drake robbery last New Year's Eve.

"Are you one of the detectives investigating that robbery?" she asked. "Maybe you saw me then."

"No, I work mostly homicide," John lied. He was getting bored and just wanted to get laid. "Listen, MJ, I got to work tomorrow, early, so whadda ya say I take you home and we see each other another time?"

"Sure," she said.

John had had a few drinks too many, but he was still able to drive OK. When he got to her house, he reached over and kissed her. She responded, but when he reached for her breast, she pushed his hand away.

"No, John, not yet. I don't do it on the first date."

"OK," John said. "I'll call you tomorrow, if that's OK."

"Sure." She kissed him good night and got out of the car.

Cappolino was pissed, but he thought, What the fuck. I'll go home and bang the wife.

For the next two weeks, Cappolino saw MJ every night, and they became lovers. MJ was falling in love with this handsome "police detective" and was telling her parents and friends all about John

Saverese. MJ had an uncle, her mom's brother and also her god-father, who was a police sergeant in Queens. His name was Tom Daley. One day, while having a casual phone conversation, MJ's mother mentioned to her brother that MJ was dating a cop.

"Oh yeah? What's his name?" Tom asked.

"John. John Saverese, I think."

"Oh no," said Tom, laughing. "Another I-talian in the family."

"Oh, Tom, that's not nice. Look how Walter takes care of me and the kids."

Tom laughed again, and they said their good-byes. The next day at work, Daley put in a call to his old partner, Al Andreason, who worked in HQ.

"Al, Tom Daley here. How you doing?"

"Daley, you old fucker, I heard you died."

"Ha ha, very funny, you dopey squarehead." They both laughed. "Listen, Al, I need you to look up a guy for me. Detective named John Saverese. He's dating my niece, and she's falling hard. I don't want her to get hurt, and we both know how cops do."

"Sure, Tom, hold on." Andreason worked in personnel, so finding this kind of info was routine and easy, especially as all person-nel records were now computerized. A few moments later, he said, "You sure of the name? Do you know how old he is?"

"No, but my niece is twenty-four, so maybe thirty, I don't know. Whadda ya got?"

"Well, the only Saverese I got is a Paul, and he is a lieutenant in the Bronx. He's about fifty-five years old and has thirty years in the business."

"OK, you sure?"

"Tommy, please."

"Yeah, sorry, Al. Thanks, and take care."

"We should get together for a beer."

"Yep, we should," Tom said, but they both knew the only time they would get together would be a retirement party or a funeral, the latter being more likely than the former.

Cappolino was still waiting to hear about getting made. He would never think of calling Big Pete or even Tommy, for that matter, but he called Rocco several times to make an inquiry. Rocco, being Rocco, would pretend not to know who he was. "Johnny Cappolino," he'd say. "Do we know each other?"

"Fuck you, Rocco, you little weasel," Cappolino would say, and then Rocco would just hang up.

Cappolino was starting to tire of MJ. He was now down to seeing her one or two nights a week, and each time they stayed in a cheaper hotel. After sex, he would pretend to get a call and tell her he had to go on a case.

"How come we never go to your place?" she finally asked. "How come we don't go out anymore? We just come here, you screw me, and then you leave."

John was getting angry. "How come this, how come that—is that all you can fucking say?" He wanted to smack her in the head, but he was a rarity among wise guys in that he never struck a woman, not even his wife. But he was furious with his situation with the crew. He had been earning for Tommy Ruggerio and his fat old man for several years now and had squat to show for it. "Fuck them!" he yelled at no one in particular.

"Johnny, what's wrong? Maybe I can help you."

"You, you dumb shit? You want to help? I'll tell you how you can help. Go tell your uncle the cop that you're fucking one of the guys who did the Drake hotel robbery. Yeah, that's right. I was the guy in the Groucho Marx mask, holding a fucking gun to your head. Told you how pretty you were and called you Mary Jane in that phony put-on Russian accent when I took your purse. Remember now? And here's another thing: I'm married, and I got two kids. How about that, you dumb shit?"

MJ looked at him with shock and disbelief in her eyes. She was now sobbing uncontrollably. She just wanted to get out of there and go home. She got dressed and left and never saw John Saverese/ Cappolino again.

Too embarrassed to tell her mother or Uncle Tom what had happened, MJ said that she and John had broken up because he wanted to get married, and she felt he was too old for her. She lied and said he was almost fifty. After a day or two, she got the courage to make a call to one of the real detectives who'd interviewed her several times after the Drake robbery. She had his card in her desk at her job at Chase Bank. "Joseph Pollicino, Detective First Grade, Major Case Squad," the card read. MJ called, and a female answered the phone on the second ring.

"Major Case, Detective Bracey, can I help you?"

"Yes, Detective, my name is Mary Jane Signorelli, and I was one of the people at the Drake hotel last New Year's." She paused.

"Yes, go on, Ms. Signorelli."

"Well, I'd like to talk to Detective Pollicino. He's the one I spoke to on several occasions, and, well, is he there?"

"No, not at the moment, but I can have him call you, or you can talk to me, whichever you prefer."

"No—er, I mean that I'd rather talk to him. No offense."

"None taken. Give me your number, and I'll have him call you, OK?"

MJ gave her the number and hung up. Bracey paged Joe P. and gave him the ten-two code to call the office.

Joe was having lunch with Lieutenant Bosso when he got the page. They were grabbing a burger at one of the many Greek diners where Joe knew the owners. They usually got the police discount. "Got a page from the office, boss," Joe said. "I'm gonna hit the head and call from the pay phone in the back."

"Yeah, sure, Joe. And I guess I'll get the check," Dio chuckled.

Joe P. gave Dio the finger gun and winked. "You're the best boss ever."

When Joe P. came back to the table, Dio was picking up his change from the check.

"Want me to leave the tip, boss?" Joe asked.

Dio just gave him the stare and got up. Joe knew that that meant he'd given the waitress her tip when he paid the check. Joe smiled and said, "One of the hostages from the Drake called me. She told Bracey she has some new information."

"Which one?" asked Dio. Dio knew the name and pedigree of everyone involved in the robbery, except of course the perps.

"Lady named Mary Jane Signorelli. Lives in the Bronx in the fiftieth precinct. Was at a party on New Year's Eve and got separated from her friends and went into the hotel to use the can, right before the robbery."

"Yeah, I remember reading the DD five," he said, referencing the police report.

Back at the office, Joe P. placed a call to Mary Jane Signorelli at her home in the Bronx.

"Oh, hi, detective, thanks for getting back to me," she said.

"Detective Bracey told me you had some new information about the Drake?"

"Yes, but I don't want to talk here. My parents are home, and er, it's kinda private. Can I come to your office?"

"Sure, I'm here until midnight."

"I'll be there in an hour or so. I'll take the subway."

She was there in forty minutes. "Caught all the train connections," she explained.

As soon as Joe saw her, he remembered her. She had a full head of thick, dark-red hair and a slim figure. Joe recalled thinking she must be half Irish; she sure didn't look like a Signorelli. She'd seemed a bit naive to Joe when he first interviewed her back in January. He remembered her saying how nice the robbers were, even though they had foreign accents.

Joe escorted her into one of the interview rooms. He'd pulled the DD5s on her previous interviews and read them while he was waiting for her to arrive.

MJ told Joe all about meeting and dating John Saverese, who'd told her he was a detective from Queens, and how they'd dated for about three months. Joe could see she'd been hurt by this guy and wondered why she was telling him this. He wished she would get to the part about the Drake.

"Well, after about a month or so, we stopped going out," she said.

Joe looked at his notes. "You said you dated this Saverese for three months, Miss Signorelli."

She hesitated. "Well, yes, but after a month, he always said he was working a case..." She stopped and started to well up. "So we would just go to a hotel and have sex."

"Oh, I see. Would you be more comfortable if I asked a female detective to join us?"

"No, it's OK."

"OK, go on."

"Well, after about six weeks of just going to hotels for sex, I told John that I wasn't happy with the way the relationship was going. He went off on me and called me names, bad names, and said he was involved in the robbery at the hotel."

"And what made you believe him?"

"He told me about the fake Groucho Marx disguise and the fake Russian accent he'd used, and then he told me that he'd read my name off my license when he went through my purse. And then he told me he'd followed me to Xenon, where we met, and he picked me up."

Joe was reading back over the initial interview when something caught his eye. "When we spoke in January, you told me your uncle was a cop in Queens. Is that correct?"

"Yes. Tom Daley, my mom's brother. He's a sergeant in Queens."

"Did you talk to him about this John Saverese fellow?"

"No, but I think my mom did. Why?"

"No reason. Just covering all the bases."

Joe P. asked MJ if she wanted a soda or some coffee.

"Do you have tea?" she asked.

"Yes, I think so." He excused himself and left the room. He asked Detective Bracey if she would get the witness a cup of tea.

Bracey gave him a look. "Hey, Joe, it's 1994, even though your brain still thinks it's the '50s." She smiled.

"Oh, I'm sorry, Dot. I'll get the tea, but I gotta pee real bad."

Bracey smiled again. "I'll get the tea, but I'm making a beef with EEO against you. They're gonna make you come to my house and do my dusting." She laughed as though that was the funniest thing ever.

"Also, Dot, can you call HQ and get a line on a sergeant by the name of Tom Daley? That's D-A-L-E-Y. He's in patrol in Queens."

"Sure. Anything else? Maybe you need a hand in the can."

Dot Bracey was one ball-breaker but a good detective. That was why Dio had her in his squad.

Joe P. got back to the interview just as Bracey was giving MJ her tea. He continued the interview, and after about ten minutes, Bracey came in and handed Joe a note. "Sgt. Thomas Daley, 114th Pct. Tax #861225," it said. The tax ID number was issued to everyone who was sworn into the NYPD. It was used as a positive identifier more often than the shield number.

"He's on the desk now if you need to talk," Bracey said.

Joe looked up. "Thanks, Dot, you're the best. Excuse me, Ms. Signorelli, I'll be right back, and then Detective Bracey here will give you a ride home. Right, Dot?"

Bracey gave him a withering look.

Joe dialed the number for the 114th Precinct. After about ten rings, a male voice answered. "One fourteen. Officer Gonzales."

"This is Detective Pollicino at Major Case. Is Sergeant Daley on the desk?"

Joe could visualize the young cop covering the phone and telling the desk sergeant, "Hey, Sarge, Major Case wants you."

The next voice Joe heard said, "One fourteen, Sergeant Daley."

"Hey, Sarge, Joe Pollicino over here at Major Case."

"Yes, what can I do for you?"

"Well, you know your niece was a victim at the Drake hotel robbery on New Year's, right?"

"Yeah. What's that got to do with me? She OK?"

"Yeah, she's fine. As a matter of fact, she came in tonight with new info on our case."

Daley was quiet, waiting for Joe to continue. "Did she or her mom ever mention that she was dating a cop?" Pollicino asked.

Daley didn't know how much this detective knew. Had he spoken to Andreason? Daley decided to tell the truth. He'd done nothing wrong.

"Yeah, her mom mentioned it casually."

"Did you check him out?" Joe asked. Again, there was a long pause. "Look, Sarge, it would not be unusual for one of us to check out some cop dating someone in our family. Shit, I've done it for my daughters, cop or not," Joe lied. "I'm Major Case, not Internal Affairs Bureau."

"Yeah, well, my sister, MJ's mom, mentioned the guy to me. She was concerned, so I made a call."

Joe did not ask to whom, nor did he care. Probably someone in personnel. It was against department policy but done all the time. Again, the pause.

"So, what did you get?" Joe asked.

"Eileen, my sister, told me the guy's name, and when I checked it out, it came up empty."

"You recall the name, Sarge?"

"Yeah. Didn't my niece give it to you?" Joe didn't answer. "Saverese, John Saverese. The only Saverese in the system was a Paul, and he is an old-timer in the Bronx, close to fifty, so I knew it was 'fugazy.'"

"Did you say anything to your niece?"

"Nah. I told my sister, but I guess she didn't tell MJ. Anything else, detective?"

"No. Thanks, Sarge," Joe said, and they each hung up.

Joe P. briefed Dot Bracey on what he knew and asked her to drive MJ home. "Use your feminine touch to see if you can get any more info out of her. Oh, wait, I forgot, you have no feminine touch."

Bracey shot him the bird as she grabbed the keys for the pool car and left with MJ Signorelli. On the drive home, Dot made small talk with MJ, asked about her family and job. "Did the guy you were dating ever take you to any clubs or bars where the clientele looked or dressed like him?"

MJ shot her a look like she didn't understand. "You mean like Guido bars?"

"I'm not sure. That term is unfamiliar to me," Bracey lied.

"Yes, there was one. He seemed to know a lot of guys there, which I thought was strange for a police officer."

"Do you remember the name or where it was?"

"Yes, it was called Parisi's. It was in the East Sixties."

Bracey just shook her head and continued driving. Bracey knew Parisi's was a known mob hangout.

Joe P. called his contact in the Organized Crime Control Bureau, Lt. Jay Stendrini. Jay was a legend in OCCB and one of the most knowledgeable detectives in the division. He was considered an expert witness in any trial involving gambling, and he lectured not only at the NYPD but also at many other police agencies on the inner financial workings of organized crime. He'd authored a white-paper report titled "Gambling and Vice, the Greases that Oil the Wheels of Organized Crime." He was an adjunct professor at John Jay College of Criminal Justice and had been a guest lecturer at every session of the FBI National Academy over the last ten years.

When Joe P. called, Jay gave his standard response. "Joey, baby, whaddya need?"

Joe told him he had a fresh lead on the Drake hotel caper and explained that they now thought again that it was an OC job, not a Russian-mob job. Joe asked him if he knew any wise guys who used the alias John Saverese.

"Let me check on it. I'll get back to you."

"Great, Jay, thanks."

"How's my boy Dio doing? I hear there is gonna be a captains' class in about two months." Besides being an expert on OC, Jay Stendrini, everybody's friend, was the most informed cop in the department, with the exception of the commissioner.

CHAPTER FOUR

Joe P. briefed Dio verbally as he handed him his DD5 on the MJ Signorelli interview. He also mentioned the conversation with Stendrini.

"Shit, I haven't seen or talked to Jay in a dog's age. How's he doing?" Dio asked.

"Great. He sends his regards."

Just then someone in the squad room yelled out, "Hey, Joe, call on line two."

Joe picked up. It was Stendrini. "My boy, we got lucky."

"What do you got, Jay?"

"John Cappolino, an associate of the Ruggerio crew, uses the alias John Saverese. He used it several times when he got popped, once in Atlantic City and once upstate in Newburg. Both times for drug sales. Currently on probation for the AC bust last year. I pulled his sheet. He was busted with another Ruggerio associate named Giacomo 'Jerry' Falana. Falana died earlier this year of cancer. Goddamn fuckin' shame," Stendrini said sarcastically. "I also have some info here that his Ruggerio connection is Bobby Bruno, a made guy in the Ruggerio crew."

"Anything else, Jay?"

"Nope, that's about it."

Dio motioned to Joe P. to hand him the phone, and Joe said, "Hold on, Jay, the boss wants to say hello."

"Hey, Jay, how the hell are you?" Dio said.

"Great, Dio, doing just fine. You?"

"I'm good."

"My sources tell me the department got funding for a captain's promotion and you're second on the list, so it should be soon. I'll let you know as soon as I hear."

"Thanks, Jay, you're the best."

Dio called a squad meeting and updated the assembled detectives on the new information and what they would be doing going forward. He told the squad that he wanted to start twenty-four-seven surveillance on John Cappolino starting now. He assigned detectives Bobby Izzo and John Belardi to find Cappolino and, once they did, to stay on him like stink on shit.

Detectives Ed Brady and Mike Kennedy would relieve Izzo and Belardi. Each team was issued a packet with Cappolino's photos, as well as photos of all his known associates in addition to Bruno and other known members of the Ruggerio crew. Falana's photo was included, but it had a large X drawn through it and was marked "deceased."

Unknown to the detectives, every member of the Drake hotel crew had his picture in the packet, with the exception of Rocco DeAngelis. As far as the NYPD was concerned, Rocco DeAngelis did not exist.

Later that day Dio got a call from Chief Dan Courtney, head of the OCCB's Narcotics Division.

"Hi, Chief, how you doing?" Dio said.

Courtney was a no-nonsense commander, straight as an arrow. "Bosso, I hear your Drake hotel case is focusing on John Cappolino, among others in the Ruggerio crew."

"That's right, Chief. Is there a problem?"

"Could be. My DEA/NYPD Drug Task Force got two A-one felony cocaine buys on him. We got an undercover working him for an even bigger purchase—three to five kilos, going down this week. I'd like you to hold off until we pop him. Then, once we do, I'll let you interview him. Chances are, if he's involved in your case, you can offer him a deal or turn him over to the feds. We get him on one more A-one and he's facing life, plus Big Pete Ruggerio has a standing order that if any member of his crew, made or not, gets pinched for dope, he's dead."

"Sounds good to me, Chief. I'll pull my guys off the tail. Oh, Chief, anybody else in Ruggerio's crew involved in your operation?"

"Bobby Bruno and Danny Carbone. We got them both on audio and video with Cappolino discussing drug sales."

"OK, Chief, consider it done."

Dio did not like having to back off his case, but he really had no choice. Courtney outranked him, and drugs and large drug busts got more play in the department and the press than the old-news Drake hotel caper. In addition, most of the people victimized at the Drake had received payouts from their insurance companies, and Dio figured they'd probably claimed more in losses than they'd actually incurred.

About a week after the conversation with Chief Courtney, the Narcotics Division made the bust of Cappolino, Bruno, Carbone, and several other low-level street dealers in an operation called White Heat. The NYPD and most other law enforcement agencies gave names to their major investigations, mainly for the good publicity it would bring the department. A press conference was held, and all major TV networks covered it. Chief Courtney and the narcotics officers involved in the takedown were positioned behind a large table where several kilos of pure cocaine, numerous weapons, and large stacks of currency were on display for public view. Courtney stated to the press that this operation had put a large dent in the drug trade operated by members of the Ruggerio crew, and he and the members of the NYPD Narcotics Division would continue their all-out effort to eradicate the scourge of drugs from the city.

Big Pete Ruggerio was furious that members of his crew had broken his no-drugs rule and that his name and photo were plastered all over the TV. He called a meeting of his inner circle: his son Tommy; his consigliere, Frank Alonzo; and underboss Freddy "Fuck Me" Boaise.

"Who else in our crew is involved with this shit?" Pete yelled.

"Not sure, Pop," replied Tommy.

"Fuck me," said Freddy, "I told those fucking assholes no drugs, but did they listen?" Freddy was lying, of course, because he was getting a big tribute from Cappolino and in fact was bumping some up to Big Pete, but that was the way of the mob. Like in real life, shit flowed downhill.

"I want all those guys gone as soon as they make bail, you hear? No bullshit. Gone."

"What about Bobby, Pop? He's a made guy."

Big Pete looked over at Alonzo and Fuck Me, and they both just nodded in unison. That was that.

"Sure, Pop, I'll take care of it."

"No, I already gave it to the Duke to handle. That Russian prick owes me one."

Bobby Bruno and Danny Carbone made bail, and they both went to Tommy to plead their case. They swore they would do their time, even if it meant life, although they were facing a lot less time than that. Tommy told them he would talk to Big Pete. Cappolino, on the other hand, knew he was a dead man unless he could make a deal. He was denied bail, which he had no problem with, and was placed in protective custody. His lawyer, another mob mouthpiece named Bruce Goldstein, went to the DA and said his client wanted to deal. The DA assigned to the drug case was an up-and-coming ADA named Jill Ruane. She told Goldstein she would list

Tommy never bothered talking to his father about Bruno and Carbone, but he told them the old man wanted to sit down with them. They were told to meet him and Big Pete at Louie's All-Nite Diner by JFK airport at eleven o'clock the next night. When they arrived at the diner and started to walk inside, two large men wearing ski masks appeared from behind the building and immediately opened fire. As Bruno and Carbone fell to the ground, dying, one shooter calmly walked up to them and fired two more shots into each guy's head.

"Good-bye, Bruno. Good-bye, Carbone."

The shooters got into a waiting vehicle and drove off.

John Cappolino and his attorney, Bruce Goldstein, met with ADA Ruane. Cappolino was looking to make a deal. Since Bruno and Carbone were dead and the rest of the drug ring were in jail, Ruane said, what could Cappolino possibly give her that she didn't already have?

"If you want any kind of deal, John, I need you to give me the Ruggerios," she said. "That's it. Nothing else will save your sorry ass. You want to do a deal with me, it's got to be the Ruggerios."

"I don't know nothing about the Ruggerios. I swear on my kids. I mean, sure, I know who they are, but I swear I never talked to either Tommy or the old man."

"Well, that's too bad, John, because unless I get them, you get life."

"How about I give you all my drug connections?"

"We know your drug connections, and we already have most of them in jail or have arrest warrants on them."

"No, I mean the ones in Florida, where all the shit is coming from."

Goldstein chimed in. "Ms. Ruane, my client has good information about the large quantities of cocaine coming through the port of Miami. I'm sure your colleagues in the US Attorney's Office and the FBI or DEA would be interested."

Ruane knew if Goldstein took his offer to the feds, they would swoop down and take her case away. "Is there anything local you can give me, John? If you do, I'll go to the feds on your behalf. But you have to give me something."

Cappolino leaned over and whispered in Goldstein's ear.

"How about the Drake hotel?" said Goldstein.

CHAPTER FIVE

Dio was in his office when he got a call from ADA Jill Ruane. He did not know her personally, but he'd heard about her, and from what he heard, she was good.

"Lieutenant Bosso, ADA Ruane here. I just had a nice conversation with John Cappolino, and I understand your major case squad had some interest in him regarding the Drake hotel robbery back in January."

It sounded to Dio like she wanted something, so he just said, "Go on, Ms. Ruane."

"Well, Lieutenant, here's the deal. I'm turning Cappolino over to the feds. He has more information for them on the drug case, and truth be told, I don't want to come away from this with nothing."

Dio knew once the feds got wind that Cappolino had information for them, they would take over without even giving Ruane as much as a courtesy call, but he played along. "Yes, I see."

"Well, Cappolino claims he was part of the crew who did the Drake. He's willing to deal if we drop the state charges and give him to the feds, where he can deal for witness protection."

"OK, Ms. Ruane, I'm still listening."

"Please, Lieutenant, call me Jill."

The next Monday was August 1, eight months since the Drake hotel robbery. Dio, Joe P., and Det. Dot Bracey were at the DA's office at One Hogan Place in lower Manhattan for a meeting with ADA Jill Ruane, one of her clerks, a court stenographer, Cappolino, and Bruce Goldstein. Ruane, who looked to Dio to be in her early forties, was tall, about five ten, with pulled-back brown hair and no makeup. She reminded Dio of a nun he'd had in grammar school. Ruane nodded to the stenographer to begin.

"We are here today to interview Mr. John Cappolino in regard to his involvement with the armed robbery of the Drake hotel, which took place on December 31, 1993," Ruane began. She continued to name all those present. Cappolino then gave a detailed description of the planning and execution of the Drake hotel robbery. Both Dio and Ruane knew he would hold something back, as this was a give-and-take situation. During his narrative, he never named any of the participants. When he was done, Ruane started the questioning.

"Mr. Cappolino, can you tell me who first approached you about the robbery?"

"Yeah, Bobby Bruno."

"The late Bobby Bruno?"

"Yeah."

"And what did Mr. Bruno say to you?"

"He told me that there was a job going down and asked if I wanted in."

"And?"

"I said, 'Yeah, sure, count me in.'"

"You mentioned several other members of the robbery crew—Danny Carbone, also deceased; Jerry Falana, also deceased; Al Rende; Ambrose 'Sammy' DeCrezenzo; Jingo Walker; and Frank Ferrerra. We know that Rende and DeCrezenzo are in Sicily, and we have the US Marshals Service looking for Walker and Ferrerra. Hopefully we will find those two before Ruggerio's hit men do. Were there any members of the Ruggerio family involved in the planning or execution of this crime, Mr. Cappolino?"

Cappolino looked at Goldstein, who said, "My client wants to know if you mean by name."

"Your client knows what I mean," Ruane shot back, sounding annoyed. "Was there any member of the Ruggerio crime family involved, either in act or deed? Was there, Mr. Cappolino?"

He hesitated. "Yeah, just Rocco."

"Rocco who, Mr. Cappolino?"

"I'm not sure of his last name, but he was the main guy. He hired me; he explained every detail and told all of us what our assignments would be. He even told us to wear disguises and speak with foreign accents. He was the one running the job."

Ruane looked at Bosso, who shrugged. She asked him to step outside.

"You know anyone in the Ruggerio crew named Rocco?" she asked.

"Could be an alias."

They went back inside. "Tell me more about this Rocco, Mr. Cappolino," Ruane said.

"Like I said, I only met him two or three times before the job. He seemed to know what he was doing. Very confident, very smart about the job."

"Can you describe him?"

"Yeah, he was a little skinny guy, maybe late thirties, early forties, five five or five six, a hundred forty or a hundred fifty pounds. Strange little guy. I swear, I never saw him before or since."

Dio whispered to Joe P. Joe got up, excused himself, and left the room.

ADA Ruane suggested they take a break and reconvene in thirty minutes. While they were out, Joe P. had taken a ride over to police

HQ at One Police Plaza and gone up to Lt. Jay Stendrini's OCCB office.

"Hey, Joe, how you doing? What do you need?"

"Jay, you ever hear of a Ruggerio-family guy named Rocco, no last name?"

"Come on, Joe, that's like walking into an Irish pub and asking for Paddy O'Toole."

Joe just shrugged.

"Not off the top of my head. Let's see what I got on file." He swung around in his desk and switched on his computer. "We got all OC mug shots on computer now, but I kept the old photo books as a backup in case somebody fucked up entering shit into the system." Unfortunately, Rocco was a common name for Italian males. "Got a nickname or alias, Joe?"

"Yeah, most people call me Joe P.," he said with a grin.

Stendrini shot him the bird. "You're funny, Joe, real funny. Most of these Roccos are either dead or in prison. Nothing on the computer, let me check this old photo-mug-shot book. Stendrini paged through the photo book. OK, here's one. It's a mug shot for a burglary arrest back in 1976. Rocco DeAngelis, male, white, twenty-one. DOB Feb. 7th, 1955. Five feet five, hundred thirty-five pounds. Got pinched for breaking into a jewelry store. Can't tell you why he's in the OC file, but I can print this out for you with a photo."

"Sure, Jay that would be great."

Joe looked at the photo of a funny-looking young guy with a skinny face and a nose that seemed too big for him. "You know this guy, Jay?"

"Nope, never heard of him. But he's here in the OC book."

"Any family affiliation, Jay?"

"None listed."

"OK, buddy, thanks a lot."

Joe looked at the mug shot again. What he found most interesting was the date of birth. February 7, 1955. The same DOB as Dio Bosso.

When Joe P. got back to the meeting with ADA Ruane, Dio and the ADA had just resumed their meeting with Cappolino and Goldstein. Dio handed the photo to Ruane. She in turn asked Cappolino, "Mr. Cappolino, do you recognize the man in this photo?" She handed him the picture.

"Yeah, that's him, although he's much older now, say around forty. But it's him. Funny-looking fucker, ain't he?" Cappolino chuckled.

Back at the Major Case office, Dio assembled the team and brought them up to speed with what he'd gotten from Stendrini.

"OK, let's get a team out and pick this guy up. Do we have an address?" Dio asked.

"Yeah, boss, it's on the back on the photo. He lives in Brooklyn, the same house he lived in all his life. I checked with property records, and he bought it 1970 and then transferred the ownership to a Marie and Dennis Quigley. She's his sister, and her husband is a smoke eater" (cop speak for fireman).

"OK, have Alison and DeAngelo sit on the house, pick him up, and bring him in."

"Sure thing, boss. Notice anything else about him?"

Dio looked at the photo front and back and then looked at Joe. "Shit, we were born on the same day."

Rocco was lying low and spent a few days in Atlantic City. Both Big Pete and Tommy spoke to him and told him that Bruno and Carbone had to go. They could not take any chances now that Cappolino had become a rat.

"What about the rest of that crew?" Rocco asked.

"Rende and Sammy D. took off for Sicily. Walker and Ferrerra are in the wind, but I got people looking for them. That leaves you, Roc."

Rocco said nothing.

"Pop and I know you'll stand up, right, Roc?"

"Yep," was all he said. Rocco was not sure if Big Pete and Tommy had put out a contract on him like they had on the others. Either way, he was tired of AC, and he took a bus back to Brooklyn. Even then Rocco eschewed driving. He got back to the basement apartment in his sister's house, and as he was putting the key in the door, he felt a presence behind him. For a second he thought, This is it, but then he heard, "Police, don't move," and he breathed a sigh of relief.

CHAPTER SIX

The two detectives from the Major Case Squad, Steve Alison and Len DeAngelo, drove Rocco to the Major Case office on the sixth floor of One Police Plaza. They left him in an interview room for about an hour and then returned with another detective, who did the talking.

"I'm Detective Pollicino, and I am going to ask you a few questions." He read Rocco the Miranda warning and then asked Rocco if he understood his rights.

"Lawyer," Rocco said. Joe P. tried to get Rocco to confirm his name, address, and DOB, but all Rocco would say was "lawyer."

After about fifteen minutes, Joe gave up and pointed to a phone on the desk. Rocco dialed the number for Lyman Solniker and, with his hand over his mouth, whispered where he was.

Lieutenant Bosso was in the adjoining room behind the two-way mirror and thought, What a strange little man. Rocco was transported to central booking, fingerprinted, photographed, and placed in a holding cell. When Solniker arrived, he told Rocco that they were charging him with the Drake hotel heist—robbery in the first degree, thirty counts kidnapping, thirty counts unlawful imprisonment, and criminal possession of stolen property. Solniker told him all the evidence had been obtained by a sworn statement from John Cappolino, who was going to testify against Rocco and the others involved in the Drake robbery. Rocco just nodded as if to say OK. He then took Solniker's legal pad and wrote, "Big Pete—Tommy?"

"Their names are not on the indictment," Solniker said. "And Rocco, you can talk to me in here. The cops can't listen in." Rocco just nodded. Solniker continued, "The DA told me he would offer you a deal if you would testify about your knowledge of the Ruggerios' involvement in the Drake robbery and any other criminal activity involving Big Pete and Tommy. It's not you they want, Rocco, it's the Ruggerios. Cappolino was willing to testify against them, but fact is, he knows nothing about them, so they want you to consider their offer."

Rocco once again reached for the legal pad. "Fuck them and fuck you," he wrote. "I'm no rat. I took an oath."

Rocco was remanded without bail, and for the next several weeks, he was interviewed by Joe P., ADA Ruane, the FBI, and even Dio Bosso, the man responsible for his arrest and incarceration. In each interview Rocco had his lawyer present, and in each interview, he did not respond to any questions except to verify his name and date of birth—but even then with only a nod. During his time alone with Solniker, he would talk, but only to say, "You be sure to let Pete and Tommy know that I ain't saying shit. I'll do my time, but I ain't gonna be no fuckin' rat like that Cappolino cocksucker."

The case against Rocco was a slam dunk. Cappolino testified, and Rocco knew he was a dead duck. Rocco still feared that Big Pete could have him clipped in jail, but Tommy convinced his father that Rocco was strictly old school and believed in the Cosa Nostra code of omertà.

Tommy could not have been more correct. When at trial, Rocco had a chance to address the court prior to sentencing. "Your honor, the DA, the FBI, the police—everybody has wanted me to rat out my friends and family. I am a soldier. Soldiers don't rat. Even if I knew things, which I don't, I would not tell you. Thank you."

Judge Matthew Damico was not impressed. He sentenced Rocco to the max—twenty years.

Rocco spent two weeks at Rikers Island, the New York City jail situated in the East River between the boroughs of Queens and the Bronx. This was where Rocco was most fearful that Big Pete would have him clipped. Rikers housed prisoners who were either waiting to be transported to an upstate prison or still on trial. While in Rikers he received only one visitor—Dio Bosso. Dio was curious and wanted to see if he could learn more about this strange little man who, for over twenty-five years, had managed to stay under the radar of the NYPD and the FBI. Perhaps it was the birthday connection that drew Dio to Rocco. When they first met in Rikers, Dio brought Rocco a nice Italian hero he'd bought at a family-owned Italian deli on 108th Street in Corona.

At their first meeting, Dio did all the talking as Rocco ate his hero. Dio thought, For a little guy, he can sure put it away.

"Rocco, why don't you talk to me about yourself? I know you're connected to the Ruggerios, and truth be told, I don't care." Dio wanted to learn how Rocco had been able to avoid detection for all those years.

After eating his hero and wiping off his mouth, Rocco just looked at Dio and belched.

On February 7, 1995, Dio and Rocco's fortieth birthday, Dio decided to take a trip to the Clinton Correctional Facility in Danamora, New York, about six hours north of the city. Dio left early in the morning so that he would get there around one o'clock, spend an hour, and head back to the city. A call to the warden facilitated his getting into the prison, and the staff had Rocco in a private visitation room. When Rocco saw that his visitor was Dio Bosso, he gave sort of a half smile and nodded.

"Happy birthday, Rocco."

"You drove all this way from New York to wish me happy birthday?"

"Yeah. It's my birthday too. Maybe that's why I'm so fascinated with you Rocco—two people born on the same day, similar background but completely different lives. I find it intriguing, don't you?"

Dio did not expect an answer and was not surprised when Rocco just shrugged. Dio tried to make small talk with Rocco about prison life, about his sister and her family. When all he got was more shrugs, he started to think, Why am I wasting my time with this guy?

"OK, Rocco, have it your way. Hopefully we will both still be alive twenty years from now, when your sentence is complete." With that he exited the interview room without looking back.

Rocco sat there for a minute or two thinking that maybe, just maybe, he should have been a little more receptive to the man responsible for his incarceration.

PART THREE

Palm Beach Gardens

CHAPTER ONE

After Rocco was paroled, one of the first things he wanted to do was to meet with Tommy Ruggerio. Tommy was now the boss of his late father's crew, but he was not designated a capo in the Gambino crime family. This meant that Tommy still had to kick up tribute to the new Gambino boss, Lino Trentino. If he were a capo, he would get a piece of the money kicked up by all gang members. Tommy's headquarters were in the back room of Big Pete's Pizza, "the Home of the Big Slice," on Seventy-Third Street and Eighteenth Avenue in the Bensonhurst section of Brooklyn. Big Pete owned several Big Pete's pizzerias in Brooklyn and Queens. The Bensonhurst pizzeria was the same location where his father had run his crew. The first thing Rocco noticed was that the place hadn't changed at all in twenty years. Same wood paneling on the walls, same linoleum on the floor. Same pictures of Frank Sinatra and Pope Paul XI.

Tommy greeted Rocco warmly, and after the small talk was done, Tommy came right to the point. Although Rocco was well respected by Tommy Ruggerio and his crew, there was not much for an aging mobster to do. "Look, Rocco, since my old man died, I have been struggling to maintain whatever action I got. Between the Gambino people and my dwindling crew, it's getting harder and harder. I got to kick up ten G's a month to Lino. My guys are getting popped by the feds because they are greedy and getting more and more involved with the drug trade." Tommy stopped for a minute. "Look, Rocco, there may not be much for you here, plus I'm sure you would like some time to think about the future."

Yeah, that's why I'm here, thought Rocco, but he said nothing, just nodded.

"Listen. My kid brother—you remember Vinny? Well, he's down in Florida, and he runs a pretty successful topless club and restaurant."

Rocco remembered the kid—always cooking up meatballs and sausage and making specialty pizzas before they became fashionable. By the time he was in high school, Vinny was managing several of the pizzerias in Brooklyn for his dad.

"Why not take some time and go down there and visit him?" Tommy asked. "He's got a nice place with plenty of room, and I'm sure he would love to see you. You were always a guy he admired." Rocco again didn't say anything; he just nodded, thinking Tommy was giving him the brush-off. Tommy got up and walked over to a safe behind his desk. Opening it, he withdrew a stack of bills and gave it to Rocco. "Here's ten G's. I'll call Vinny and tell him you're coming down. He's gonna be happy to see you, Roc, I know he will."

Rocco looked at the stack of C-notes Tommy had handed him. "I don't know if I can go there. I'm on parole and staying in a halfway house."

"Don't worry, I know some people. I don't see it being a problem. What do you say?"

"Yeah, well, I guess so."

Tommy got up and put out his arms to give Rocco a hug.

Well, Rocco thought, I guess this meeting is over.

Rocco had to report to his parole officer, Brian Smyth, who signed off on his move to Florida.

He told Rocco that this unusual move was a favor to Tommy Ruggerio and that he expected Rocco to stay clean and not get into any trouble. Staying clean was not a problem for Rocco, who never did drugs and drank very little alcohol. Not breaking the law…well, that would be a challenge, as Rocco was a career criminal, and planning and executing a big job was his life's blood. But, he thought, what other options do I have? None, zippo, zilch. Plus, the thought of a warm climate appealed to him. After twenty years in Danamora, which was located in upstate New York, he'd had enough of cold and dreary weather.

CHAPTER TWO

W hen Rocco got down to Florida, Vinny acted as if he were the second coming of Christ, bragging about what a stand-up guy Rocco was and how he'd done a double dime because he'd refused to rat out guys in his crew, including Vinny's father, Big Pete.

Rocco didn't fit in with the local guys in Vinny's circle, nor did he try. Most of them were local guys in their late twenties and early thirties who like to fish or play golf when not hanging at the club. Most were into some sort of recreational drug use—coke, weed, or molly. Vinny's club was named Club Inferno, featuring the "Hottest Ladies" in South Florida, or at least that was what the billboard said on I-95. The club was pretty big and consisted of a large main room where seminaked or naked ladies pole danced on a stage behind a circular bar while the male customers stuffed dollar bills into their G-strings. To the side of the bar were several banquettes where one could get a lap dance. If a client wanted something extra, he would have to pay for a private room upstairs. There was also a sports lounge inside the club, where several big-screen TVs featured every sporting event imaginable. The club had a direct link to every major racetrack in the country, and bets could be made on horse and trotter races. Of course, the club got a piece of the action. Vinny also ran a weekly high-stakes poker game, and this was where Rocco felt he could be productive and start to earn some money.

They played the card game every Thursday, starting at six o'clock and going all night. Any form of poker was played, dealer's choice, so they played five- or seven-card stud and various types of Criss Cross. The dealer anted ten bucks, and bets and raises were in five- and ten-dollar increments, max on three raises per card, no check and raise. It was a good game, one where unless you were really unlucky, you could keep your losses to under a G.

At first Rocco just sat around and watched the game. Twenty years in the can had made him leery of such a high-stakes game. Most of the other guys in the game were regular working stiffs. Frank "Frankie Wheels" Wheeler was a used-car dealer. Norm Penny was a security-alarm installer who constantly talked about all the high-end systems he installed and how much he knew about the latest technology in home alarms. Howie Wolstein owned a couple of strip-mall buildings and collected rent on several low-end rentals he and his wife, Myrna, owned. Doc Rossman was a chiropractor who made no bones about how he had been bilking Medicare and other insurance carriers for decades. Billy Barth, known as Billy B., was a limo driver who was a huge fan of any team from Pittsburgh, his hometown. Two other players were brothers, John and Jim Larkin, who owned a couple of McDonald's franchises in Palm Beach County. The last regular player was Boris, a nasty-looking Russian who claimed to be connected to the Russian mob in Brooklyn's Brighton Beach section. He was always trying to buddy up with Rocco, citing their mutual organized-crime connections. Rocco was not a chatty guy to start with, but he did not like or trust Boris, or any Russkies for that matter. Maybe it had something to do with growing up in the '60s during the Cold War. All in all though, not a bad bunch of guys for a weekly poker game. Rocco would figure out some way to use them or the game itself to his advantage.

After a month or so in Florida, Rocco started to adjust to his new life. He got a kick out of Vinny, who idolized him and was always upbeat, smiling and seeming to enjoy his life away from New York. Although he ran the club and was the owner on paper, the club belonged to Tommy and was run by three women who worked there. Vinny enjoyed golfing and fishing, hanging out at the club, and "dating" a different dancer every few months. He had his bookkeeper, Janelle Fishman, put Rocco on the books as an assistant manager so he could show his parole officer a pay stub. Whenever Vinny fished or golfed, he would invite Rocco to join him. Vinny had a thirty-eight-foot Grady White fishing boat he kept at the dock behind his condo at the Heron Club on the Intercostal Waterway in Palm Beach Gardens. Rocco had no interest in either sport, and on the one occasion he went fishing, he got so seasick that Vinny had to take him back to the dock. He had even less interest in golf.

Vinny was very different from his older brother or father. Not soft, but not hard like Tommy and Big Pete. From the time he was a little kid, he'd enjoyed cooking and making pizza. After high school he'd gone to Johnson and Wales College of Culinary Arts in Rhode Island, where he'd not only refined his cooking methods, he'd also learned how to operate and manage a restaurant. When he graduated in 1986, he'd gone back to managing Big Pete's pizzerias, which now included seven locations throughout the city. It was Vinny who'd come up with idea to self-supply the "shops," as they referred to their pizzerias. They'd bought a small dairy farm in upstate New York and started making their own cheese; they'd also "acquired" a small packaging company and made their own takeout boxes. Of course, Big Pete used his "charm" to ensure that most other pizzerias in Brooklyn and Queens also bought their ricotta, mozzarella, and takeout boxes from the Ruggerios.

Vinny lived in a gated community called the Heron Club. Like most gated communities in Palm Beach Gardens, the Heron Club boasted two golf courses, a fitness center, and a clubhouse. The club was considered older in that most of the 525 assorted homes, condos, or golf villas had been built in the 1970s and needed some remodeling. Vinny had had his three-bedroom condo on the Intercostal Waterway completely remodeled when he bought it in 1997.

Vinny gave Rocco his account number to use at the club if he wanted to buy some sports apparel. Rocco didn't get the hint. He wore black pants and black shoes, with the "gangster" socks and a dress shirt open at the collar. Even the time they went fishing, that was what he wore. What a strange little guy, Vinny thought, but I love him.

On the first day, Vinny took Rocco to Club Inferno, where he introduced him to Janelle Fishman, Darla Cummings, and Kris Keefer. Janelle pretty much ran the front of the house, which included overseeing the dancers, bartenders, and cocktail waitresses. Janelle also did the books for the club. Rocco noticed that the bartenders were former cocktail waitresses and the waitresses were former dancers. Like a progression, he thought, or maybe a digression.

As with everyone else he met (not only here but everywhere), Rocco made a less-than-stellar impression on the club employees. When Darla asked Janelle what she thought of Rocco, Janelle just rolled her eyes. So Vinny figured as long as Rocco didn't enjoy golf or fishing, he might as well let him hang at the club and see if he could keep himself busy there. Little did Vinny know that was exactly what Rocco had been hoping for. He did not want to interfere with Janelle and Darla's management style, and he told them so. When Janelle asked, "Well, what exactly does Vinny want you to do here?" he replied, "I work for Tommy."

CHAPTER THREE

Rocco's days were pretty much the same. He would get up around eleven, shower and shave, get dressed in his black pants (he had four pairs, all exactly the same) and a dress shirt over an "Italian T-shirt." He had heard some guys refer to them as "wife beaters," but he didn't get it. He finished the look with socks and black shoes (of which he owned three different pairs, all slip-ons). He would get to the club around twelve thirty or one.

At first, he was surprised that the club had a pretty good lunch crowd. He soon learned that Kris Keefer ran a pretty good kitchen, and Darla, who did most of the food and beverage purchases, followed Vinny's instructions to buy the best. On average, the club did seventy-five to a hundred lunches a day and another two hundred to two hundred twenty-five dinners at night—plus the sports bar offered a bar menu. Kris had a staff of fifteen, mostly Latino males, some legal, some not.

Rocco would stay at the club through the dinner hour, always watching, always trying to learn something. He was enjoying it, and he started to interact more socially with Janelle and Darla. There was also at least one bouncer working the club, and each night the club employed an off-duty Palm Beach Gardens police officer or Palm Beach County sheriff's deputy, armed and in uniform for security. This not only kept problems to a minimum but also served as good public relations between the club and local law enforcement.

Vinny tried to make friends with PBG police chief Tom Pellitiere and PBSO sheriff Rick Romaine. Both these men were seasoned professional law enforcement officers, and they knew that the club was connected to the New York mob, so they kept their respective distances. They both liked Vinny and enjoyed him when they met at a charity golf outing or other social event, but that was it. They also knew that the club, while doing well, was probably laundering money for Vinny's brother in New York. They were not wrong, but as long as there were no problems, the officers thought, they'd let the feds worry about the financial crimes.

Rocco was enjoying this new lifestyle, but he still had an itch for a caper. Sure, I'm making a few bucks here, he thought, but I need to do something. He wondered if maybe the guys in the card game, which he was now playing in on Thursday nights, might be able to "inspire" him. He knew that on most weekends he would see Norm Penny, Jimmy Larkin, and Billy the limo guy in the sport lounge, making bets on various games and just hanging out. Vinny was usually there too. One night Rocco noticed that Vinny was drinking more than usual. Rocco went over to him.

"Hey, Vinny, how you doin'?"

"I don't know, Roc. My brother is coming down next week, and he's bringing that Russian fucker, what's-his-name, with him."

"You mean Rudukas? The Duke?"

"Yeah, that prick. Last time he was here, two of his goons got into it with a couple of regulars. Sent two guys to the hospital. It cost me a couple a G's to get them out of it and not even a fucking thank-you from Tommy or Rudukas."

Rocco thought about the time he'd torched that Russian's car back in Brooklyn before he went away, and he smiled to himself.

"What's with these fuckin' Russkies?" Vinny went on. "They treat my girls like shit, they don't spend a fuckin' dime, and the Duke is always asking Tommy to sell him the club, like it's his."

It is his, Vinny, Rocco thought. You know it, I know it, and so does everybody else. He told Vinny to take it easy. "I got a car coming. You want to ride home with me, Vinny? Looks like you had a rough night."

"Nah, I'll have Stu drove me home." Stu Rogers was the head bouncer, a reformed alcoholic and drug addict—although Rocco knew that if you ever said "reformed" to Stu, he would say, "Not reformed, I still have the sickness" and would go on about finding Jesus and sobriety, blah, blah, blah.

"OK, Vinny, I'll see you later," Rocco said.

Vinny just nodded and walked toward his office in the back.

CHAPTER FOUR

A loud banging on the door brought Rocco out of a dreamless sleep. "What the fuck is going on?" he said as he got out of the bed. The banging went on, and now it was joined by an alarm bell. If this were Brooklyn, he would have gone for his gun, but he knew security was pretty tight at the Heron Club, so he cautiously went to the front door and waited for another knock. "Yeah, who's there?"

"It's the police, sir. Please open the door."

Rocco looked out through the side window—the door had no peephole—and saw a Heron Club security vehicle and a Gardens police car. He opened the door and was greeted by a uniformed cop, who said, "I'm Officer Ed Leopold. Do you live here?"

Rocco, barefoot and wearing only boxers, looked at the cop and wanted to say, "No, I broke in here to take a fucking nap, you fucking moron," but he didn't. "I'm staying here. Why?"

The security guard, whose name tag read "Stabinsky," spoke next. "Is this the residence of Mr. Vincent Ruggerio? I told the officer that Vinny—er, I mean Mr. Ruggerio—lived here."

Leopold put up his hand as if to stop Stabinsky and said, "Well?"

"Well, what?" said Rocco.

"Does he live here or not?"

Leopold seemed to be getting angry, so Rocco egged him on. "Don't you believe this security guard here, Officer?" he said mockingly.

"Never mind," replied Leopold. "I'm here to make an official notification that a Mr. Vincent Ruggerio, whose driver's license indicates that this is his address, was killed in an auto accident on Military Trail and PGA Boulevard."

Rocco was stunned for a second. He looked at Stabinsky, who just shook his head.

"Sorry," was all Leopold said. "I need a name for the official record."

Rocco, not wanting to give his own name, said, "Tommy Ruggerio. Vinny's brother."

"Oh," said Leopold, "sorry for your loss. Could you come down to the morgue to make a positive ID?"

"What happened?"

Leopold looked at his clipboard. "I wasn't at the scene, but from what I heard, your brother was a passenger in a car driven by a forty-six-year-old white male named Stuart B. Rogers when they were broadsided by a speeding car that witnesses claim ran the red light at PGA and the Trail. Mr. Rogers suffered two broken legs and some internal damage. His car was traveling south on PGA, turning left, when the speeder T-boned Rogers's Cadillac on the passenger side. If it's any consolation, your brother was killed instantly."

"The other driver?" Rocco asked.

Leopold shook his head. "Drunk, illegal, unlicensed, and uninsured, I'm sorry to say."

"How is he?"

"Alive. Minor injuries. But don't worry, sir." Leopold now took a more sympathetic tone. "He will be punished to the fullest extent of the law and then deported back to wherever the fuck he came from."

Rocco just shook his head and thought, Shit, I gotta call Tommy.

Tommy, his wife, Maria, and their twin daughters, Jennifer and Denise, flew in to West Palm Beach Airport for the wake and funeral. Tommy handled everything from Brooklyn through Janelle and Darla. He insisted that Cosmo Sessa, the family undertaker, fly down and personally see to it that Vinny had an open casket. Sessa had buried both of Tommy's parents, as well as most of the deceased members of the Gambino family. He was a master embalmer, and the word was that no matter how bad a guy got shot up, if you wanted an open casket, call Cosmo.

On the day of the wake, Club Inferno was closed for the first time since it had opened in 1999, and after the funeral and burial, Tommy hosted a luncheon at the club for the three hundred or so mourners.

Tommy kept pretty much to himself during the entire funeral. Maria and his daughters seemed to be at his side constantly, so Rocco did not have a chance to speak to him alone. Not that he had anything to say, but he was curious and concerned, once again, about his future. Plus, Janelle, Darla, and everyone else at Club Inferno were asking Rocco what he thought would happen.

Toward the end of the luncheon, Tommy caught Rocco's eye and motioned him to the office.

"I want you to keep an eye on the place going forward," Tommy said. Rocco knew what he meant.

"What about Janelle and the others?"

"I'll talk to Janelle."

Rocco just nodded, and Tommy extended his hand. As Rocco reached for it, Tommy pulled Rocco to him, put his arms around him, and started sobbing. Rocco, an emotional cripple, did not know how to respond. He just patted him on the back, pushing his own body away from Tommy's.

PART FOUR

The Green Violinist

CHAPTER ONE

Rocco had now been in West Palm Beach, Florida, for six months. With the help of his attorney, Lyman Solniker, he was able to have his parole requirements transferred to the local probation department, and he actually liked his parole officer, Desiree Witherspoon. Rocco had never before interacted with a black female. He'd pretty much kept away from the blacks in prison, or maybe it was vice versa. Rocco was unique in that he never used the n-word. He still referred to African Americans as colored people. He never used the n-word. It was something he'd gotten from his parents.

Rocco and PO Watson met once a week initially, then bimonthly. Each time, Rocco had to pee in a cup, but it was only a formality. Rocco had never done drugs; he'd smoked a joint once but hadn't liked it. Witherspoon had no problem with alcohol, and Rocco only drank wine. Although he had no official job title at Club Inferno, he had a weekly pay stub to show his PO he was gainfully employed.

Rocco started to generate income from two additional sources. He started to make book on small wages from guys at the card table, and he offered them small "payday loans" if they ran short of gambling money. Of course, there was a vigorish (vig) involved in these transactions. Most of the regulars at the club and card games were local blue-collar guys. Short on brains, they were losers, and their gambling was no different. Oh, they knew how to play poker or get a bet to a bookie, but these guys had no idea who they were dealing with when it came to hanging out with Rocco at the Inferno. Two of the guys in the game were particularly pitiful, and Rocco saw them as vulnerable and possibly useful in the heist he had been thinking about since arriving in the Gardens.

Janelle Fishman, bookkeeper at the Inferno, had been a model and dancer in her youth. Still attractive and shapely at fifty-five, she'd realized after her second divorce that she had better get a real job. Always good with figures, she'd enrolled at Florida State University and earned a degree in accounting after just three years. She and Tommy Ruggerio had had a brief affair (Tommy's trademark), but they stayed friends, and she'd gone to work for him after her dancing days were over. Janelle was also a den mother to the girls who worked the club, giving them advice about any number of things, including how to hide their earnings, most of which were in cash. The club had eight girls who danced regularly and were on payroll for tax and benefit purposes. The club did not pay health insurance but did have a 401(k) available. All these things were ways to hide most of the club's income, which was in cash. Several times a year, Tommy would also send down one of his guys with a couple of hundred large for Janelle to "clean."

Darla Cummings was Inferno's food and beverage manager and also helped Janelle with managing the girls and the club. Born in Australia, Darla was a strong female with a good head for figures as well. She, along with Chef Kris Keefer, ran the kitchen.

Darla oversaw the front of the house, and she and Keefer did all the ordering for both food and booze. The bartenders and waitresses were all female, and most would do almost anything to make money if the opportunity arose. However, most customers focused on the dancers. It was a rare occasion when a bartender got asked for a date by a customer.

Tommy found neither Darla nor Kris to be his type of woman. Why would he? He could have had pretty much any woman in the club he wanted. Dancer, bartender, waitress—they all would have loved for Tommy to take notice. They all thought, If I only had the chance, maybe I could make him love me and take me away from this. I could live a good life as Mrs. Tommy Ruggerio. But the chances of that happening for anybody were zippo. Tommy, although he would have fucked a snake if you held its head, was dedicated to his wife, Maria, and his teenage twin daughters.

Janelle and Darla thought Rocco strange but in a mysterious and charming way. When either of them would mention this to Tommy, he would simply say, "You're right, he is strange, but his strangeness is his strength. He doesn't talk much, and I know he has very little personality. But he is extremely loyal to my family, and we owe him a lot." Tommy made no bones about how Rocco had done his full twenty-year sentence after the Drake hotel robbery because he refused to talk. Word was that from the time he got locked up and until he was sent away, Rocco had only given his name, asked for a lawyer, or taken the Fifth.

Over time Rocco, Janelle, Darla, and Kris all became friends. Although Rocco had sisters, he'd never been comfortable around women like he was with these three. He wasn't interested in any of them physically, nor they in him, although he did fantasize about each of them when he lay in bed at night. After a time Rocco started to become infatuated with Darla. She was the least attractive of the three—thin but shapely, small breasts, and a nice bump in

her butt. However, it was her accent that Rocco was most attract-
ed to. He had never heard an Australian accent before and was
charmed by Darla's. He started to fantasize about her more than
about Janelle or Kris. He also felt that she seemed to be one of the
few people in the world who actually enjoyed being around him.

CHAPTER TWO

Back in New York, Tommy had formed an alliance with Sergei "the Duke" Rudukas, head of the Russian mob in Brooklyn. Rudukas, born in what was now Belarus, was a former colonel in the Red Army who had forged documents to make himself Jewish so he could immigrate first to Israel and then to the United States. His sources of income were mainly extortion, loan-sharking, and hijacking, mostly committed against the ever-growing Russian population in the Brighton Beach, Sheepshead Bay, and Canarsie sections of Brooklyn. Also on the list of the Duke's services was contract murder. Although nothing more than a brutish thug, the Duke fancied himself a lover of fine art and would often bore Tommy with histories of the Russian artists he loved.

After several sit-downs, the Duke and Tommy agreed not to interfere with each other's illegal activities, so for Tommy, this worked out OK. Besides, Tommy was getting more and more involved in legitimate businesses. He owned several car washes in Brooklyn and Queens; plus he and his kid brother, Vinny, owned Club Inferno in Palm Beach Gardens.

One night, while meeting for a drink at the Duke's club Bely Mishka, Tommy found Rudukas in a foul mood. When Tommy asked him why he seemed so down, the Duke explained, "For once in my life, I try to do something legit, and what happens? I get shit on."

Tommy had no idea what he was talking about. The Duke went on. He explained to Tommy that he had attempted to buy, at auction, a painting by the famous Russian artist Marc Chagall. Tommy had never heard of Marc Chagall, but he did not want to add to the Duke's foul mood, so he just listened. The Duke said that the painting, called *The Green Violinist*, by Marc Chagall, who had been born in the same Belarus city as Rudukas, had been sold at auction for $7.2 million to some rich politician in Florida. The Duke explained he'd had a proxy bidding for him and that the proxy had stopped bidding at $2 million. The Duke seemed pissed; Tommy felt bored. Then the Duke said half-jokingly, "You got people in Florida. Why don't you steal it for me?" Yeah, sure, Tommy thought. Hmm, maybe I can talk to Rocco about this.

On Tommy's next trip down to Florida, he gave some thought to the "offer" Rudukas had made about the Chagall painting. Shit, he thought, if anyone can get his hands on this painting for me, it's Rocco. Maybe I'll have him look into it and see what he can do. One night, when the card game was in full swing, Billy Barth (called Billy B.), who drove for a limo service, was bemoaning how cheap some of his clients were when it came to tipping. During the season (October to May), he would work six to seven days a week. Clients had accounts and were billed a 20 percent gratuity for the driver. Additional cash tips were greatly appreciated but rarely offered. He mentioned a client, a former US ambassador to France, who lived in the exclusive gated community called Old Trail Village and had just purchased a painting for over $7 million. Norm Penny, who worked for Old Trail security, chimed in that he had installed the security cameras and alarm system for the same people. They'd treated him very well, he said—even gave him and his partner lunch. Penny laughed like he was busting Billy B.'s balls.

When Rocco asked him about the house later on, Penny said the ambassador, whose named was Paul Stockwell, and his wife, Teresa (whom everyone called Tippy), lived in Old Trail Village, where the homes started at $3 million and went as high as $12 million for beachfront property. Old Trail was old money. Located in Palm Beach Gardens, the community boasted two golf courses, a marina, a state-of-the-art fitness center (nobody at Old Trail called it a gym), a spa, and a twenty-thousand-square-foot clubhouse. Penny went on about how he'd started as a security guard at the main gate and then been chosen to be trained as an alarm installer and eventually became a certified Class A installation specialist. He had a knack for the work. The security director at Old Trail Village, John Pettway, recognized this and had Penny trained in the latest technology.

It was a good thing that Norm had been grandfathered in when the company instituted drug testing for all employees. It was no secret Norm like snorting cocaine, but he seemed to be a weekend user, and from what Rocco could see, it was not a problem for him, at least not yet. If the weekly card game went all night, which it usually did, Rocco would notice Norm hitting the head for a bump to keep him going. Both he and Billy B. were what Rocco referred to as degenerate gamblers. If they saw two cockroaches on the floor, they would wager on which one would get to point A faster. Rocco felt he had a winning combination here in Billy B. and Norm, two guys who had access to the same target, someone who was vulnerable and kept a great deal of valuable art in his home. The wheels in Rocco's head started turning. But first he had to formulate a plan and then take it to Tommy.

After a few weeks of thinking this caper out, Rocco approached Tommy. Not wanting to talk on the phone (what else was new?), Rocco suggested Tommy himself come south with his next "deposit." Tommy agreed. He flew down to Florida the following week, and Rocco laid out his plan for burglarizing the Stockwells.

In the weeks before Tommy's arrival, Rocco had learned through the Internet that Ambassador Paul Stockwell had purchased at auction a coveted Chagall painting for $7.2 million, outbidding several anonymous bidders, one of whom was thought to be Sergei "the Duke" Rudukas, the Belarus-born head of the Russian mob in Brooklyn. Rocco knew that Tommy and Rudukas had discussed the possibility of pulling this off. Tommy had not told Rudukas that he had in Rocco a master thief.

Tommy wanted to know the particulars of the plan. Rocco assured him his plan was solid but still not totally formulated. He had yet to approach both Billy Barth and Norm Penny, and he needed both of them to execute his plan. Tommy acted surprised and concerned that Rocco would include "civilians" in a caper of this magnitude. If push came to shove, would these two stand up? It was a good point, and Rocco acknowledged that it would be the first time he'd used outsiders for a job. But he told Tommy he had that covered and would tell him more once the Duke was on board and came up with the dough. Rocco wanted $1 million for himself, and Tommy could negotiate his end with Rudukas. Rocco did not want or need to know Tommy's end. He just wanted the mil. He would pay Barth and Penny out of his end.

Tommy contacted Rudukas, and he was all in. He knew that if he acquired the painting, it would have no value other than the fact that he had it; it could not be sold on the open market or displayed publicly. But he seemed interested. Tommy told Rocco that Rudukas would pay him the million. He did not mention his end of the deal. Now all Rocco had to do was convince Billy B. and Penny to agree.

Later that same night, Rocco called both Billy B. and Norm and asked them to join him at the Inferno. He scheduled their meetings for about an hour apart. He did not want them to hear the plan at the same time in the event that one did not go along, although he figured that they would join in, as the amount he was going to offer amounted to "an offer they could not refuse."

Billy B. was first. All Rocco needed from Billy was for him to let Rocco know when he would be driving the Stockwells next. He then gave Billy B. an outline of his plan. Billy scoffed at first, but then Rocco told him all he had to do was get Rocco into and out of Old Trail Village undetected and he would give him $25K, which was about a year's worth of driving for Billy. Rocco told Billy that he would have to lie low after the job was completed and should tell his boss that he was planning on visiting family up north (Billy was originally from the Pittsburgh area and still had family there).

Norm was a little less enthusiastic about getting involved. While he liked the idea of ripping off the wealthy, he was somewhat skeptical they could pull this off. Rocco countered by playing to Norm's weakness, which was his ego. Norm saw himself as someone who was better than everybody else and thought the world owed him a living. After Rocco plied him with a few lines of coke and offered him $100K (about two years' salary), he wanted to hear more. Rocco laid out his plan, which hinged on the fact that Norm could disable the alarm and motion detectors in the home after Rocco had gained entry to the gated Old Trail community. Norm often bragged about how, in addition to having the alarm company's default code to use for repairs and updates, he had his own personal entry code that he could use to disable the alarm on every system he'd installed.

After several meetings and dry runs, Rocco, Norm, and Billy B. were set to go. They just needed to know when Billy would be picking up the Stockwells for an evening out. Usually they went to Palm Beach for dinner or to some other millionaire's home for a charitable fundraiser. They were rarely gone for more than three hours, but that would give Rocco enough time to get in and out of their home with the painting. The Stockwells did not have any permanent staff in the Old Trail house. They had only an estate manager, Georgiana Duvall, who managed all four of their homes but lived in New York. She would fly down to Florida whenever the Stockwells needed her for a dinner they were hosting, and then she would arrange for staff to be brought in to cook and serve the dinners.

Finally, Billy B. called Rocco on Thursday, September 17th, to tell him that he would be picking up Ambassador and Mrs. Stockwell on Saturday, September 19th, at seven, to take them to a fundraiser at the Flagler Museum in Palm Beach. The Stockwells had instructed Billy to wait for them and take them home around nine.

The stage was now set for Rocco to execute his plan. Previously he'd instructed Billy B. to purchase three burner phones to be used for all communications between him, Billy B., and Norm. He'd also instructed Norm to make a service call to the Stockwells' home to manipulate the alarm system so that it could be deactivated remotely from Norm's burner phone. If done properly, this would afford Rocco sufficient time to gain entry and remove the painting.

Rocco went online to learn the dimensions of the painting and downloaded a photo of it. He then enlarged the picture on the computer and printer Janelle used in the office. She assured him that once this was done, she would erase any reference to his search. What fantastic burglar's tools the computer and Internet are, Rocco thought. Had he had that technology back in the day, there was no telling how many more jobs he could have pulled off.

Janelle was smart enough to suspect that Rocco was up to something when he asked her how to use the computer to Google something, but being the smart lady she was, she did not ask or want to know. She was actually starting to like Rocco, and since Vinny's unfortunate accident, Rocco had taken more of an interest in running Inferno. Of course, this came from Tommy, but Rocco seemed to enjoy learning about the club and how it operated as not only a topless joint but also a pretty good restaurant and sports bar. Janelle, Darla, and Kris knew Tommy had given his blessing for Rocco to be more involved, and they had no problem with that. All three ladies, especially Janelle, were happy to have a male friend who wasn't always trying to get into their pants. She and the others talked about Rocco, and all agreed that though he was not easy on the eyes, he had a quality that they admired. Was it his strangeness? Darla especially thought he could be someone she would like to know better. Unlike Janelle, Darla had had no one in her life since her husband died several years ago. Kris, on the other hand, just saw Rocco as the boss. They all knew what the club's real purpose was: laundering money for the Ruggerio family in New York. But since Vinny had been killed in the car crash, Rocco was the de facto boss.

On Friday night, the evening before the caper, Rocco had Norm and Billy B. go through a dry run of the plans. It went well. Rocco reminded them that the most important thing to do was to act as normal as possible and to keep their mouths shut. He advised them to leave Palm Beach Gardens on Sunday after the heist. Billy

B. had already informed his boss that he would be heading to Pittsburgh to visit family. Norm had informed his employer that he was going to stay at the Hard Rock Hotel in Tampa, where, he told Rocco, he had a lady he saw a few times a year. Anyway, Rocco figured that if all went according to plan, the burglary would not be discovered until sometime Sunday at the earliest, and by then Billy B., Norm, and the Chagall would be out of town.

CHAPTER THREE

Tommy Ruggerio was scheduled to fly down to West Palm Beach with the payment for the painting—one million in cash for Rocco. Tommy flew on NextJets, a private carrier that was not required to inspect clients' carry-on luggage. Tommy used NextJets when he flew down his prelaundered money. If he had one of his trusted soldiers take it down—say, John "Johnny O." Oterio or Lou "Spanish Louie" Roque, both stand-up guys in Tommy's crew—they would have to drive. Tommy had no problems getting the money from Rudukas. Rudukas trusted Tommy, but to make sure everything went well, he sent two of his top soldiers, Ivan Blatnikov and Yuri Smolinsky, to Palm Beach Gardens to ensure that the money got handed off and the painting delivered to him. In addition, Ivan and Yuri had other tasks to perform while in Florida.

Rocco, who did not like to drive, asked Darla to drive him to pick up Tommy at the private airport at West Palm Beach International. He was surprised to see the two burly Russkies get off the plane with Tommy, rather than Johnny O. or Spanish Lou. Rocco did not say anything about it until they got back to the house and he and

Tommy were alone. Ivan and Yuri had gone out to rent a car and get a steak dinner at the club and probably a blow job from one of the girls. Of course, it would be on the house, and these "cheap Russians bastards," as Tommy called them, never tipped. Tommy told Rocco that Rudukas had insisted the two goons go with him to ensure that the Chagall got back to him. The Duke was then going to try reselling the painting on the international stolen-art network in Eastern Europe and Asia, or keep it for himself. Plans changed, however, and now Tommy was going to fly the Chagall back Saturday night on NextJets. Rocco went over the plan with Tommy, who did not offer any comments other than to ask where Billy B. and Norm lived and where they would be going after the job was done. Rocco was curious about why that was so important to him, but he assured Tommy that these two guys would be OK. He only wished he felt more confident in them than he let on to Tommy.

On Saturday night at six, Billy B. met Rocco and Norm at Vinny's condo. Inside the garage, Rocco went over the plan one final time. They checked the phones to ensure that they were fully charged. Then he and Norm, who were dressed in black from head to toe, placed cloth booties over their shoes and climbed into the trunk of the town car. They had practiced this several times, but Norm, who stood at six feet one, weighed a hefty 275, and was slightly claustrophobic, still had to reassure himself getting in and out. They got into the trunk one last time, Rocco first, as his smaller frame gave Norm more room. Closing the door, Rocco heard Norm yell, "Son of a bitch!"

"What now, Norm?"

"I cut my fucking finger on the latch. I'm fucking bleeding."

They both got out, and Rocco went back in the house to fetch a Band-Aid for Norm.

"Here, put this on, and stop whining like a fucking baby," Rocco said.

Billy B. opened the trunk lid. He chuckled and said, "You two look like of a couple of fags trying to find a hideaway for sex."

"Close the fucking trunk and let's go," Rocco said.

It was now six thirty. The ride from the condo in Palm Beach Gardens to Old Trail Village would take no more than ten or fifteen minutes.

At the security gate, they would execute the first step of the plan. Billy B. advised them by phone of their location, and Rocco and Norm held their collective breaths.

"AAA Limo for a pickup at 810 Turtle Bay Drive. Ambassador and Mrs. Stockwell," Billy B. said to the security guard, handing him his driver's license as required for entry. The guard, who recognized Billy, made an entry in his computer and told Billy to proceed, reminding him to obey the twenty-five-miles-per-hour posted speed limit, which he did. Eight Hundred Ten Turtle Bay Drive was one of the more exclusive homes within the exclusive community. A long circular driveway led to the main house. The property also contained a guest cottage, a pool house, tennis courts, and access to the beach. Unlike most of their neighbors, the Stockwells did not maintain a permanent staff or estate manager at the home. Billy B. had confirmed this to Rocco during one of their planning sessions. Instead they had a cleaning lady who came twice a week. They ate out most nights at one or two local restaurants or at the clubhouse dining room. This, of course, was one less problem Rocco had to worry about.

Halfway up the driveway and seeing no one in sight, Billy B. popped the trunk. Norm and Rocco exited, and Norm once again caught his fat fingers on the latch, this time tearing the Band-Aid off. He threw it on the driveway, causing Rocco to give him a look that asked plainly, "Are you a fuckin' idiot?"

Rocco picked up the Band-Aid and tossed it in the trunk. "Put those fucking gloves on, Norm," he whispered. They ducked into the lush shrubs surrounding the driveway, crouched down, and waited. It was still light out and would remain so for at least another thirty minutes. At about 6:55 p.m., Ambassador Stockwell came out and told Billy B. that they would be ready in ten minutes. Although Billy had driven them no fewer than two dozen times, Stockwell acted as if he had never seen Billy before. No greeting, no "how you doing." Fucking asshole, Billy thought. I would give all my pay to see your face when you discover your shit gone. Then he chuckled to himself. Not really.

Rocco didn't tell Billy what would be stolen from the house. He'd convinced Billy that the $10K first installment of the promised $25K (in about three hours, Billy thought) was more than adequate compensation for his role in the job. Meanwhile Rocco and Norm remained in the bushes, checking out a better place to hide once the job was completed, and waited for Billy B. to return with the Stockwells. They hoped that wherever the Stockwells were going, they would get bored and leave by eight thirty. Rocco knew that if all went according to plan, he would be in and out of the house in ten minutes.

The Stockwells came out about five after seven. The ambassador was wearing a tuxedo, which looked to Billy to be the same one he always wore. Mrs. Stockwell, who was about sixty-five and thin as a rail, looked like a well-kept old lady. She had blond hair pulled back so tightly her eyes seemed to be popping out of her head. She probably had $50K in jewelry on and as much in plastic surgery.

Billy B. held the door for Mrs. Stockwell, but as usual she did not thank him or even acknowledge he was there. Once they were in the town car, the ambassador told Billy, "We're going to the Flagler on the island. Do you know where it is?"

No, Billy thought, I've only been driving a limo for ten years, and I've taken you there at least a dozen times, you fucking idiot. "Yes, sir, I do."

Rocco and Norm waited until Billy's town car passed the gate. In a preset move with the burner, Billy signaled to Rocco's phone. They now began to move to the back of the house. Norm deactivated the alarm and told Rocco he had no more than three minutes to get in. Norm had given Rocco a verbal about where the alarm was located and had even drawn a rudimentary map of the living quarters. Rocco, who carried a duffle bag containing his burglar's tools, removed a suction cup and placed it on a pane on the rear door. Using a glass cutter, he cut a circular hole in the pane, removed the glass, reached in, and opened the door. Norm then entered behind him, went to the main alarm box, shut off the alarm, and deactivated the motion detectors. He knew that the deactivation would register in the main guardhouse by the front gate. But rarely did the single security guard have the opportunity to see it and make the connection that the occupants of that house were off the premises. Once the alarms were off, Rocco removed a rough replica of the Chagall from his bag. The picture Rocco had downloaded and enlarged was now in a frame similar to the original. Rocco had gone to a frame-it-yourself store, using a fictitious name and paying the fifty bucks in cash. He did not think the fake, when discovered, could be traced to him. Rocco removed the painting from the wall and replaced it with the fake. To the untrained eye, it might pass, but Rocco knew once the ambassador or his wife saw it, they would know it wasn't real. It did not matter, though. By the time they saw it, even if that happened later tonight, the Chagall would be on its way to Rudukas. They had now been inside about five minutes. Rocco wrapped the painting in bubble paper and placed it inside his bag the and used glue to replace the glass he'd removed. He then buffed the edges around the replaced glass with sandpaper to conceal the fact that it had been tampered with. Norm reset all of the alarms, carefully checked his surroundings, and exited the front door. They were out and back in the bushes in less than ten minutes. They moved away toward the back of the house and made themselves comfortable by the pool house, still out of view. Norm knew the security patrols were not permitted to check on the backs of the residents' homes. Cameras were position on the beach, and security had a patrol boat that was stationed at the jetty that led into the beach-access area. It had always seemed strange to Norm that the main gate and the beach access were the only stationary posts on the property. Once someone was allowed access, there was pretty much no security except for the one patrol vehicle. The officer assigned to the patrol vehicle had to be an EMT, and the vehicle contained a defibrillator and other first-aid gear. Norm wondered if things would change after this.

They sat in silence for the next hour and a half. Several times they saw the patrol vehicle drive by, but the guard just drove slowly, not really looking for anyone lurking in the bushes. Finally, at about 8:45 Billy texted that he had the ambassador and his wife and would be there in about twenty minutes. They waited anxiously. When they finally saw the headlights of Billy B.'s town car pull into the driveway, they got set to go. Billy pulled up to the circle and got out to open the door for Mrs. Stockwell. The ambassador was already by the front door, looking for his key in a planter by the front door. Billy remembered seeing him do that several times before. Shit, he thought, why didn't I think of that? It could have been helpful to Rocco. But that was Billy B.—not the sharpest knife in the drawer.

As soon as the ambassador and Mrs. Stockwell were inside, Billy got back in the car, drove slowly down the driveway, and popped the trunk. Rocco hopped in and shimmied to the back, with Norm following. Norm closed the lid, this time without ripping his finger, and Billy drove off, careful to observe the posted speed limit. He was nervous, and when the security guard at the gate signaled him to stop, he started to sweat, thinking, What if the ambassador discovers the burglary and calls security? I'm fucked! But before total panic set in, the guard approached the town car and told Billy he had to open the gate manually, as the system had malfunctioned temporarily. He waved him through. They were home free—at least for the time being.

CHAPTER FOUR

Once back at the condo, Rocco and Norm hopped out of the trunk, and the three made their way through the garage into the kitchen. Tommy was waiting there with the two Russian goons, Ivan and Yuri. Tommy was really excited and asked Rocco to go back to the garage with him alone. Once there Tommy told Rocco that plans had changed, and he was going to fly the painting back himself. Yuri and Ivan would be driving back on their own.

Rocco thought nothing of it at first. As long as he got his money, which Tommy had brought down with him in a large duffel bag, Rocco had nothing to say. He was not going to count the money, at least not yet. He reached in and took one wrapped stack of C-notes—$10K—for Billy's down payment and ten additional stacks for Norm's share. Rocco held back Billy's balance because he and Billy both knew he would do something stupid like try to deposit $25K into his checking account. Rocco had explained to Billy several times how to launder the money through the casinos he frequented in Hollywood and Coconut Creek, both owned by the Seminole Indian tribe of Florida.

When Rocco went back into the kitchen, the Russians were gone, and Billy and Norm were drinking a beer. Rocco gave each his dough and once again told them how best to avoid problems. Rocco was less concerned about Norm and his dough, although he advised him to be careful how he spent it. Norm assured Rocco that he knew what he had to do.

They shook hands, and before they departed, Rocco thanked them once more and said he looked forward to maybe working with them another time. Little did he know he would never see either one again.

CHAPTER FIVE

On Sunday morning around seven o'clock, Mrs. Stockwell
awoke and went down to make herself some tea and start
her day, first by calling their daughter in Philly and then by planning her social agenda for the week. The ambassador had an early-
morning tee time and was already out of the house by the time she
awoke. The Stockwells kept separate bedrooms but would sleep
together for appearances when their daughter and her family visited. They had not had sex in about fifteen years, and when they
did, it was anything but exciting. Mrs. Stockwell was stiff and cold
and never showed any affection to her husband. He, on the other
hand, had had several affairs over the years. Being an ambassador
and in the foreign service put him in the company of some very
attractive European woman who had very liberal standards when it
came to things like fucking some other lady's husband, especially
when he was a man who had money and an important position.

At first no one noticed anything amiss. Around ten o'clock, Mrs.
Stockwell went into the formal living room just to sit and look at

her collection. The look on her face when she saw the Chagall was one of disbelief that turned to confusion and then shock. Were her eyes playing tricks on her? Was she having a seizure? She could not understand what she was seeing or thought she was seeing. She gasped and walked slowly toward the painting, forgetting that in about two more footsteps, the motion detector would beep and trigger an alarm to the security command center. It did not take her more than two seconds to realize that the painting she was now standing in front of was not hers.

"My God!" she screamed. "We've been robbed!"

Panic set in, and she did not know whom to call first, the ambassador (as she still referred to him, even he was no longer an ambassador, not since Obama had been elected), police, security... She started to get dizzy and thought she would faint. She went to the alarm box and pressed a preset panic button. Then she went back to look at the fake, still not realizing the motion detector was beeping.

In the security command center by the main gate, Security Supervisor Nino Ramirez was on duty. As soon as he heard the panic alarm coming from 810 Turtle Bay Drive, he called the rover and sent him there forthwith, assuming the caller was having a medical incident. He attempted to disarm the motion detector, but for some reason that was not that important to him. He then instructed SO Bauman, who was on his break, to get out front, as he had to respond to Turtle Bay Drive. Bauman, a crusty old-timer, bitched about his break being interrupted, but Ramirez had no time to explain.

"Just get the fuck out here, and quit your bullshit," Ramirez said. "We've got an alarm, and I've got to respond."

Ramirez was at the Stockwells' residence within ten minutes of hearing the alarm. When he saw the rover there and heard no call for fire and rescue, he was relieved that this call was not a medical emergency, at least not yet. The rover that day was SO Dan Barger, who was a lot younger than Bauman and an enthusiastic, well-trained professional security officer. Once Ramirez got inside, he found Mrs. Stockwell in full panic mode, saying someone had stolen their *Green Violinist*. Ramirez and Barger had little knowledge of the art world, and they kept picturing an actual green violin. But they both knew the name Marc Chagall and were savvy enough to know the people in Old Trail had big bucks—and in some cases, like the Stockwells', mega bucks. So if they chose to spend millions on a green violin, well, that was their business. Ramirez thought about trying to preserve the crime scene, but he really did not know where that was, other than the area right in front of where Mrs. Stockwell was pointing.

"Look, look," she said. "It's a fake!"

Ramirez saw a painting of a man playing a violin. Then it dawned on him. He instructed Barger to notify Palm Beach Gardens PD, as they had jurisdiction over Old Trail. He then called his boss, Old Trail Village director of security, John Pettway. Within ten minutes two officers and a sergeant from the Palm Beach Gardens Police Department arrived at the residence and started to take information from a now somewhat calmer Mrs. Stockwell. The patrol sergeant, whose name was Art Doolan, started to ask Mrs. Stockwell some basic questions, such as who had access to the house and where her husband was. She did not want to hear this, however, and quickly informed Doolan that he had better stop asking her questions and go find who had taken her painting. Doolan tried to calm her down, but to no avail. Meanwhile the other responding officer, PO Debra Stringer, notified the Detective Division to respond, explaining as best she could that some lady in Old Trail Village claimed someone had stolen a $7 million painting.

CHAPTER SIX

The Palm Beach Gardens Police Department was a 152-person force with a chief and two assistant chiefs. One AC was in charge of the Administrative and Investigative Division and the other the Field Operations Division. Responding to the Stockwells' home that Sunday morning was Det. Sam Daniels, a thirteen-year veteran and a fairly competent investigator, or so he thought. He'd started his police career in the Juno Beach PD, and after about three years, he'd been hired by the Gardens PD, which paid more and had more opportunity for advancement. Daniels, like many other police officers, aspired to get hired by the Palm Beach County Sheriff's Office (PBSO), as that agency paid the highest salaries and was the premier law enforcement agency in Palm Beach County. But after he made detective after only five years at PBG, he gave up any interest in the sheriff's office.

Upon entering the Stockwells' home, the first thing Daniels noticed was that there were too many people hanging around. By this time Ramirez had notified his boss, John Pettway. Pettway was a retired Palm Beach Gardens sergeant and had a very good working relationship with both that organization and the Palm Beach County Sheriffs Office.. He and Daniels were on a first-name basis, but Daniels always called Pettway chief, more to be patronizing than out of actual respect. To maintain relationships, Chief Pettway would arrange to make tee times available for the deputies and cops whenever he could. This small perk went a long way. Most cops who golfed played the local muni courses and thought playing at an exclusive private club like Old Trail Village was heaven.

Daniels greeted Pettway and then told him to get everyone out except the first officer on the scene. He then went into the kitchen, where Mrs. Stockwell was sitting, crying to her daughter on the phone. The ambassador had completed his round of golf and was on his way. Daniels asked the basic questions of Mrs. Stockwell: When did you last see the painting? Who has access to the house? As there was no obvious forced entry (Ramirez had checked the doors and windows), the first line of thinking was that it was an inside job. Daniels even thought that the Stockwells might be doing this for insurance money, and without thinking, he asked if the painting was insured.

"What are you implying, young man?" shouted Mrs. Stockwell.

"Nothing, ma'am. I just need to ask these questions."

"Well, my husband will be home soon, and he is the American ambassador to France, blah, blah, blah." She neglected to say he *was* the ambassador to France, speaking instead as if it were a lifetime position. Daniels tuned her out. Over the years he'd dealt with a host of wealthy people who'd threatened him with losing his job, walking a beat in John Prince Park, and so on. He was not fazed. At that moment the ambassador got home and went straight to the fake Chagall. "What in God's name happened here?" he shouted. "Who are you gentlemen?" Then he recognized Pettway, but he only knew he was security, nothing else.

"Ambassador Stockwell, I'm Detective Daniels from the Palm Beach Gardens PD, and Mr. Pettway here is—"

"I know who he is!" shouted the ambassador at no one in particular. "Where is the FBI?"

Daniels, trying to maintain his composure, replied, "At this time we are in the process of investigating a burglary, although the value of the stolen property is very, very high. I can assure you that the Palm Beach Gardens PD will do all in its power to find the person or persons who committed this crime and return your property to you. Since this crime did not occur on government property, however, I don't believe the FBI can get involved."

"Well, we will see about that. I believe as a diplomat, I'm protected by the FBI."

"I see. I'll have to call them myself," Daniels wanted to say, It's the State Department who provides security for diplomats, you idiot, but of course he did not. "In the meanwhile why don't you and Mrs. Stockwell check to see if any other items were taken, and we will continue our investigation. I have alerted our crime-scene people to respond, and I will need this area clear, so please check your valuables, and let's be sure that the painting is all that is missing."

Both of the Stockwells seemed a bit calmer after his speech. They looked at one another and started off to the upstairs bedrooms to see if anything else was missing.

Within minutes of that conversation, another Gardens police vehicle pulled up the driveway. Now there were two marked police cars, one Old Trail security vehicle, and Detective Daniels's unmarked car parked in the semicircular driveway. Early-morning joggers and walkers started to gather and gape, and Ramirez thought, Even these rich motherfuckers want to see what's what when the cops are on the scene. Ramirez was instructed by Pettway to position his vehicle close to the road and hinder the view of the lookie-loos. Pettway also informed him to just say that the ambassador and Mrs. Stockwell were fine, no more. Several of the neighbors who claimed to be close friends became indignant when told they could not go to the house, but Ramirez reminded them that one, it was a crime scene, and two, the ambassador and his wife did not want visitors at this time. Inside the house Daniels and the crime-team detectives, Laurie Stillman and Larry Napolitano, conducted a routine, by-the-book CS investigation. They looked for prints on all windows and doors, checked all the locks on doors and windows, and took photos of the fake painting and all the access and egress points. They worked the entire lower floor and garage, which was not attached to the house and was rarely used by the Stockwells. They also checked the pool house, cottage, and tennis changing room. There were no signs of forced entry, no signs of any disturbances.

As the Crime Scene people continued their search, Daniels put a call in to his immediate supervisor, Captain Jack Harkness, who was the head of the Detective Division. He in turn wasted no time calling the chief of police, Tom Pellitiere. Pellitiere was a seasoned professional, having served over thirty years in law enforcement. After rising to the rank of director of the Vermont State Police, Pellitiere had retired to Jupiter, Florida, where after a year he was contacted by a national search company asking if he would be interested in applying for the position of chief of police of the Palm Beach Gardens PD. The current chief, an avid boater and fisherman, had died suddenly of a massive heart attack while reeling in a large yellow-fin tuna. The chief had died, and the fish was cut loose. Pellitiere took the job when the council gave him full control to run the department the way he saw fit, as well as the budget and the tools to upgrade the once-tiny town of Palm Beach Gardens with the police force it now needed for an ever-growing population. In the past fifteen years, several high-end, private gated golf communities had been developed. In each community, management called upon Chief Pellitiere to assist in the implementation of state-of-the-art security systems and guard operations. He'd also been instrumental in forming a gated-community-security-directors' information network and had assigned a sergeant to co-ordinate and disseminate pertinent crime statistics to the group.

Pellitiere arrived at the Stockwells' residence about nine thirty, less than three hours after the theft was first discovered. He waited until the ambassador and Mrs. Stockwell returned from their inventory and then greeted them as if they'd remember meeting him before, but it did not register with them. He could have been the man in the moon for all they knew. The good news was that nothing else seemed to be missing, but the chief assured them that if they found later that anything else had been stolen, it could be added to the report. That seemed a little condescending to the ambassador, but he just shook his head, still in disbelief that something like this could happen to him. Pellitiere excused himself and called Daniels and Harkness aside. "I want you to talk to anyone and everyone who might have some information on this," he said. "I want you to interview all the security people on duty the last twenty-four hours. I want you two to canvass the neighbors, no one else. This is yours, Daniels, and Jack, you can be sure we are gonna get heat from all levels. This guy is a big-shot ambassador, and he knows a ton of the right people." It was not like he was telling Daniels and Hill anything they didn't already know; he was just doing the chief thing. "Let's make sure all the bases are covered here, OK?"

After Pellitiere left, the CS team finished up. "I think we're done here, Cap," Detective Stillman said to Harkness. "We will have to get prints from the residents for the purpose of elimination, but there are no signs of forced entry."

"What about the alarm system?"

"We're going to stop at the command center and check it out. According to Ramirez over there"—she pointed to the security guard standing out by the front of the driveway—"the alarm did not go off, indicating that the perp had the code or the alarm was not set."

"OK, see what you can find. And oh, by the way, did you check the grounds?"

The two Crime Scene detectives looked at one another. Stillman answered, "Er, no, Cap, we were gonna do it now. You know, on our way out."

Yeah, sure you were, Captain Harkness thought. Fucking amateurs.

By early afternoon all of the work that could be done by the responding officers was done. Harkness remained on the scene while Daniels canvassed the two homes next to the Stockwells'. He checked the rear of the home, which included two fenced-in tennis courts and a set of wooden steps that led to the beach. CS had checked the beach, with negative results. No footprints in the sand, no indication that entry was gained from the ocean.

Daniels came back to the house, and he and Harkness sat down and started to put together a case history. "So here is what we got so far. The Stockwells leave here by limo around seven on Saturday. They return three hours later and find a valuable Marc Chagall painting missing and a cheap replica left in its place. Questions: Who knew they would be out and the house unoccupied? Who had access to the house, including the alarm code? Was the fake painting left as a delay tactic to give the perp time to get away, or was it some private joke? And what about insurance fraud? What is the possibility of an inside job?"

CHAPTER SEVEN

B ack at the condo, Rocco saw Tommy and the painting off on the NextJets that left from Palm Beach International's private airport. Not wanting to drive at that hour—it was ten thirty at night—Rocco asked Darla, who was still at the club, if she could drop by and give him and Tommy a ride. It was all of twenty minutes, and no one spoke until Tommy got out of the car and had Rocco walk him to the plane.

"Be careful, Roc," Tommy said.

"I'm always careful, Tommy. Why do you think I'm still doing this shit?" Rocco chuckled. But Tommy's tone was more serious, and at first Rocco didn't get it.

"No, Roc, you mean a lot to me, and I don't trust these Russian cocksuckers. If not for the fact that I cleared close to a mil on this deal, I would not have gotten involved. These fucking guys don't give a fuck, Rocco. They're not afraid of us, the cops, or the feds, for that matter. You just gotta kill the motherfuckers if they get too pushy. Fortunately, Rudukas and I get along. He knew my old man—they made money together—and

Big Pete helped him get his wife and kids here. But these fuckers aren't loyal like us. You just can't trust them. So all I'm saying is be careful.

"One other thing, Roc. I'm thinking about selling Inferno. With Vinny gone, there is really no fun for me coming down here, plus my daughters will be going to college next year."

Tommy had always said he would retire before the feds or the enemy put him away. The Ruggerio family was more than 60 percent legit now, so Tommy felt he would not need a money-laundering operation going forward. He shared with Rocco that he planned on taking care of the guys in his crew. He'd arranged it so that all sixty-five made guys and ten to twelve associates would have a voice in who would take over. Most agreed Spanish Lou Roque would be the best candidate. Lou was not 100 percent Italian, as he had a Portuguese grandmother. But his mother was related to the Gambinos, and he was born Louis Alphonso Roccha. After his uncle Paul (Paulie the Pigeon) turned state's evidence back before Lou was born, the family changed its name to his Portuguese grandmother's name, Roque. Good thing most crime families did not have historians among their ranks. No one could remember how Lou got the moniker Spanish Lou, either, but no one seemed to care. He was a stand-up guy to everyone in the crew.

Tommy pressed on. "Just be careful. Oh, one more thing. I want to sell you the condo, so you got a permanent place if you want to buy it. Think about it. Let me know, and I'll have my realtor set it up."

"Sure, Tommy, it sounds fine."

They hugged good-bye, and Tommy walked on the jet, never looking back. Shit, Rocco thought, something ain't right. To him Tommy seemed frightened—so unlike him. Nevertheless, Rocco got back in Darla's car, and they headed out of the airport.

They didn't say much on the drive back to the condo, and when they got there, Darla asked Rocco if he had any beer.

"Sure. You want one?"

"If you'll join me."

Darla knew Rocco was not a drinker, and it surprised her when he said yes. They went inside. Rocco sat on the sofa while Darla went to the fridge and retrieved two Heinekens. Darla spoke about nothing while Rocco half listened, half thought about what Tommy had said and the way he'd said it. It was like he'd been trying to tell Rocco something without telling him something.

Darla asked Rocco if she could light a joint.

"Sure, go ahead," he said. "I don't like that shit, but be my guest."

Darla pulled out some rolling papers and a baggie of weed, about a dime's worth, if Rocco recalled. Darla rolled a joint like she'd been doing it all her life, took a hit, and offered the joint to Rocco.

"I just told you, I don't like that shit."

"This ain't that shit," she replied, with a twinkle in her eye that made him want to kiss her. He did, and she responded. They separated and kissed again, this time longer and softer than the first time. Rocco had not been with many women in his fifty-five years, and none in the last twenty-five. The first thing most ex-cons did after seeing their parole officer was go out and get laid, but not Rocco. It just wasn't something he needed—until now, maybe. He felt his dick get hard almost immediately, and he took a hit of the jay, figuring it would relax him. After about ten minutes of kissing, Darla got up, took him by the hand, and led him to his bedroom. She undressed him, and when he was fully naked, she undressed herself slowly, dancing as if she were on the stage at Inferno. Darla was probably over fifty, thin as a rail and white as a ghost, but her small breasts were still firm and her butt tight and round. She danced in a playful and sexy way, and then, getting down on her knees, she took his penis into her mouth and started to suck and lick it. Rocco almost swooned and fell back on the bed. Darla then mounted him, and for the next several minutes, they made love in a way Rocco had never experienced before. Afterward they lay side by side, kissing and petting until they both fell asleep.

CHAPTER EIGHT

Billy Barth got home Saturday night and was still high on adrenaline. He counted and recounted the ten G's over and over again. He could not believe that besides this he had fifteen G's more coming. He started to think, Even if Rocco doesn't pay me—but I know he will—this is the best day of my life. It's like someone gave me a $10K tip for driving them. Which, in fact, that is what this was, no?

Billy showered, changed clothes, and then drove to the Seminole casino in Coconut Creek, where he went to the twenty-five-dollar blackjack table and got $1,000 in chips. He gave the pit boss his players' club card so he would get credit for playing. Most casinos had this system of tracking players and how much they played. Billy wanted to take only two grand with him, but he feared the place might get burgled and decided to take the whole $10K. He put some in each of the front pockets of his jeans and some in his wallet. The wads of cash were still bulky and made him feel like a big shot. He played about thirty minutes of conservative blackjack and lost about $150. He then went to the cashier's window, cashed in his chips, and put his "clean" money into his zippered back pocket. He went and had a steak dinner at the New York Prime restaurant and washed down his twenty-four-ounce T-bone with a couple of Coors Lights. He remembered Rocco's advice: keep a low profile, don't go overboard. But shit, he thought, I got almost ten grand and fifteen more coming next week. I'm gonna enjoy it!

After dinner Billy repeated the same routine several more times, buying $1,000 in chips, playing for about an hour, and then cashing in and going to another table. Around one o'clock, Billy had washed about $5K and felt it was time to head home. He had the number of an escort service he used whenever he had enough extra cash to pay for a hooker. It was usually $200 for the hour, but the girls, especially when Billy called, rarely stayed more than twenty minutes. Most guys who were half-shit-faced when they called had to struggle to get it up, popped their rocks in fifteen strokes, and then wanted to go to sleep. Wham, bam, thank you, ma'am.

Driving home, Billy dialed the escort service and asked if Tanya was working.

"Yes, I am, baby," she replied.

He gave his address and said he would be there by two thirty. At about two fifteen, Billy pulled into the space for his condo in a modest community called Paloma of Palm Beach Gardens unit 114B. He got out but didn't notice the black SUV parked behind his space in the visitors' parking area. Billy was still on cloud nine, as he had been ever since Rocco had handed him his ten grand and told him to come back for the balance before he hit the road to Pittsburgh. Billy planned on putting about $7K into his bank account Monday before driving to Pittsburgh, telling anyone interested that he'd had a good night at the casino. But, as Janelle had told him, no one cared unless the deposit was over $9,999. Then the bank was required by law to make a report.

Billy put his key into the lock and turned the door open. He entered and immediately felt a hand, a rather large hand, cup itself over his mouth, blocking out his scream. He tried to kick a breakaway, but a second hand came out of the darkness and hit him hard in the stomach. Doubling over, he felt dizzy and nauseous, and within thirty seconds, he started to black out. He could smell the chlorophyll on the rag held over his mouth by that rather large hand. His last thoughts were, what's happening to me?

Yuri and Ivan carried Billy's limp body to the bed and undressed him down to his shorts. While Yuri started to randomly throw his stuff around and empty his dresser to make it look like a burglary, Ivan removed a large bayonet from a sheath and stabbed Billy several times in his stomach. As the blood poured out of Billy's dying body, Yuri took all the cash from Billy's jeans. In less than five minutes, Billy's life went from bright lights at the top of the world to total darkness.

Outside of Billy's condo, a black town car pulled up. A small young black woman wearing a short miniskirt, a tank top, and a large afro wig got out, walked up to unit 114B, and gently rapped on the door.

Ivan and Yuri were still inside and stopped what they doing, which was just getting ready to leave. Yuri peeked out the window and saw the hooker. Perfect, he thought. Here is our "killer." He motioned to his partner, placing his finger over his lips.

The hooker knocked several more times and then started to bang impatiently on the door. "Hey, motherfucker, this some kinda joke? You called, I'm here, so open up or I'm outta here." After a minute she reached into her bag and dialed the guy who'd dropped her off, Deshaun Gillings, who was neither her pimp nor her boyfriend but who fancied himself to be both.

Deshaun answered on the first ring. "Waz up, baby? You done already?" he said half-jokingly.

"No, this motherfucker is either passed out or not here. Pick me the fuck up. I ain't waitin' no more."

In about two minutes, the black town car pulled up. She got in the back, and they drove off. Inside the condo, Yuri found Billy's cell phone and flipped it open. It was on vibrate, and the last call was to the same number that had just called him. In his contacts the number was listed under "PUSSY." Yuri and Ivan had their cover—not that they'd ever felt they needed one. They had been doing hits for Rudukas for over twenty years now, starting back in Russia when they were soldiers in the Red Army. They'd also killed a couple of Italian wise guys for the Ruggerios back in 1994 outside of some diner in Queens. They waited a few minutes and then, after scanning the parking lot, exited unit 114B, got in their rented car, and drove off. One down and one to go.

CHAPTER NINE

Norm Penny drove home from Rocco's condo in his Ford F-150, which was twelve years old and needed some work. A new truck was what kept Norm's thoughts cheerful and upbeat. He was going over in his mind all the neat shit he could buy with the hundred large that was in his blue duffel bag on the floor of the passenger side. Would he get a Dodge Ram or stay with Ford? Or would he give up on trucks and get a nice car like a Caddy or BMW instead? Well, if he did that, he would have to continue working.

All these thoughts went through his mind as he drove back to the house he owned in Tequesta, about a twenty five minutes north of where he worked. Lots of good thoughts were going through his mind. He had a shitload of money in the small duffel bag on the floor, he was off for a week, and he was heading over to Florida's west coast in the morning. He would tell Linda, his sometimes girlfriend, that he would be there on Tuesday. That would give him Sunday and Monday to go to the casino, get a hooker, and celebrate before meeting Linda.

"This is it with her," he said out loud. "I'm gonna tell her that it's over. I can't do this cross-state commute any longer, and truth be told, I don't want *her* to move to my side." Now, if he could only tell her that without her kicking the shit out of him, he would be OK.

Yuri and Ivan headed back to the Marriott in the Gardens, where they were staying. They got a message from Rudukas that Tommy and the goods had arrived in New York, and the painting was now in his possession. He wanted to know the status of the work he'd ordered them to do. Ivan texted back, "One down, one to go."

By the time Norm got home, it was close to midnight. His house was a small two-bedroom that he'd inherited when his mother died about seven years ago. Norm had no mortgage, but the money he made covered the taxes and utilities, with more than enough left over. Norm now had some cash, but not to put into the house. Sure, it probably needed a new roof, some updating, but fuck, he was going to enjoy living good with this money. Odds were he would probably gamble most of it away after he bought the new truck.

Norm showered, and he yelped as the hot water touched the cut where he'd caught his finger on the trunk door getting in after Rocco. Didn't I have a Band-Aid on this fucker? he wondered for a second. Then he showered, shaved, and went to bed.

Around eight o'clock, Norm got up, dressed, and threw a couple of clean pairs of underpants and socks and some other clothes into a suitcase. He couldn't use the duffel bag because it was full of his money. Maybe I'll buy some new clothes, he thought, but he knew he wouldn't. Norm wore a uniform at work. He owned two pairs of jeans, about a dozen or so T-shirts, and a couple of pairs of shorts and socks. He was not what one would have called a slave to fashion.

He packed his shit into the truck and then drove over to his favorite diner and ordered some eggs and sausage. He called Linda on the way over to the diner, telling her he would be there Tuesday around noon. She sounded about as enthusiastic about that news as someone being told she needed a root canal. As Norm drove north on US-1, he did not notice the black SUV behind him.

Inside the rented Explorer, Ivan looked at the GPS locator he held on his lap. It showed Norm's truck as a green circle. The night before, while Rocco was paying out Norm and the late Billy B., Ivan and Yuri had gone outside and placed GPS tracking devices on each of their cars. Following Billy had been easy because he only lived a few miles from Rocco. But they'd had to drive around Tequesta for about an hour to get within range of the device they'd planted in Norm's truck. They were not sure what Norm would do next, but Rudukas's instructions were to kill him and dump his body several miles from where Billy would be found so that the two cases could not be connected.

After about an hour or so, Norm left the diner, got back in his truck, and headed west toward the turnpike and interstate. He left his suitcase in the truck but took the duffel bag. The Russian hit men figured he had the money in there. They followed, trying to formulate a plan as to when and where to clip this motherfucker and get on their way back to Brooklyn. The $8,500 they'd taken from Billy B. was nice, but they knew Norm had gotten a much bigger payday.

After about an hour on back roads and checking the map in the rental, they figured he was heading across the state. Yuri remembered hearing Rocco telling these two idiots to lie low, and they knew there was a casino in the Tampa area that was owned by the same Indians as the casino Billy B. had gone to last night. After about an hour and a half of driving, Norm pulled his truck into a

Cumberland Farms gas station. He got out and pumped his own gas—then reached in, grabbed the duffel, and went inside.

"For sure that's the money in that bag," Yuri said, and Ivan nodded in agreement. They gassed up themselves, taking care to use a pump away from where Norm had topped off.

While Norm was inside the convenience store, Ivan walked by his truck and slashed his back drivers-side tire. The Russians hoped it would not go completely flat until they were well clear of the gas station.

Norm exited the building, got back into his truck, and pulled out, and they followed about one minute behind. They were on Route 60W, which led to Tampa, so they knew they could give him some space. They had driven about five minutes when they saw Norm's truck on the side of the road and Norm standing there looking at his flat rear tire. They pulled up about twenty feet behind his car, and Ivan exited the passenger side of the SUV.

At first Norm was happy someone had stopped to offer assistance. He then recognized Ivan, and in the few seconds of life he had remaining, his thoughts went from "What a coincidence!" to "*Oh shit.*" He was still wondering what was going on when the bullet Ivan fired from his nine-millimeter Glock entered Norm's head about one inch above his left eye. Norm fell back, dead before his body hit the ground.

Ivan pushed his body off the road into a small ditch adjacent to the road. Yuri, back in the rented SUV, was surprised no other vehicles drove by, but it was Sunday morning. Ivan removed Norm's wallet from his pants pocket, took his cell phone, and got into his truck. He pulled away, driving slowly on the flat tire. Yuri exited the rented SUV and, looking down at Norm, fired two rounds from his Glock into Norm's already-dead body.

"What the fuck you doing?" shouted an agitated Ivan to Yuri. "You want to make noise so cops can find us?"

"Want to make sure he's dead," replied Ivan in his thick Russian accent.

A few hundred yards up the road, Ivan pulled Norm's truck off to the side and wiped down the steering wheel. Yuri pulled up next to him. Ivan threw the duffel into the SUV and then took the registration and insurance card from the Ford's glove box and placed them inside the blue duffel bag with the phone and wallet. He then got back in the rented SUV and said to Yuri in Russian, "Let's go home."

They drove away slowly, and after about a mile, they pulled to the side and checked inside the duffel. Sure enough, there was Norm's payday. They then set their GPS for I-95 North and headed home. Mission accomplished and over $50K each richer. Yuri planned to dump Norm's stuff somewhere along the way, but after placing it in the duffel bag, he fell asleep and forgot about it.

CHAPTER TEN

By late Sunday afternoon, all of the crime-scene personnel had departed the Stockwells' residence. By now the entire 750-home community of Old Trail Village knew about the robbery at the ambassador's residence and were questioning how this could have happened, where was security, where were the police, and so on—the usual response from people who thought the entire world revolved around them. Most upset were the Stockwells, who were calling every important person in their respective contact files and demanding immediate action. The Stockwells' combined net worth was somewhere north of $150 million, so the financial loss of the theft was not as difficult to accept as the affront of this happening to them at this home, the most secure of their four residences. Besides the house in Old Trail Village, they owned an apartment in Central Park South, a small cottage in the south of France, and a ski house in Aspen. In the latter two, they had employees who lived nearby and checked on the homes regularly and prepared them for the Stockwells when they went there.

One call the ambassador made was to his personal lawyer and friend, John W. Powers, a senior partner at the law firm Powers, Booth & Anderson. JW, as his friends called him, was a powerful lawyer, a very competent litigator, and well connected in political circles. He contributed to both the Republican and Democratic Parties and as a result was only a phone call away from the most powerful people in the country. JW had recommended that the Stockwells insure their extensive art collection with Lloyd's of London, on whose board JW sat and who assured them fast response and quick results.

Jeremiah Clifford was the general counsel at Lloyd's of London and a personal friend of JW Powers. Upon hearing from JW of the crime perpetrated against one of their most important clients, Lloyd's quickly dispatched the senior investigator for the eastern United States, one Dio Bosso, retired deputy inspector of detectives from the NYPD. Bosso was in his New York apartment when he got the phone call at one o'clock on Sunday, just as he was sitting down to watch his beloved Giants take on the Washington Redskins. At 4:40 he was on a flight from JFK to West Palm Beach.

He booked himself a room at the Marriott in Palm Beach Gardens (the same hotel where the Russians had stayed) and started to make calls. His first call was to Clifford to let him know he was in Florida and would start his investigation immediately. Then he called his administrative assistant, Ann Thompson, and instructed her to find out all she could about the ambassador and his wife, the stolen artwork, and anything else that might help him. Thompson knew what to do; she had been with him at Lloyd's since she'd retired as a senior police administrative aide at the NYPD. She had worked for Bosso when he was in charge of the Major Case Squad, and when he made Deputy Inspector he was able to get her a promotion too.

Next, he called his go-to guy, Joe Pollicino. Joe P. was a retired first-grade detective who'd worked with Bosso going back over twenty years and now worked for Dio at Lloyds. He gave Joe a run-down on what he knew and told him to get him the names of all the law enforcement and security players he would need to contact and speak with over the next few days. He told Joe to get on an early flight to West Palm Beach in the morning. He then did what he always did before starting an investigation: he got a yellow legal pad and started to write down the steps he needed to take to make sure everything was done correctly.

PART FIVE

Dio Bosso, 2002–2010

CHAPTER ONE

A few years ago, Bosso, who had been a cop a long time, had had no plans of retiring. He knew how the NYPD worked, and with his reputation and connections in the department, he would surely make it to at least full inspector, maybe even chief. In the NYPD every promotion—from police officer to sergeant, lieutenant, and captain—was based on a competitive civil-service test. After that, the positions of deputy inspector, inspector, deputy chief, assistant chief, and beyond were by appointment by the police commissioner. Bosso had made captain in 1995 and had been appointed to the rank of deputy inspector by Police Commissioner Mike Widman in 2002 but, in a rare move, had been allowed to keep his command of the Major Case Squad. Widman had not wanted to make any changes that would upset the post–9-11 changes that were finally seeing results against international terrorism. Six months later he'd offered Bosso another promotion, to inspector. Widman told Dio he would have to go back to patrol in uniform, as he needed to fill several slots in that division. There were not many openings above DI in the Detective Division at that time. Bosso thought he would wait and bide his time. He was fifty-five, not that young for a deputy inspector, but he was widowed, with a married son and no real hobbies. "No, thanks," he said. "I'll stay here."

About a year after that, he got promoted to deputy inspector, and when he was still in command of the Major Case Squad, two of his detectives were murdered while transporting a prisoner to central booking. The prisoner, one Javier Lopez, had been locked up by a uniformed cop for the armed robbery of a bodega. Good arrest for the cop, but a series of mistakes by the young officer and a bad decision by Bosso had cost two detectives their lives.

The arresting officer, a rookie cop named Bill Gray, had been processing his prisoner in the Major Case Squad room because the processing room at One Police Plaza was being painted. He'd been completing his paperwork when he accidentally slipped while escorting the prisoner to the men's room and got a nasty gash on his head. Fortunately, Gray's partner was also on the escort, so Lopez just took his leak and said to himself, "Fuck that cop."

Bosso heard the commotion and came out of his office and asked what was going on. "The kid slipped on the bathroom floor," said Detective Alison. "Looks like he cut his cruller open."

"Call an ambulance. Get him over to Saint Vincent's and have that checked out," said Bosso.

"No, I'm OK," said Gray, but he stopped his protest when Bosso gave him the long stare. Most detectives knew the stare. If Bosso wanted to get a point across or reprimand a slight, he would just stare at the offending party without saying a word, glaring over his reading glasses and giving the individual a chance to realize the futility of a debate. Young Rookie Gray was not aware of this, but he knew that Bosso was fair and that he was the boss.

"Aren't you and DeAngelo going to court?" Bosso asked.

"Yeah," replied Alison

"OK. When the bus comes, get the kid in, and you guys can drop the perp off at central booking."

Alison and his partner, Len DeAngelo, got Lopez from the holding cell, cuffed him, and marched him out of the station house. They placed him in the back seat of the squad car, and off they went to central booking, about a ten-minute ride from the Major Case office on the tenth floor of One PP.

Alison and DeAngelo were discussing where they would go to eat after they finished lodging Lopez and meeting with an ADA on a case they were about to wrap up. When Gray, who was on foot patrol, heard the robbery-in-progress call over his police radio, he was two blocks away and responded. He practically ran into Lopez running away from the scene. When Gray, service weapon in hand, ordered Lopez to freeze, he did so, dropping the nine-millimeter used in the bodega robbery to the pavement. Gray spread-eagled him on the ground and rear cuffed him. Making a classic rookie mistake, he did not search Lopez. He assumed the gun he'd picked up from the ground was the only one Lopez had. Unbeknownst to Gray, Lopez, who had several outstanding warrants both in New York and in Puerto Rico, had a small two-shot derringer stashed in his crotch. While the detectives were discussing dinner, Lopez removed the weapon from his crotch. The sound of gunfire rang in Len DeAngelo's ear and in the split second as he turned around and saw his partner's head explode, he was also shot. The bullet from the derringer entered the left side of his neck near the carotid artery. The car, which was still moving, struck a vehicle in front of it and came to a stop.

Pedestrians, hearing the shots, started to run—nowhere in particular, just the normal panicked stampeding people did when they heard gunfire. No one bothered to try to stop Lopez, who reached over the front seat and removed DeAngelo's nine-millimeter Sig Sauer from its holster and took the car keys, noticing a handcuff key on the ring. Lopez, now one hand free of the handcuffs, ran from the unmarked vehicle into the crowded streets of lower Manhattan, carrying DeAngelo's nine-millimeter. Pedestrians got out of his way as he ran toward the nearest subway.

Back at the shooting scene, people started to gather around the unmarked car and looked on in shock and amazement at the two detectives. DeAngelo was still alive and was able to call a ten-thirteen (officer needs assistance), shots fired, into the portable. Within seconds sirens could be heard approaching. Transit Officer Diane Budion was on patrol at the Lafayette Street station of the D train when she heard the ten-thirteen call from central dispatch. As she went to the exit stairs, she noticed a male figure running down the stairs toward her. He stopped when he saw her. In an instant she drew her own Sig Sauer nine-millimeter service weapon.

"Police! Freeze!" she commanded.

Lopez, out of breath, stopped short and raised DeAngelo's nine-millimeter toward the uniformed female. He was about fifteen feet from Budion, and civilians around him started to scatter. Budion fired three quick rounds. The first two caught Lopez in his chest and the third in his right arm as he fell dead to the ground. Budion, a three-year veteran of the force, had never fired her weapon in the line of duty before, and in fact she was only working patrol this day on an overtime tour. Her normal assignment was crime analyst in the personnel bureau of the Transit Division.

After Lopez fell, she screamed into her radio. "Ten-thirteen, ten thirteen! Lafayette D train station, shots fired!" Several of the patrol cars responding to the scene of the first ten-thirteen were redirected to respond to Lafayette.

CHAPTER TWO

The aftermath of this event was not pretty. Two detectives murdered by a prisoner being transported to central booking—how could this have happened? Who was at fault? In the NYPD such incidents demanded someone take the hit for it. After a postincident investigation, it was determined that the arresting officer, probationary police officer Michael Gray, was the most negligent for not properly searching Lopez. He was allowed to resign rather than be dismissed for negligence. The murdered detectives could have been faulted for not searching Lopez before placing him in their vehicle and for not rear cuffing him as procedures dictated. But that was not going to happen. DI Bosso, who'd directed the detectives to take Lopez to court, took the brunt of the fallout. He knew his career was over, and any chance of further advancement within the department was now out the window. While he was not charged with any wrongdoing, he knew department politics, and he knew that he would be transferred to an administrative assignment, probably in the patrol bureau.

Once the investigation was completed, Bosso met with his immediate supervisor, Inspector Bruce Ross, and the chief of detectives, Dennis Ryan. At that meeting Bosso was told there would be no charges, but he would lose his command and be reassigned to the Patrol Division. He went from that meeting to the pension section, where he "put in his papers"—cop speak for retirement.

CHAPTER THREE

B osso was greatly disappointed by his sudden fall from grace within his beloved NYPD. After it became public knowledge that he planned to retire, he was summoned to Chief Ryan's office at One Police Plaza.

"Dio," Chief Ryan said, "why not wait this out? You and I both know this will pass. So you do a year or so back in patrol. Then, if I'm still here—and I see no reason why I won't be—I'll reassign you to the detective bureau."

"I don't know, Chief. Twenty-five years is about all I wanted to do when I got sworn in. So maybe it's time."

Bosso did retire then. He took about a month off, and he and his wife, Celia, traveled to Europe, first to Italy and then to Spain, France, and England. It was their first time out of the country to-gether. Their only child, David, had married and lived and worked in Seattle for United Technology. Shortly after their return from Europe, Celia was diagnosed with pancreatic cancer. Within six months she was gone. Dio was brokenhearted. First, he'd lost the job he passionately loved, and then he'd lost his beloved Celia.

After the funeral, which many of his former colleagues attended, Chief Ryan introduced him to Jeremiah Clifford, the general counsel for Lloyd's of London. Clifford offered his condolences and said, "I know this may come across as insensitive, but I asked the chief here if I could meet you, as I'm leaving for London tomorrow. Lloyd's is looking for someone like you to head up our US investigative division. I don't expect an answer now, and once again, please forgive me for bringing this up at this time. But our current chief investigator died suddenly, and my chairman has tasked me with finding the right replacement. The chief here is an old friend, and he recommended I speak to you. I've done my due diligence, and I believe you are the right man for the job. I'll leave you now to your family, but please contact me as soon as you feel we can discuss this further."

After Celia's funeral, Dio contacted Clifford in his London office. He said he would take the job, provided that he be able to keep a New York City office and hire his own staff. He knew he would need to spend time at Lloyd's HQ in London, and in fact he spent his first six months there, acclimating himself to the company's policies and operations. He was amazed to learn the amount of wealth that some Europeans had and how much money they spent on insuring their assets.

By the time Dio Bosso arrived in Florida, he had received via e-mail all the information he needed about what had occurred at the Stockwells' residence, as well as the names of all the key players he would need to meet, interview, or work with. He never doubted Ann Thompson's ability as an administrative assistant. Although in her midfifties, she still took computer classes to keep her current with the latest technological developments. This skill was something Dio depended on her for, as he was still somewhat uncomfortable within the ever-changing digital world.

Dio always traveled with the same old black attaché case he'd had since his days on patrol. It was a gift from his beloved Celia.

Only now, instead of arrest reports and other police forms, the case held his laptop, a supply of plastic gloves, plastic baggies, a magnifying glass, several pairs of tweezers, pens, legal pads, and USB chargers and cords for his cell phone and computer.

CHAPTER FOUR

On Monday, two days after the heist, Mal Thomas arrived at AAA Limo Service at 7:30 a.m., his usual time. He was surprised to see Billy Barth's Ford Focus in the spot where Billy normally parked his assigned town car, number twenty-six. As he walked into the office, he shouted at Heather Winters, dispatcher and office manager at AAA Limo, "Where the hell is twenty-six? And why hasn't that idiot Barth brought her back yet? It's scheduled to go out with Glenn later."

"I know, boss. I saw his car there. Don't worry, I already called Billy. He probably got home late and—"

"He should have brought it back yesterday. Call him again."

She did and once again got his voice mail. She left a second message.

CHAPTER FIVE

D io got up around six, showered, shaved, and dressed in slacks, shirt, tie, and (yes, even in Florida) a sport coat and went down to eat some breakfast. As he sat eating his scrambled eggs and sausage, he went over the notes he'd made the night before. On a separate sheet of paper, he wrote down the mini bios Joe P. had given him on the police and security personnel he would need to interact with. Ann had furnished him with bios on Ambassador Paul Stockwell and his wife, Teresa. His first stop would be to their home, the scene of the crime.

He telephoned the Stockwells, and Mrs. Stockwell answered on the third ring. Dio introduced himself and inquired when might be the best time to come by and speak to them. Mrs. Stockwell said they both would be home all day. The ambassador, she said, had important phone calls to make, and she would not be going to her Monday book-club meeting.

"Great," Dio said. "I assume I'll need access to your residence, and I also want the detective assigned to work with us on this." (He did not want to refer to the burglary as "your case.") "I will reach out to the Palm Beach Gardens PD and let you know what time we will be there."

Dio then called the number Joe P. had given him for Det. Sam Daniels. To be sure, Dio always felt a little anxious when calling on local law enforcement on a case. It was different when he was in the NYPD, but now he feared that the detective on the other end of the phone would be thinking, What the fuck does this civilian know about how to handle my case? Dio knew that was how he and most of his fellow detectives had felt about outside or private investigators. If he were doing a case in New York City, making that call would have been no problem. Still respected by almost everyone in that agency, he'd have had no problem picking up the phone. Here it would be different, if the locals thought like him. Anyway, he dialed Daniels, and after a brief introduction, he asked if Daniels would be available to meet with him later that day at the Stockwells' residence. Surprisingly, Daniels did him one better.

"Why not stop over here at my office? We can go over what we've got, and then we can visit the scene together, if you don't mind. My department ride is in the shop for routine maintenance."

"Er, sure," Dio said, surprised at how friendly Daniels seemed.

What Dio did not know was that Daniels had gotten a heads-up from Chief Pellitiere that he would be getting a call from the ambassador's insurance company and had better cooperate 100 percent. "Plus," Pellitiere had added, "the guy they're sending down is a retired NYPD deputy inspector. He ran the Major Case Squad, and my sources tell me he is not only an excellent investigator, but he's also a good guy."

"No problem, Chief," Daniels had replied. "I'll treat him with kid gloves."

Pellitiere hadn't said anything, just hung up.

CHAPTER SIX

B y eight o'clock, Ted Glenn was getting ready to leave his house, when he got a call from Heather at AAA. "Ted, Mal wants you to swing by Billy's condo and see why he hasn't brought back twenty-six. He starts on vacation today, so I'm thinking he's gonna drop it off and change cars on his way to Pittsburgh, but Mal is getting more pissed by the minute. So stop by and, if necessary, leave your car there, use your key, and take twenty-six. Your first job is a pickup on the island at nine a.m. for an airport drop-off."

"OK, babe," Ted replied. Heather was one of those unliberated types of women you could still call babe or hon or sugar without her filing a sexual-harassment lawsuit. Plus, at about fifty pounds overweight, a single mom with two teenagers and three dogs, she was not offended by such terms of endearment. As Ted pulled into Billy condo complex, the first thing he saw was car twenty-six parked in spot 114B, Billy's. He parked his car in the visitors' spot, walked to twenty-six, and peered in. It looked OK. Then he went to Billy's front door and knocked.

"Hey, Billy, open up. It's me, Ted." There was no answer, so Ted figured Billy had probably tied a big one on and was sleeping it off. He dialed Billy's cell phone, and it went right to voice mail.

Ted waited a few minutes. Then, looking at his watch, he said to himself, I'd better get going if I want to be early for that 9:00 a.m. Using his key, he opened twenty-six and backed it out, then put his car in spot 114B, got back in twenty-six, and drove away. Had Ted tried to open the door to Billy's condo, he would have found it unlocked, and soon he would have found his friend's lifeless body on the bed. He would also not have made his nine o'clock pickup. Ted called Heather and reported that Billy was not answering his door or phone, but he had twenty-six and was on his way to the island for his pickup.

CHAPTER SEVEN

After breakfast Dio got into his rented Chevy Impala and drove over to the Palm Beach Gardens PD office on PGA Boulevard. The building was attached to the PBG Fire Department and Rescue Company. He parked in the visitors' section and walked into the main lobby, where he was greeted by an attractive female officer.

"Good morning, may I help you?"

"Yes," responded Dio. "My name is Bosso. Detective Daniels is expecting me."

"Oh, yes, Mr. Bosso. Please, right this way."

He followed her through a door that she accessed with her ID badge. Bosso looked at her butt, but he did not think anything more than that it was nice. He had lost any interest in women or sex since Celia had passed almost three years ago.

Sam Daniels greeted Bosso with an outstretched hand and a big toothy grin. He was a big man, probably six four, and his frame was much wider than Dio's lean six-one build. "Well, sir, it's nice to meet you. Let's go and sit in one of the interview rooms. It will be more private."

Dio looked around and saw only one other person in the squad room, but he said, "Sure."

"Want some coffee or a soda or something?" Daniels said.

"No, thanks, I'm good."

"So, what have we got so far?" said Daniels. It wasn't really a question, but he was asking it as an intro to Bosso. They went over the early report submitted by the responding officer, as well as the initial crime-scene report. They even had the report that Security Officer Ramirez had submitted to his employer. Yes, the PBGPD and Old Trail security were deep into the digital age.

Bosso was impressed at how efficient this all seemed. Now, he thought, if they can actually do some real police work, we'll be fine. Daniels then gave Dio a history of the Gardens, as the locals referred to this city within Palm Beach County. Dio listened, but he was not really interested in the history lesson. When they got to the main gate of Old Trail Village, SO Ramirez was on duty. He waved Daniels through, but Daniels stopped and introduced Dio Bosso. He said that Bosso would need unfettered access, just like Daniels had. Ramirez said he just needed to see Bosso's ID and put him in their system. Once that was done, they proceeded to 810 Turtle Bay Drive. Three years ago, Bosso would have been impressed with the homes here, but after joining Lloyd's and conducting security surveys on the homes and palaces of some of the world's wealthiest people, he was not fazed. Yeah, they were real swanky places. But for Bosso, who'd grown up in an apartment with his immigrant parents, older brothers, and a maiden aunt, plus the occasional "cousin" from Italy, any place with a lawn was upscale.

At the house they were greeted cordially by Mrs. Stockwell. Once the intros were completed, she excused herself and went back out toward the pool area. The first thing Dio wanted to see was where the stolen painting had hung and the location of the alarm keypad. Daniels informed him that Old Trail Village Security was in the process of checking all of its tapes for the entire day of the crime. He has been in contact with Chief Pettway and would introduce Bosso to him after they were done here. Bosso only half heard what he was saying, and he was getting the feeling that Daniels talked an awful lot, sometimes saying nothing. As Daniels went on, Bosso walked around the house, looking for something—he did not know what—but something. He once again asked Daniels, "No signs of forced entry?"

"Nope, I had Crime Scene go over this place twice. No prints either. We printed the Stockwells for elimination purposes." He dropped his voice. "My guess is these folks forgot to put the alarm on when they left."

"And then what?" asked Bosso. "Someone just walked on by, tried the door, and took the Chagall?" He gave Daniels the stare, but Daniels, seeming to realize that what he'd said sounded dumb, just shrugged. Bosso pointed to the alarm box by the front door. "Is this the only keypad?"

"No," said Daniels. "There is one by the back-patio door. Come, I'll show you."

They went to the back door, and Bosso went outside and started to look around. He bent down and rubbed his finger over what appeared to be some sand on the paved patio floor just below the glass door.

"Be careful. That sand could be from a fire ant colony," said Daniels. "Those fuckers sting like hell."

"It's not sand," said Bosso. "It's glass." He reached into his attaché case and removed a magnifying glass, the kind used by Sherlock Holmes. He studied each door pane with the magnifier. "Here's your point of entry." He pointed to the fourth frame from the top, just parallel to the alarm panel inside. He then took a digital camera from the case and took several photos, first of the glass debris on the floor and then of the panel itself. The naked eye could not see the ten-inch circle cut in the glass, but with the aid of the magnifying glass, it became quite clear that this was how the burglar had gained access.

Bosso then used his trusty Swiss Army knife to scoop up bits of glass and place them in a baggie. "Here," he said to Daniels. "Can you have your lab people analyze this? I want to be sure it's glass."

"Sure, no problem," replied a somewhat-dumbfounded Daniels.

"So here is how the perps got into the house. Now we need to find out how they got onto the property."

They continued surveying the house and grounds. In the front of the house, just to the right of the driveway, Bosso noticed a few shrubs that seemed to be pushed a bit to the side, as if someone had squatted there. There were several impressions in the soft turf but no footprints He took some photos of the area and measured the length and width of the impressions but said nothing to Daniels. He assumed the impressions in the turf had been caused by shoes or boots covered with some sort of protective cover similar to the booties a worker would don to avoid tracking mud or dirt into a home. Bosso also observed that two of the impressions were larger and deeper, indicating that (a) more than one person was here, and (b) one was a much bigger person, judging by the length and depth of the impression.

After they completed the survey, Bosso told Daniels to go see if Mrs. Stockwell was available to talk to them. He purposely said "them," not wanting to further embarrass Daniels. Since the glass door discovery, Daniels had remained silent. It was obvious to Bosso that he had achieved his goal of getting Daniels to realize that this was not his investigation, and from here on in, Daniels's role would be that of a Gardens PD liaison. But Daniels would get the credit should the case be solved.

CHAPTER EIGHT

Ted Glenn's airport run was over by ten o'clock. Mal instructed him to come back to HQ, drop off twenty-six, and take Billy's car back to his condo. Mal figured that maybe Billy had decided to fly to Pittsburgh and forgotten to change up the cars. After all, Billy was, in Mal's eyes, a fucking moron.

Ted dropped off twenty-six and took Billy's spare keys (all AAA drivers had to leave a set of their keys in the office so cars could be jockeyed around as spaces were needed). When Ted pulled into Billy's condo complex, he noticed two of Billy's neighbors walking their dogs. They were almost in front of Billy's when Ted got there.

"Hey, folks, good morning," he said. "I work with Billy, and I'm trying to reach him. Did either of you see him this morning?"

"No, I haven't, but that's his car right there in his spot," the male dog walker said.

I know, you fucking idiot, thought Glenn. "Yeah, I just parked it there."

"Oh. Er, no I haven't seen him, have you, Lucy?"

"No, I haven't," said the other dog walker.

"OK, thanks."

Ted walked up to Billy's door. After banging on it, he decided to turn the knob. "Shit, it's open," he said aloud.

CHAPTER NINE

Dio drove Daniels back to the cop shop on PGA. Daniels tried to pick Dio's brain to see what he thought about the burglary.

"Looks the perps got in through the glass door and disarmed the alarm system. But how did they get on the property?"

"It does seem that way." Dio was not sure how much he wanted to tell Daniels, but then he thought, Maybe I should not be such a dick with this guy. He seems OK. Maybe not the sharpest, but we are on the same side, if not on the same team.

Daniels went on while Dio was in thought, not paying attention. As they drove to the gate, Dio stopped and waved Ramirez out. "Officer, do me a favor," Dio said. "Could you pull all of the tapes from Friday afternoon—say around four p.m. through this Sunday?"

Ramirez looked at Daniels. "I don't know. I have to check with Mr. Pettway to get—"

"Just do as this gentleman asked," Daniels said. "I'll talk to Pettway." He used the chief's last name to set a tone with Ramirez. He also wanted to show Bosso that he had juice in spite of Bosso making an ass out of him, or so he figured.

Bosso, on the other hand, knew he was a better investigator than most. Shit, he'd been doing this stuff for over thirty years. He thought about saying something to Daniels to soothe his bruised ego, but then he said to himself, Nah, fuck 'im.

CHAPTER TEN

When Ted Glenn opened the door to Billy's pad, he was first taken by the mess the place was in—lamps turned over, drawers left open and ransacked.

"Billy? Billy, you here?"

Glenn walked down the hall to Billy's bedroom. Through the half-open door, he could see Billy's right leg hanging over the bed. He knew that something was wrong. He pushed the door open slightly. Then he saw all the blood on the sheets and the cold dead body of his friend Billy Barth. He ran out the door, yelling to the dog walkers, who were still in conversation, "Call 911! I think Billy's dead."

"What?" said Lucy. "What?"

"Just call!"

Ted ran back toward the condo and then figured he'd better wait for the cops.

Although Billy B lived in Palm Beach Gardens, his condo complex was part of unincorporated Palm Beach County, therefore the investigation of Billy's homicide would by conducted by Palm Beach County Sheriff's Office. The PBSO was the premier law enforcement agency in southeast Florida, with over 2,400 sworn officers and 1,500 civilian employees. They were well paid, well trained, well equipped, and well managed. The sheriff was elected to a three-year term, and the current sheriff, Rick Romaine, was a seasoned thirty-year veteran of law enforcement. He'd started out his career in his hometown of Baton Rouge, Louisiana but joined PBC after he and his wife moved to her native Wellington, Florida. He was one of the few officers who'd transferred directly into PBSO without first doing a stint in some local department. Back then the powers that be had known they had a winner in Romaine. He was a good deputy, made rank fast, earned his bachelor's and master's degrees at night, and had the good looks and political savvy to get to where he was today. The first officer on the scene was Deputy Jay Shelley, a five-year veteran. He was met by Glenn and the dog walkers, and he could see Glenn was visibly shaken. Shelley calmed him down enough to get him to relate what he knew. He then radioed for backup, ambulance, and a patrol supervisor. He figured he would need the detectives and the Crime Scene people, but that was not his call. Only the patrol sergeant could make those calls.

He went up the walkway to condo 114B, putting on the rubber gloves that all deputies carried in today's post-AIDS world. Entering the house, he made mental observations of what he saw and then drew his service weapon and went to the bedroom where the witness told him he'd found the body. Although Shelley assumed that the perp was no longer on the scene, he had to proceed as trained. Once he confirmed that, he went back outside to secure the crime scene.

Just then he saw his patrol supervisor, Sgt. Gary Baxter, arrive, followed shortly by PBC fire and rescue. These "rubber men" love coming out to a job, whether they are needed or not, Shelley thought. He briefed Baxter, and they both entered the condo.

Shelley did the talking, telling Baxter what he knew. When they got to the bedroom, Baxter went in to get a better look at the stiff.

"OK, Jay, go out and get statements from the limo driver and the two neighbors. Let's try to get some positive shit for the detectives when they get here, OK?"

Shelley didn't know if Sergeant Baxter was trying to comment on his performance, but he blew it off. "Sure thing, Sarge," he said, and out he went.

Baxter moved closer to the body and gently touched the forehead to get an idea of how long the man had been dead. The body was stone cold. Baxter then exited the condo and told the fire-and-rescue guys they would not be needed. He didn't bother telling them why. He radioed dispatch, relating what he had and requesting Homicide, Crime Scene, and the medical examiner. He then instructed Shelley to place yellow crime-scene tape around the entire perimeter of unit 114B.

CHAPTER ELEVEN

When the call came in on the Billy Barth homicide, Det. Lydia Martinez was the next up. She and her supervisor, Sgt. Chris Clarkson, responded to the scene. Martinez was a seasoned eighteen-year veteran of the PBSO. Hired when the sheriff's office needed to hire more minorities, she'd proven not to be a token hire. Raised by parents who'd fled Castro's Cuba in the '60s, she'd been born in Miami and been raised in the Old World Spanish way. Her father had been a prominent banker in Cuba before the revolution. Both he and his wife had been educated in private Catholic schools in Cuba, and when they arrived in America, they'd seen to it that their three children, two boys and a girl, went to private Catholic schools as well. They could afford this because her father had been able to leave Cuba with most of the money he had made, plus what his parents left him.

Lydia, his last child, had come late in his life and was the only one born an American citizen, unlike her siblings, who'd been born in Cuba. As a young girl, Lydia had been a good a student but found it hard to fit in with the other girls in her classes. More

146

of a tomboy, she'd played both volleyball and basketball and been a member of the swim team. Early on she'd expressed an interest in the military and law enforcement. She'd attended the University of Miami and joined their ROTC program.

Upon graduation she was commissioned a 2LT in the US Army. In 1990, at the age of twenty-two, she was the XO of a squad of military police stationed in Kuwait during Operation Desert Storm. She'd been thinking about a career in the army, when her mother passed away from a major heart attack, and only one month later, her father was seriously injured in an auto accident. Returning home on leave in 1991, she heard that the PBSO was looking to hire minorities to show that it was not a predominately white-male agency (which in fact it was). She applied and scored in the top 5 percent on the written, physical, and medical exams. Her military background and being bilingual added points to her position on the list for appointment. Once she'd fulfilled her military obligation, successfully completed the mandatory Florida police academy training, and passed the background check, she was appointed to the next class. She was discharged from active duty in December 1992; she still had a four-year reserve commitment but was able to get into the next six-month police-academy class. She graduated fourth in the class of two hundred and was the top female. She was immediately hired by the PBSO, and after only two years on road patrol, she was assigned to the Detective Division, first to a gang task force and then to a two-year stint in sex crimes, and then finally ended up in the Homicide Division.

In each assignment, Martinez received training in the area where she was assigned. Many of those training programs were conducted by the FBI or other federal agency. It was during these seminars that she became friends with many other female police officers from all over the country and of all ranks. After corresponding with these colleagues, she, along with two other detectives, one from the NYPD and one from the LAPD, formed a national fraternal organization named Women in Policing. The organization now boasted 7,500 members, and Martinez was its national vice president.

As an army reserve officer, she'd been assigned to a military police command and was deployed twice in a three-year span, once to Afghanistan and once to Iraq. She was now a captain and commanding officer of her reserve unit. Martinez had never married and had little time for relationships, but she did date on occasion. At forty-two, she was still attractive, with dark, piercing eyes, thick, curly black hair, and a shapely figure, which she maintained by working out at the PBSO gym whenever she could.

When she arrived on the scene, Detective Martinez got a briefing from Sergeant Baxter, who pointed out Glenn as the one who'd discovered the body.

"Who are the other two?" she asked.

"Neighbors. I had my uniform take their info and a brief statement."

"Good," she said. "Keep him here to keep lookie-loos away. And I'm sure the media will be here momentarily, and I don't want them anywhere near the scene."

Technically Baxter outranked her, and some might have been rubbed the wrong way by Martinez's bossy way of saying things. But Baxter was smart enough to realize that she was doing her job, just as he would do his. He also knew Martinez was a very capable investigator. Like most other males that came into contact with Martinez, he fantasized about what she would be like in bed. Martinez donned plastic gloves and entered the condo. As she was heading in, the crime-scene unit arrived at the complex. Martinez surveyed the living room. At first, she suspected it might have been a burglary gone bad, but when she went to the bedroom and saw how savagely Billy had been killed, she ruled that out. Most burglars were nonviolent and rarely broke into an occupied dwelling. She rolled the body over and noticed about six or seven stab wounds on the victim's torso. As she bent down near his face, she could smell something mint-like coming from his mouth, but she could not place it. She then searched the pockets of a pair of jeans she saw thrown on the floor. She retrieved his wallet and opened it up to reveal a Florida driver's license bearing the name David W. Barth, DOB 8/3/68. She looked under the bed and found a flip phone. She opened it and saw that it was not locked. There were several incoming calls, two from a local 561 exchange, the next four from an 800 number, and one from a 561 exchange at 2:35 a.m. There was an outgoing call to that same number at 1:30 a.m. She would keep the phone and run all the numbers for as far back as she deemed necessary.

Crime Scene entered, and Martinez instructed the techs to photograph and dust the living room, first printing the body to eliminate his own prints. She estimated the victim had been dead about eight to ten hours, judging by the body temperature and the lividity of the wounds. She also instructed the crime-scene detectives to swab the victim's mouth to determine the source of the minty smell she'd detected. The medical examiner could pinpoint that more correctly.

She returned outside. Looking around, she did not see a camera on any of the buildings or street lamps. Then the meat wagon from the ME's office pulled up. Martinez instructed the attendant to have the ME on duty notify her when he did the cut—cop talk for an autopsy.

Martinez summoned Sergeant Baxter to bring the guy who'd found the body back to the front of the house. Ted Glenn was telling the sergeant that he had to get back to work; he had a pickup at the airport at two o'clock and—

Martinez cut him off. "Call your dispatcher, and tell them you're gonna be here awhile. Then I want you to come with me to my office." She pointed to her unmarked police car. He tried to protest, but Sergeant Baxter told him to clam it.

"Do you want us to find out who did this to your friend?" Baxter asked.

"Well, yeah, I guess so, but I—"

"Listen," Martinez said. "What's your name again?"

"Glenn, Ted Glenn."

"OK, Mr. Glenn, let's you and I get into my vehicle, and I'll try to get you out of here shortly."

Reluctantly he complied and walked behind her to her sedan. She opened the passenger door for him and motioned for him to get inside.

"So, let's start by you telling me how well you know David."

"Who?" He stopped himself. "Er, well, first of all, we never called him David. He was known as Billy—Billy B. to all of his friends and coworkers. He worked for AAA for about seven years and was one of the top drivers, meaning he always got the primo assignments. He had several regulars who asked for him."

Martinez asked if they socialized—"You know, went out for beers."

"Oh, no," Glenn replied. Glenn was married with a couple of kids. "And Billy liked to, you know, go to the dogs—the kennel club—and the casinos, and he liked to bet on games."

Martinez inquired if it was unusual for Ted to check on him, but he did not understand the question. She put it another way. "Why were you here today, Mr. Glenn?"

"Oh. Well, Billy started vacation today—" He stopped himself. "Oops, sorry, I didn't mean it that way."

"Yeah, I know, go on," she said.

"Well, he finished up Saturday night and was supposed to bring number twenty-six—er, that's his car—back to the office. When it wasn't there, and his car still was; Mal, the owner, had me drive over here and make the switch."

After some more routine questioning, Martinez thanked Ted Glenn for his help and told him that she might want to talk to him again. "Oh, by the way," she said. "Did Billy have a girlfriend or any family here in Florida?"

"Girlfriend? I don't think so. He hung out in that topless place a lot—you know, Club Inferno over on Congress. Mal would know more about his family than I do."

She gave him her card with the usual instructions to call her any time of the day or night if he thought of anything else. "And make sure you give Sergeant Baxter your contact info," she added.

"I already did that," he said.

"Thank you. By the way, Mr. Glenn, do you know if David—I mean Billy—was going anywhere on his vacation?"

He had to think a minute. "Yeah, I think Mal told me he was going to Pittsburgh. That's where he is from."

"OK." She would need to interview this Mal guy and then call the Pittsburgh PD to make a notification to Barth's next of kin.

While Martinez was interviewing Glenn, the crime-scene team finished up, and the ME's crew put the body into a body bag and carted it away in the meat wagon. Martinez then left the crime scene and decided to visit Barth's employer AAA Limo before heading back to the Homicide office at PBSO HQ on Gun Club Road. While in her vehicle she dialed the last number Barth had called at 1:30 a.m., the same number that had called him at 2:30 a.m.

The call went to voice mail after two rings. A female voice said, "Hi, baby, you've reached Tanya. Leave a message." The speaker sounded young and black, and her voice had a sexy tone to it. Martinez figured Tanya was a "lady of the evening," as she liked to refer to hookers. People like David W. Barth used these services a lot. Martinez was just hoping that this was not why he was murdered. Then again, it would make her job of clearing the case much easier. Now she had to ID and locate "Tanya." When she arrived at

AAA Limo headquarters she interviewed owner Mal Thomas and dispatcher Heather Winters who could not add anything to what Ted Glenn had told her about the late David W. Barth.

Back at homicide office Martinez typed a few reports and then briefed her supervisor, Sgt. Bobby Dixon, on what she had. Dixon was a short, muscular, ex-marine. He was the only African American in the Homicide Squad he was all cop and all cops were one color—blue. His police career had started in the former Belle Glade Police Department, a small, understaffed, and underfunded agency that was eventually absorbed into the PBSO. As a young officer still on probation, on foot patrol in Belle Glade, Dixon had been approached by a woman who told him that her drunken husband had beaten her and chased her out of their house. The woman looked to be about fifty but was probably a lot younger. Dixon could see she had a swollen right check and a bruise under her left eye.

"I'll call an ambulance," he said. "You should have that eye checked out."

"No, I don't want no ambulance. I just want you to take that motherfuckin' husband of mine to jail!"

"OK, ma'am. Where is he now?"

"He be in that bar there," she said, pointing to Rickey's, the local gin joint on Main Street. Dixon called for backup, but like everything else in Belle Glade, portable radio service was bad. As he walked with her toward the bar, a rather large black man came out and started yelling at them.

"Bitch, I told you not to call the fucking cops! Now you're really gonna get an ass whuppin'."

They argued back and forth as Dixon tried to keep them apart, still trying to call for assistance. Now half the bar had emptied out into the street, and the situation was starting to get a bit dicey. People were screaming at Dixon, some taking the woman's side, some just hoping to see some action. Dixon tried to get the crowd back into the bar and to ask the bartender, a guy named Jake, to call 911.

When he heard that, the husband, who was later ID'd as Charles Watts, became more enraged and turned his anger from his wife, Debra, toward Dixon. As he charged at him, Dixon drew his nightstick rather than his weapon, a move he would regret initially but that over time he came to realize was the best decision he could have made. He and Watts got into a struggle, with Watts trying to grab for Dixon's weapon. Dixon was able to apply a choke hold with his nightstick on the much bigger, somewhat stronger man. As they struggled, Debra Watts had a change of heart and started yelling at Dixon to let her husband go. She came around behind Dixon and jumped on his back, trying to pull him off her husband. As she did so, Dixon's nightstick was pushed harder into poor Charley's throat and crushed his windpipe. He died within minutes. Dixon was eventually exonerated by both the Belle Glade PD and the Palm Beach County State Attorney's Office. A short time later, Belle Glade was absorbed into the PBSO. The good news for Dixon was that he now had a job in a much larger, better equipped, and better paid police department. The bad news was everybody in the PBSO referred to him as "the Belle Glade Strangler."

CHAPTER TWELVE

Back at the Homicide office, Martinez started to do the part of her job she liked the least: paperwork. She had to obtain case numbers from crime scene and the ME and had to notify the state attorney's office. She knew most of the ASAs who worked Homicide, and she knew that if she presented her case to them in a professional, by-the-book fashion, they in turn would present a winnable prosecution to a judge and jury. She then had to map out a strategy of what her next steps would be and sit with Dixon and Lt. Frank Pooley, both of whom were good detectives, good supervisors, and most of all who did not interfere with her methods.

CHAPTER THIRTEEN

After dropping off Detective Daniels at his office, Dio returned to Old Trail Village to start reviewing the tapes. Chief Pettway was there waiting for him and introduced himself to Dio. He did not tell the security chief what he'd found at the crime scene as to the point of entry. Pettway was a big man—not as big as Daniels, but it seemed to Dio that the guys down here, or at least these two, avoided the gym, not the buffet table.

After some small talk, Pettway led Dio to his office, which was on the second floor of the command center's main entrance. The command center itself was a two-story modern structure and, from what Dio could see, had state-of-the-art digital video and communications. Pettway explained to Dio that Old Trail Village ran from Donald Ross Road on the south to Fredrick Small Boulevard on the north and from US-1 east of the ocean. There were two entrances. The main gate, where they were now located, was accessed off Donald Ross Road and a service entrance located off US-1. There was also a marina with access to the ocean. All deliveries to the clubhouse and golf operation—food, beverages, and so on—plus the landscaping contractor used the service entrance. Residents, their guests, UPS, FedEx, and other services, like limos, were permitted through the main gate but needed to show a photo ID, which was entered into the security system. Pettway further explained that each resident's vehicles (most had two; many had three and four) had decals affixed to their windshields that allowed them unfettered access. The access system only recorded the time a vehicle departed the campus from the residents' (right) side of the two-lane entrance roadway. Pettway explained that posted signage indicated that residents could enter or exit from the outside lane, while guests and deliveries had to use the inside lane to stop and produce a valid driver's license before being allowed access.

Pettway wanted to continue describing his operation in detail and to explain how the homeowner association (his employer) and the golf, fitness, and dining-room operations relied on him as security director to stay involved with their operations. But Dio said politely, "Look, Chief, I got a lot to do today, so how about you just let me review the tapes for now? Maybe later on we can meet, and you can tell me all about the operations you oversee here at Old Trail Village."

"Oh, yeah, sure, I got a bunch of stuff to do anyway. Meeting with the board and general manager and whatnot. The residents here are very security conscious and require a lot of hand-holding. Plus, this robbery has everyone on edge, and I need to be on top of things."

It seemed to Dio that Pettway was concerned about his cushy job here, and the fact he'd called the theft a robbery rather than a burglary led Dio to believe this guy's skill set was less than he made it out to be. As a former police officer, Pettway should know have known the difference: a robbery is a theft when force is used or implied.

Pettway finally left Dio alone after giving him instructions on how to work the digital joystick to review the tapes. Dio didn't want to show annoyance, but he was getting pretty steamed at Pettway's insistence on explaining every little detail of the system. Finally he left. Dio first ran through the period from 8:00 a.m. Friday through 8:00 a.m. Sunday, viewing the tapes of the comings and goings at the back gate. Pettway had left Ramirez in the command center to assist Dio and answer any questions he might have. He didn't really think he needed to review the tapes from the service entrance, but he did so anyway. Nothing he observed seemed out of the ordinary. In viewing the main entrance tapes, he noticed more activity on Friday than on Saturday. He started to really focus on any activity that occurred after five o'clock Saturday afternoon, when the Stockwells were getting ready to leave. He asked Ramirez to join him at this point so he could help Dio ID anyone who might appear.

At 5:45 a black Lincoln Town Car stopped at the gate. The driver handed the security officer on duty his license. Dio froze the frame and asked Ramirez if he knew the driver.

"Yeah, I think that's the guy who picks up the Stockwells. I can get his name from the system if you want."

"OK, but let's wait until I go through the entire evening."

Only two other vehicles entered Saturday evening after the limo. Both were guests of other residents who had been called in. At 8:45 Dio observed the Stockwells pulling back in. He could see the ambassador lower the back window as the town car slowed at the gate. It was waved in, but Dio could see it was the same guy driving. He asked Ramirez to pull the driver's ID. Ramirez did so and handed him a photocopy of the Florida driver's license. David W. Barth. Maybe I want to talk to this guy, Dio thought. He asked Ramirez the name of the limo company Barth drove for.

"AAA Limo in West Palm," Ramirez replied. "Most of the residents here use them. They're pretty good—on time, drivers always in a shirt and tie."

Dio held up a hand without looking away from the screen. "Thanks, Officer, that's good for now."

Ramirez frowned and went back to the front of the command center. Dio wrote down the information on his pad. He included the names and addresses of the two residents who'd had guests that night, and the guests' names too. He thought he would have Joe P. conduct these interviews tomorrow.

CHAPTER FOURTEEN

On Monday morning Polk County Sheriff's Deputy Don Bronte had just started his seven-to-three-thirty shift when he received a call to investigate a possible abandoned vehicle on State Road 60 about half a mile west of the 7-Eleven. As he was coming from the east, he stopped by the 7-Eleven and pulled his cruiser up to the gas tank to top off. The PCSO had a contract with the 7-Eleven to gas the three cruisers assigned to that sector, as they were too far from HQ to gas up there. The three deputies assigned to that sector, Bronte and two others, always got a coffee and donuts included in their stops. Bronte was an easygoing type of guy, and why not? This was a very nice detail as police jobs went. No heavy lifting, mostly traffic enforcement and road accidents. Most of this rural county's crimes were domestic disputes, which were handled by a two-person team consisting of a male and female deputy. Each of the county's five sectors had two such teams. Any other crimes, such as drug enforcement, robberies, and homicides (which were rare—Polk County had had five last year, all drug related), were handled by detectives.

Bronte drank half his coffee and ate a donut while chatting with the young girl behind the counter, whose name tag said "Rachel." Like most of the local ladies, she was overweight, had a couple of tattoos and piercings, and probably had a couple of kids and no husband. She was bemoaning the fact that her boyfriend's truck wouldn't start, so she'd had to give him her Camry so he could get to his job as a laborer in Polk County, which meant she had to Uber it to work. Looking at her fat belly, he wanted to ask her if she were pregnant but then thought, Every time I ask that question and get a "no" response, I feel like a jerk. So he let it go. Bronte went back out to his cruiser and drove west on Route 60 to investigate the possible abandoned vehicle. He was hoping that it was gone by now, that the owner, who'd probably run out of gas or had some other mechanical problem, had returned with a friend and gotten the vehicle running again. The thought of having to do some police work, albeit minor, did not appeal to him. About half a mile past the 7-Eleven, he could see a silver truck off to the side of the road. He slowed down to avoid hitting a flock of vultures off to the side. "Probably feeding on some roadkill," he said out loud to no one. He pulled behind the truck and noticed the rear passenger-side tire was flat. He activated the emergency light on top of the cruiser. The truck, he noted, was an older, late-'90s or early-2000s, Ford F-150. He wrote down the license number and called it in to dispatch. Bronte now cautiously approached the vehicle with his right hand on his weapon. Once he verified the vehicle was unoccupied, he reported back to dispatch. Dispatch responded that the vehicle, a silver 1999 Ford F-150, was registered to a Norman J. Penny, 122 Norfolk Drive, Tequesta, Florida. Bronte, looking at the rear flat, reported the same to dispatch. The guy probably got a flat and went to get help, he thought. But why would he not go back to the 7-Eleven, only a half mile behind? Then Bronte figured maybe the guy hadn't seen the 7-Eleven, or maybe he'd flagged down a ride, but the ride would take him to the gas station.

Bronte decided to search the vehicle. He looked under both seats and checked the glove box but did not find a registration or insurance card or anything else of value. He could tell by the coolness of the engine hood and the heat of the interior that the Ford had not been driven in a while. He popped the hood. The engine seemed cool to the touch, adding to his hypothesis. He requested that dispatch send a tow truck. He wanted to get the truck off the shoulder before the Monday traffic started to build. In the meantime he would go back to the 7-Eleven and ask the fat-chick clerk if she knew anything.

Rachel, who now gave her full name as Rachel Smith, told Bronte that she'd come on duty at six o'clock and had served about a dozen or so customers since then. Most of them had bought gas and either coffee or water. No, she hadn't noticed anything out of the ordinary, and yes, she knew or at least recognized the faces of all of those customers. "Oh," she added, "except for the big dude with the funny accent," who got two coffees and four donuts. She did not recall seeing any other strangers.

Bronte, in a stroke of actual good police work, inquired about the video cameras located outside. Rachel indicated that the cameras worked, but only the manager, who would not be in until ten, could access them. Bronte then noticed the tow truck heading west and hopped into his cruiser to follow. Again, he had to slow down as he passed the dozen or so vultures and crows feasting on the roadkill.

CHAPTER FIFTEEN

D io put a call in to Joe P. and gave him the names and addresses of the people he wanted him to interview. These included the Barretts, guests of Mr. and Mrs. Martin Kilmister, who lived in Juno Beach, and Dr. and Mrs. Poissant, guests of Mr. and Mrs. Bertram McCooey, who lived in Jupiter. Dio wanted Joe to interview both residents and their guests. He also wanted Joe to visit AAA Limo and interview the Stockwells' driver, David W. Barth. He briefed Joe on what he had so far and said he wanted him to interview the only visitors who'd come through the main gate between five and nine on Saturday night. "See if they saw anything, especially the driver. He was at the scene twice that night. Who knows, he may he seen something suspicious."

"Got it, boss," Joe P. said. "I'll get on it right away."

A lot of veteran detectives would have been offended by Bosso telling them what questions to ask and what to look for, but Pollicino knew this was his boss's style. Bosso was a micromanager. If a detective under Dio Bosso's command had a problem with that, all he had to do was say so, and Dio would have him transferred to the precinct of his choice.

Joe P. called both the Kilmisters and the McCooeys and spoke to the husbands. Yes, they said, they knew of the robbery at the ambassador's and were very concerned. They would be happy to furnish the names and phone numbers of their guests, and they would call them and let them know to expect Joe's call. The Kilmisters' guests, Hank and Susan Barrett, had come for dinner on Saturday and stayed from about six to ten o'clock. They hadn't seen anything or anyone suspicious on their ride in and out of Old Trail. Joe P. did not know it, but the road the Barretts took to the Kilmisters' was different from the road to the Stockwells' residence.

The McCooeys' guests gave Joe got a similar response. Dr. Poissant said he and his wife, Christine, only stayed long enough to pick up the McCooeys and then they went to dinner at the club. Pollicino then called AAA Limo. The phone was answered by a rather pleasant-sounding woman, but Joe detected something in her voice that sounded off, especially when he stated why he was calling and said he wanted to speak to David Barth.

"Excuse me," she said, "aren't you from the police?"

"No, ma'am, as I said, I'm an investigator, and I'm investigating a crime that your driver Mr. Barth may be able to assist me with. Can you tell me the best number to reach him?"

"You'd better hold on a minute." Cupping the phone, she called to Mal, "Mal, there's a guy on the phone claiming to be an investigator, and he wants to talk to Billy B."

Mal gave her a look and picked up the phone, saying harshly, "Who is this, please?"

"My name is Joe Pollicino, and I am an investigator with Lloyd's of London. I am investigating a crime, and I believe David Barth may be able to help me. Is this Mr. Barth?"

"No, my name is Mal Thomas, and I'm the owner of this limo company. You should talk to the police. I can't tell you anything." He hung up.

Joe felt this was odd, especially since he'd told Thomas who he was. Why would he not talk to him? He called back, and once again the female picked up the phone.

"AAA Limo Service," she said.

"Listen, ma'am, this is Mr. Pollicino again. I just need to ask a few questions, please—"

"Mal said you should call Detective Martinez at the PBSO," she said, and hung up.

He held the receiver away from his face and looked at it, thinking, This is fucking weird. I'd better call Dio.

Joe told Dio about the first two calls to the guests and their responses. He then told Dio about the strange response he'd gotten from AAA and gave him Detective Martinez's name and number.

"OK, Joe, take a ride down to AAA—you have the address—and see what's going on. I'll see if I can track down this Detective Martinez. Maybe Daniels knows him."

Dio put a call into Detective Daniels, who answered his phone on the first ring.

"Sam? Dio Bosso here. I need your help."

Daniels, wanting to be involved, responded, "Sure, Dio, how can I help you?"

"Do you have reach into the PBSO?"

At first Daniels didn't get the word "reach," but after a second or two, he said, "Sure, we work a lot together on cases. What do you need?"

"You know a detective named Martinez over there? Seems he has something to do with AAA Limo. I had my investigator call them to set up interviews with the guy who drove the ambassador and his wife, and they referred him to this Martinez guy."

"First of all, he's not a guy, if it's the same Martinez I know," said Daniels. Dio could sense the gloat. Point for Daniels. "She works Homicide, and she's one tough piece of work. Good rep, army vet—the real deal, if you know what I mean."

"Could you reach out to her and see what's going on?" Dio asked.

"Sure. Anything I can do. I'll get back to you," he said, and he hung up without waiting for a response, just like Dio had done to him. Touché, Dio thought.

CHAPTER SIXTEEN

After the tow truck removed the F-150, Deputy Bronte tried to find a phone listing for Norman Penny at the Tequesta address given by dispatch. He was not surprised there was no listing. Few folks today had landlines; everybody had a cell phone.

Finally, he became curious about the feasting vultures and crows. "Must be a fucking deer or cow over there," he said aloud to no one. With his overhead lights on, he reversed and hit his siren, scattering the feeding flock away. He exited the cruiser and walked over to the embankment.

What he saw not only shocked him but made him go pale and nauseous at the same time. The body in the ditch had half its face eaten away, and the clothing had been torn by the sharp beaks of the scavengers. "I'll bet my next paycheck this is Norman J. Penny, or what's left of him," he said out loud to himself. He then went back to his cruiser and put the call in to dispatch.

Detective Tom Redstone was a seasoned twenty-seven-year veteran of the Polk County Sheriff's Office. Redstone was a rare breed, one of a handful of Florida law enforcement officers who'd actually stayed at one agency for their entire careers. For Redstone it worked. He'd been born and raised in Bartow, the Polk County seat. Both his parents had been born there too. His dad, now retired, had been a deputy there for twenty-five years, his mother a schoolteacher who'd passed last year. Redstone was married to his high school sweetheart, Peggy Carrolton, and they had five kids. The only time Redstone had lived outside of Florida was the four years he'd done in the navy after high school. When he and Peggy traveled, before and after the kids, it was always to Disney or the Keys.

Redstone got the call about the body in the ditch directly from Bronte. As Redstone took notes, Bronte gave him what he had, including the job concerning the F-150 and the info on Penny, whom he figured was for sure the stiff in the ditch. Redstone instructed Bronte to call the tow company, redirect them to the sheriff's office garage, and instruct the tow driver not to touch anything after dropping off the truck. Redstone would have the police garage handle the truck as evidence for the time being. He also instructed Bronte to set up a crime scene around the body, with yellow crime-scene tape cordoning off the area from where the body was to where the truck was found. Finally, he told Bronte to stand by, as he was on his way. Redstone knew he had to give Bronte detailed instructions. Not because Bronte was stupid; no, he was just a bit lazy.

Redstone grabbed his jacket and said to his partner, Det. Mike Danton, "Come on, Mickey. We got a body."

CHAPTER SEVENTEEN

Sam Daniels checked his Rolodex under PBSO and called Lt. Frank Pooley, whom he'd known for about ten years. He and Pooley were neighbors and played golf together on occasion.

"Hey, Frank, Sam Daniels here. How you doing?"

"I'm good, Sam. What's up?"

"I'm working this burglary at Old Trail Village. You know the seven-million-dollar Marc Chagall painting that was stolen over the weekend?"

"Yeah, I heard about it. How can I help?"

"Well, I'm working with this hotshot investigator from Lloyd's of London named Bosso, and he wants to interview the limo driver who drove his victim to and from an event on Saturday night. The vic is Paul Stockwell, former ambassador to France under Bush One and Austria under Bush Two. Super wealthy super influential, if you get my drift."

"Yeah. Go on Sam."

"Well, when Bosso called the limo company, they would not give him any info on the driver. They referred him to Detective Martinez."

"Was the driver's name David W. Barth?" Pooley asked.

"Yeah, I think so." Daniels actually was not sure, but he didn't want Pooley to know he'd never asked Bosso the driver's name.

"Well, if he's the same guy, then nobody's talking to him." Before Daniels could ask why not, Pooley said, "He was the victim of a homicide early Sunday morning. Looks like a home invasion, but it's still too fresh to call. Martinez caught the case."

Holy shit, Daniels thought. "Listen, Sam," Pooley continued, "I'll tell Martinez that it's OK for her to talk to you, but I don't know about this other guy. What's his name again?"

"Bosso, Dio Bosso. He works for Lloyd's of London, but I hear he was a detective commander in the NYPD."

"Whatever. You can bring him along. I'll call Martinez, but it's her call if she wants to talk to this guy or not. Here's her cell." Pooley gave Daniels her number and then hung up.

Daniels called Bosso and related what Pooley had told him about Barth. Holy shit, thought Bosso. He didn't say anything, just let Daniels speak and tell what he knew of the Barth homicide.

"Listen, Sam, can you call this Detective Martinez and set up a meeting as soon as possible?"

"Well, Dio, her boss, my friend Lt. Frank Pooley, said he would reach out to her and tell her to talk to me. I'll see if it's OK if you come along." Daniels didn't mention that Pooley had OK'd Dio's attending the meeting with Martinez; once again Daniels wanted to sound important.

"OK, Sam, thanks. Get back to me and let me know when we can meet Detective Martinez. By the way, do you know her first name?"

"Yeah. Lydia."

After Dio hung up, he called Joe P. and filled him in on what he knew. Joe was about five minutes from AAA Limo.

"What do you think, boss?" Joe asked. "Any connection?"

"Too soon to tell, but you'll find out."

When Joe P. got to AAA, several people were hanging around the front of the small storefront. The large picture window had "AAA Limo Service" printed in large gold letters centered over an image of a stretch limo. "Palm Beach County's Premier Limo Service," it said. Joe entered and saw several people milling about inside. He asked for Mal Thomas and was greeted by a tall, heavy-set man with a gray ponytail and a Rolling Stones T-shirt. The one with the tongue.

"Mr. Thomas, my name is Joseph Pollicino." He handed him a business card. "As I stated on the phone, I am with Lloyd's of London. The deceased Mr. Barth drove my clients on Saturday evening. Their home was burglarized during the time they were out, and I was wondering if you could help me by answering some questions."

"I already told that lady cop all I know," said Thomas.

"Well, sir, could you tell me?"

"Sure, I guess so. Why don't we step into my office?" He pointed to a small office off the main room. "Heather, tell everyone to get out of the office and back to work. We got a business to run here."

Heather, the dispatcher and office manager, was dabbing her eyes. Joe P. could tell she had been crying a lot since hearing about the murder of David Barth.

Once inside the small office, Mal continued, "Like I told the lady cop, Billy had that job Saturday night. His pickup time was six o'clock. He was to drive the ambassador and his wife to the island for a charity event, wait, and bring them home."

"You referred to Mr. Barth as Billy. Wasn't his name David?"

"Yes, but everyone called him Billy or Billy B."

"Oh, OK. Was that his only assignment that night?"

"Yes." Mal went on to say that Billy had been planning to go on vacation after Saturday to visit his family in Pittsburgh, so when he hadn't brought the car back, Mal figured he'd forgotten, so he'd sent Ted Glenn, another driver, to retrieve car twenty-six. Mal continued to answer Joe's questions, each response started with "Like I told the lady cop, blah, blah, blah."

Looks like she knows what she's doing—asking all the right questions, Joe thought. He concluded his interview. "Thanks, Mal." On the way out, he asked Heather if she could add anything to what Mal had given him. "No, I told the lady cop everything I know." She started crying again.

I am probably getting all I can get from these two right now, Joe thought. I can always circle back here if I need to. Or I can check with the "lady cop."

By now Daniels had reached Martinez, and she reluctantly agreed to meet with him and the guy from Lloyd's around five o'clock on Tuesday in her office. The call from Lieutenant Pooley was the reason she'd agreed to the meeting. Normally she did not want to discuss her cases with officers from other departments, and she knew Daniels and thought he was an asshole, as he was always trying to hit on her. "Like I would really be interested in someone like him," she would say aloud to herself. She was also opposed to meeting with the civilian, but at this point in the investigation, she liked the Gillings, Tanya pim/bodyguard as the doer. So what harm would it do to talk to Daniels? Besides, Lieutenant Pooley had made the request.

Daniels got back to Bosso and told him that *he* had arranged the meeting with Martinez for five o'clock on Tuesday at the PBSO Homicide office. Meanwhile Martinez was working the case in her usual fast-paced manner. From the interviews of Thompson, Heather, and Ted Glenn, she was able to establish the victim's movements from the time he'd called in to AAA at 5:45 p.m. until the 8:45 p.m. drop-off, when he'd called to say he had completed his assignment and was heading home. Martinez now had to find out Barth's actions from that point in time until he'd met his death early Sunday morning.

In checking his cell phone, which she had recovered from the crime scene, she saw that, other than the several calls to and from AAA or Ted Glenn, Billy had not made any calls on his phone other than to the 561-884-1324 number he'd dialed at 1:30 a.m. Sunday, the same number that had called him back at 2:30 a.m. The ME's initial report gave time of death (TOD) as between two and three o'clock, which was consistent with the phone records. So where had he gone between 8:45 and TOD?

She retrieved all of his calls from the previous three months and saw two other calls to the number, which was listed in his directory under "PUSSY." These calls were usually between midnight and two. From Ted Glenn she learned that Billy like to gamble and frequented the Seminole casinos, one in Hollywood and the other in Coconut Creek. He was also was a regular at Club Inferno; she made a note to contact the topless joint as part of her investigation.

Martinez asked one of the other detectives, Tommy Raftery—the computer cop, as he was called by the Homicide detectives—if he could check the local dating websites to see if he could match the number. She checked the one credit card Billy had but saw no other activity for Saturday night. The last charge was forty-two dollars for gas on Friday evening. She'd learned from Heather that drivers paid for their vehicles' gas when they drove.

Martinez knew the security chief for the Seminole casinos, a former FBI agent named Tommy Sullivan. She called, and Tommy, as usual, was happy to hear from her. Sully, as he was called, was forever trying to get a date with Martinez; he'd been trying ever since he'd first met her several years before. He tried to ply her with free concert tickets and comps of rooms and dining, throwing the whole full-court press her way, but she was not interested. However, she never said no outright. It was always, "Well, let's see what happens." She was used to guys and sometimes girls coming on to her. But Martinez had little interest. Her job was her life—or so it seemed to those who tried to date her.

She asked Sullivan if he could pull the tapes of the main entrance of both casinos for the time frame of nine o'clock Saturday through three o'clock Sunday and transmit them to her electronically. She knew that if Billy had gone there directly, she'd have enough of a span to eyeball him going in. Within an hour she had the tapes, and she downloaded Billy's driver's license photo for a comparison. It did not take her long to hit pay dirt. Within twenty minutes of viewing the tapes, she spotted Billy Barth entering the Seminole casino in Coconut Creek at 10:30 p.m. Saturday. She knew the hotel had video on all the gaming tables and the cashier's cages. In gaming-industry jargon, those cameras were referred to as "the eye in the sky." State law prohibited cameras in the restrooms and dining facilities.

She called Sullivan again and asked him to send her tapes from the cashier's cages during the same time frame, but only from Coconut Creek. Bingo—she had Billy going to the cage three times during the requested time frame. Each time it appeared he cashed in chips for over a thousand dollars. She looked back at the entrance tapes and saw him leaving the casino about 1:15 a.m. Looks like he had a good night, she thought, judging by the number of trips to the cashier. So maybe someone had followed him home. But looking again at the tape of him leaving, she saw nothing suspicious. Now she was back to thinking maybe it was the pimp/bodyguard Gillings and the hooker, Tanya, who had robbed and killed him. There was no sign of forced entry. It was possible that Ted Glenn had stolen the money, but after considering that possibility, she ruled it out. Glenn had been visibly shaken by his friend's murder.

Early Tuesday morning, Martinez received a call from Detective Raftery. He told her that in addition to checking the dating websites, he'd also check the number on Barth's cell phone through AT&T, Barth's carrier.

"I got a listing on that phone number you gave me," he said.

"OK, good. Shoot."

"It comes back to a Thelma Jackson, 11496 Southwest Hickory Road, in West Palm Beach. That's west of the turnpike in district three. I also found that same number listed for an escort on the Backpage website personals under 'Women Seeking Men,' coming back to a woman named Tanya. The picture accompanying the listing showed a scantily clad young black girl. The ad said, 'Young, sexy, hot-chocolate lady with an open mind. Out call only two hundred roses.' I just e-mailed you the link to Backpage that gave the number. Happy hunting, and if you need me to go undercover on this, you know I'm there for you." He chuckled as he signed off.

Martinez wanted to make a witty comeback, but she could not think of anything in time. She chuckled too. "Yeah, sure, Raft. What a guy. Thanks." Now she had a name to go with the number. She opened the e-mail from Raftery and went on Backpage to see for herself what Tanya looked like.

CHAPTER EIGHTEEN

By late Monday evening, Detective Redstone had completed the basic steps on the Penny homicide. He got a positive ID from the prints taken by PCSO Crime Scene. The ME had determined TOD to be sometime between 11:00 a.m. and 1:00 p.m. Sunday. The cause of death was the nine-millimeter slug that blew out the back of Penny's head. The single bullet entered just above the nose and exited through the back of the skull. Penny had died instantly; the two other shots were "make sures," the signs of a hit or a murder for hire. The ME also stated that the two slugs taken from the deceased's chest had been fired from a different nine-millimeter. Redstone recovered two shell casings from the second weapon, but the slug from the head shot was too of no forensic use.

Two shooters, Redstone thought. Why? Was this some kind of hit? Who is this guy Penny?

CHAPTER NINETEEN

Rocco spent all of Sunday at the condo. He expected Billy to come by for the rest of his payout, so he called Darla and invited her over to spend the day, but she told him she had things to do at Inferno, as well as some personal errands. She could come over around seven, if that would work. He was planning on going to Inferno himself and said maybe he would see her there. Already he felt like he was being blown off by her, and the same old self-doubt about his relationship skills, or lack thereof, was starting to creep into his consciousness. He was thinking about what Tommy had said about getting out of Florida, selling the club, and selling the condo to him. Did Rocco want to stay there? He had close to a million clams, so money would not be an object. He was confident enough that his Spartan lifestyle would enable him to live comfortably on the mil without having to pull another job if he chose not to.

He spent the next several hours counting the money. The money was all in $100 bills in bundles of ten thousand. So he would count twenty to fifty bundles at a sitting, put those stacks in Ziploc bags, and put them back under the hidey-hole Vinny had shown him in the closet of the master bedroom. The uncounted money he placed in a large gym bag, also in the floorboards.

Do I need to count each stack? he thought. You bet your ass I do. I don't trust those fucking Russkies.

It was getting close to five. Where the fuck is Billy B.? he said to himself.

CHAPTER TWENTY

Redstone had his partner, Det. Mike Danton, interview the staff of the 7-Eleven and review all the tapes for the previous forty-eight hours. Sure enough, Penny's truck was seen pulling up to pump #1 and getting gas for his vehicle. He was also seen entering the 7-Eleven and exiting a few minutes later with a bottle of water he'd purchased. Rachel Smith, who'd been working the register, told Detective Danton what she'd told Deputy Bronte. However, she didn't remember serving Penny until Danton showed her his driver's license photo.

"Oh, yeah, I remember him now. He told me he was on his way to the casino in Tampa." She also recognized the big creepy guy with the funny accent.

"Do you think you could recognize him if you saw him again?" he asked.

"I think so. I'm pretty good with faces."

Redstone had the office check to see if they could find any next of kin for Penny. All they could find was that he had a current security-guard's license and a security-installer's license. His driver's license was clean, and he had no criminal history other than a marijuana-possession violation dating back to 1985, when he was seventeen.

So why would someone want to kill this guy? thought Redstone. Was it a random killing? Do we have a couple of psychos on our hands? Will there be more murders?

All these thoughts were running through Redstone's mind when Danton called in and reported what he'd found. Danton had stopped viewing the 7-Eleven tapes once he saw Penny enter the shop. Therefore, he never saw the big creepy guy with the funny accent walk by Penny's truck and bend down by the rear drivers side tire while it was being gassed up.

Redstone called the Tequesta PD and gave them what he had. He requested they send an officer to Penny's Norfolk Drive address to see who else might live there. If no one did, Tequesta was to interview some neighbors and learn of any next of kin. He also asked them to get a search warrant for the house, and he or his partner would drive over to be there when the warrant was executed. He said this assuming Penny lived alone, and his assumption was correct. The Tequesta PD's detective on duty was Gabe Manna, and he was only too happy to comply with Redstone's request. Tequesta was a small town in southern Martin County. It had a fifteen-member PD and very little crime. Every few years the chief had to persuade the town council not to have the department absorbed by the Martin County Sheriff's Office.

In the meanwhile Redstone made all the notifications to his department and started to complete the paperwork for this homicide. Redstone was meticulous in his work and case preparation. Several years ago, in his very first case as a detective, a robbery suspect had been let go at trial due to Redstone's sloppy handling of evidence. He'd sworn then he would never be embarrassed again in a court of law by a defense attorney, and he never was.

CHAPTER TWENTY-ONE

By the time Rocco had recounted the money from Tommy and placed it in the hidey-hole, it was near seven. Rocco did not want to call Billy B., but he took his money with him when he went to the club. He would call him from the pay phone outside the club and have him meet him there. He figured Billy had tied one on and probably felt like shit about now. He chuckled. But Rocco would soon learn that Billy B. would never feel shitty again.

CHAPTER TWENTY-TWO

Ted Glenn, busting at the seams to tell someone about what he'd witnessed, stopped in the Inferno during one of the long breaks he had between runs. He got to the club around twelve thirty to find the regular Sunday football crowd packing the bar. Even though several girls were dancing on the stage, most of the customers were watching football on the four large-screen TVs in the sports-lounge area. On a normal Sunday, Rocco would have been there taking action on the games. However, today was different. He didn't need to hustle a few rednecks to make a buck. Meanwhile Ted was looking for Kris Keefer, the only person he knew who worked there. He asked one of the bartenders if she would ask Kris to come out from the kitchen, as he had something important to tell her.

When Kris heard about Billy B. from Ted, she was at first shocked and then broke down and cried. "He was such a peaceful guy," she said. "Who would want to hurt him like that? Oh my God."

She went back into the kitchen and immediately told Darla what Glenn had told her. "Darla, you'll never believe this, but Billy B. is dead. Murdered in his condo. The cops think a hooker killed him." This was not actually what the cops thought, but it was what Glenn told Kris, wanting to impress her with his being in the know.

"Oh, dear me," Darla said. "That poor man."

The two ladies chatted. Darla, who knew Rocco was on his way, figured she could wait to tell him the news when he arrived. Rocco came in around six thirty and went immediately into the office to put Billy's money in the safe. While he was in there, Darla walked in, and right away Rocco felt uncomfortable. He didn't know what to say to her or how to react to whatever she might say about him blowing her off earlier in the day. He was surprised to hear her say, "Rocco, I just heard that the limo driver Billy B. was killed last night."

Rocco was stunned by this but tried not to show it. "What? What are you saying?"

"Yez," she said. She pronounced esses like zees. "His coworker just told me. The coppers think it was a hooker."

Rocco sat down on the sofa, and Darla could see he was more shaken up than she'd expected he would be. Certainly, she thought, this is not the first person he knew who was murdered. For all I know, he may have murdered people himself.

"OK, Darla, thanks. I need a minute alone here. I'll be out later."

Darla left him alone, somewhat disappointed that he had not asked her about "them."

Rocco's first thought was that Billy had been killed by some hooker he'd brought back to his condo. He'd probably been drunk, flashed his wad of dough, and gotten killed for his efforts. Rocco was trying to think whom he could call to find out more info, but unlike Vinny, he did not cultivate friendships with the off-duty cops who worked at the club. He never suspected that Billy's unfortunate demise had anything to do with last night's piece of work.

CHAPTER TWENTY-THREE

Dio picked up Sam Daniels at the Gardens PD office at 4:45 p.m. Tuesday, three days after the heist. They headed to the PBSO Homicide office on Gun Club Road to meet Detective Martinez. On the way Daniels briefed Dio about his relationship with the sheriff's office. Although Barth lived in Palm Beach Gardens, his condo complex was part of unincorporated Palm Beach County, which is why PBSO was investigating this homicide. Dio could once again see Daniels was trying to tell him how important he was, how well connected, and so on and so on. Dio tuned him out and just nodded, thanking God that this was a short ride.

After signing in at the sheriff's office, Daniels led the way to the second-floor detective squad room. Upon entering, Dio could see several cubicles in the center of the room and glass-walled offices at the far end. Each had a nameplate on the door. On the right was Lt. Frank Pooley, commanding officer, and on the left side was Sgt. Robert Dixon, executive officer. There were two small interview rooms on the opposite side of the room. It was very different from the NYPD squad room, where there were several desks, file cabinets, and information boards scattered about. Of course, Dio had not been in an NYPD detective squad room in several years, so now things might be more modernized.

Daniels led him over to Martinez's cubicle. As they approached, she stood up and greeted them. She knew Daniels, of course, and said, "Hey, Sam, how are you?" Then, without waiting for a response, she reached her hand toward Dio and said, "Lydia Martinez."

"Dio Bosso."

"Nice to meet you. Is your name spelled 'Deo' or 'Dio'?"

Once again Daniels thought, Why didn't I think to ask him that?

"It's D-I-O, short for Diomede, my grandfather's name."

"Oh, I see," said Martinez. "You want some coffee or a Coke? We can talk in the interview room." She pointed to one of the rooms on the side.

"I'm fine, thank you," said Dio.

"I'd like some coffee," Daniels said.

Martinez gave him a look. "Sam, you know where the break room is. Why don't you help yourself, and Mr. Bosso and I will get started."

Daniels once again felt he was being dismissed, but he said, "Sure, OK. I'll be a sec."

Martinez rolled her eyes as Daniels walked off, and Dio gave her a knowing smile. Right away he felt good about this meeting, although he realized it might have nothing to do with his investigation. As they walked to the interview room, Martinez made small talk about his career.

"I hear you're retired from the NYPD—a detective commander."

"Yes," he said, but he did not want to continue along those lines where he would have to talk about the double police homicide that had cost him his career. He figured she knew that about him already, if she'd done her due diligence on him. "Twenty-five years. Now I work for Lloyd's of London."

"Yes, I know. So, you're investigating that seven-million-dollar art burglary at Old Trail Village. Pretty ritzy place, eh?"

"Yes, quite, but you probably know the place better than I do," he said.

"Well, yes, I know the area, but most of these gated communities have their own in-house security and experience very little crime."

Just then Daniels joined them and sat down next to Dio, and Martinez ended the small talk. "How do you figure my homicide has something to do with your case?" she asked Dio.

Dio looked at Martinez across the table. "Well, I'm not sure. Barth, the victim in your homicide, was a limo driver, and his last assignment was chauffeuring our victims, Ambassador and Mrs. Stockwell, on Saturday evening. I thought he might have seen something out of the ordinary or overheard any conversation they might have had during the ride. I reviewed the video tapes for that evening, and I saw him coming in for the pickup and drop-off."

Martinez liked his right-to-the-point manner and how he did not try patronizing her like so many other male cops (like Daniels) tried to do. She got the impression that if she had been a male detective, Bosso would have talked to her the same way. She liked that, and there was something about this lanky older man she found attractive. She also found it unusual for her to think like that about anyone.

She told them what she had so far. "The deceased finished his work for AAA at eight forty-five on Saturday, went home, changed clothes, and went to the Seminole casino in Coconut Creek, about a forty-five-minute drive from his condo in the Gardens." Dio gave her a puzzled look, which she picked up on right away. "That's what we locals call Palm Beach Gardens." She went on to say that video she'd obtained from the casino indicated that he'd apparently had a good night at the tables, as he was observed cashing in chips for around $3,000 during the course of the evening. He'd eaten a steak dinner at the casino's steak house and paid cash. He'd left at 1:25 a.m. Sunday.

"We checked the credit card that we found at the scene, but there were no charges for his last seventy-two hours other than gas for forty-two dollars. His cell phone indicated several calls to and from his employer. The only other call during the time he signed off from work until his body was found was to an escort service. As we speak, my partner"—she really had no partner, but she did not want to use the word colleague—"is checking that out. There is a possibility that Barth called for a date, and when the hooker saw the amount of money he had, she decided to rip him off. Usually these girls that do out calls, as this woman does, according to her Backpage ad, are accompanied by their man. If robbery was the motive here, then it's possible she called her man, and they killed Mr. Barth together."

Before Dio could ask, she said, "There were no signs of forced entry and no defensive marks on the body. The ME's report indicated no drugs in Mr. Barth's blood, just a couple of beers, and his steak had not fully digested yet."

Daniels chuckled. "Well, at least his final meal was a good one, ha."

Martinez gave him a look and shot Dio a glance. He just half smiled and thought, This guy is a real fucking clown.

"There was one other thing," Martinez added. "When I checked the body, I detected a mint-like smell on the vic's mouth. I asked the ME to swab the area and see what it could be. Maybe he brushed his teeth before the date, but I want to be sure." Martinez then stood up to signal the meeting was over.

Dio had some questions, but they were not really germane to his case, and if she didn't want to give any more info, he understood. He thanked her, they exchanged cards, and he and Daniels left.

Martinez went back to her cubicle, fanning his card, and smiled.

"Well, what do you think?" asked Daniels when they got back into Dio's rental.

"About what?"

"You know—Martinez. She's hot stuff, don't you think?"

Dio did not want to go there. He just gave Daniels the stare, which of course Daniels did not get. "Yeah, she seems to be a good detective," was all he would say.

Daniels asked if Dio wanted to grab a bite, but Dio declined without giving a reason. He dropped Daniels back at the Gardens PD, and as Daniels got out, Dio said, "Sam, thanks so much for your help. I really appreciate it." He felt Daniels needed a little jerking off to keep him interested.

"Oh, no problem, Dio. It's my case too," he said with a grin.

"OK, Sam, have a good night."

When Dio got back to the hotel, he met with Joe P., and over dinner at the hotel restaurant, they went over what they had so far. Dio had a great deal of confidence in Joe's work, but he would still ask him questions about a case to be sure Joe was doing everything Dio thought he should be doing. Joe had answers for all of Dio's questions about his interview at AAA. There was only thing he couldn't answer. "Did you happen to look at the car Barth was driving Saturday?" Dio asked.

"No. I'm not even sure it was there."

"OK," Dio said.

CHAPTER TWENTY-FOUR

Rocco was still trying to figure out what had happened to Billy B. By now everyone who worked at Inferno knew about poor Billy. Most thought the hooker scenario was the most likely explanation. Rocco went back into the office and retrieved Billy's $10K.

"Well, I guess he won't be needing this anymore," he said aloud to himself. The thought of giving it to Billy's next of kin never entered his mind. As far as he was concerned, the money was his. He then told Darla to call him a cab, as he wanted to go home.

"I should be out of here by midnight," Darla said. "Do you want me to come over?"

"No, not tonight," Rocco said and walked out to the bar. He looked into the lounge, where the Sunday-night football game was on. The twenty or so guys in there were shouting at the TV as someone made a touchdown. Rocco, who had zero interest in sports except to cover bets, just shook his head and went outside to wait for his cab.

CHAPTER TWENTY-FIVE

M artinez did not give the info she had on the escort Thelma
Jackson, a.k.a. Tanya, to Daniels or Bosso. She arranged for
Detective Jerry Wilson from Vice to place a call and set up a date
with Tanya for Wednesday evening. They gave the Holiday Inn by
the airport as the meeting location and secured a room from the
management. The hotel itself was known for prostitution and drug
sales, but management cooperated with the sheriff's office. Being
part of a national chain, it had an image to maintain, but it also
had to keep its seventy-five rooms booked, so the short-term stays
used by trysting couples were a welcome bonus.

At five o'clock on Wednesday, Martinez and Sergeant Dixon
briefed the other detectives who would assist on this operation. A
few guys carped about how having four detectives assigned to lock
up a hooker was a bit of overkill. Martinez, who ran the briefing,
explained this was part of a homicide investigation, and she wanted to apprehend not only Tanya but also whoever dropped her off
at the hotel. Hopefully it would not be an Uber driver.

Martinez assigned Jerry Wilson, who'd made the original date with Tanya, to be inside the room. He would make the arrest after an offer of sex for money was made. Det. Jerry Nathan and his partner, Det. Lee Bush—the two were known as Franks and Beans to the members of the Homicide Squad—would be outside the hotel and would hopefully detain and ID the driver of the vehicle Tanya arrived in. Martinez and Dixon would be in an adjoining room and would oversee communications. Dixon got two uniformed deputies from patrol, and Martinez had them posted about one block from the hotel as an additional backup for Franks and Beans.

At 5:50 p.m., Tanya called the cell phone assigned to Detective Wilson. This phone, issued by the PBSO, had the capability of recording all conversations. Wilson confirmed the date, gave Tanya the room number, and told her to knock three times. Franks and Beans positioned their unmarked car by the entrance in order to observe all vehicles coming and going in the parking lot.

At 6:30 p.m. Nathan (Franks) transmitted that he'd observed a petite black female, early twenties, wearing a miniskirt, tight-fitting top, spike heels, and fishnet stockings, exit a black late-model town car. He recorded the plate and was prepared to follow, but the car backed into a space at the side of the hotel. The driver was described as a black male, early thirties. Nathan was unable to give more description than that. Detective Bush (Beans), who was driving the unmarked vehicle, pulled around the hotel to be in the best location to stop or follow the vehicle. They, along with Martinez and Dixon, agreed this guy was either Tanya's pimp or her muscle and would be waiting for her to come out. Most escorts booked and got paid for an hour, usually $200 to $300.

When Detective Wilson opened the door, Tanya's first thought was, Thank God he's not some big fat fuck or drunk asshole or any number of the weirdos, losers, and old geezers who hire hookers. But as she well knew, those types went with the territory. She expected she might even enjoy fucking this good-looking, well-built customer.

Tanya always wanted the money up front, and Wilson counted out $200 in twenties and tens. Then he said, "This is for an hour, right? Anything I want?"

"I don't do Greek, but other than that, I'm yours, baby," she said with a sheepish grin.

"OK, good. Why don't to go into the bathroom and shower real quick? I'll pour us a drink."

"OK, baby, whatever you say."

Wilson wanted to be sure that her purse was out of her reach when he announced her arrest. When she came out of the shower, just wrapped in a towel, Wilson had his badge and handcuffs out.

"Shit, motherfucker, I knew you was a fucking cop!"

Just then Martinez and Dixon came into the room. Wilson cuffed her and pushed her down on the small chair next to the bed.

"Those cuffs too tight?" Martinez asked.

"Fuck you bitch," Tanya replied.

Dixon retrieved her purse and the $200 in marked money. Wilson wrote "JW" in very small letters on the back of each bill for ID purposes. He also removed a switchblade from the purse and placed it in a baggie, as it could have been the murder weapon. Everything was done as if it were a major case, when in fact the most serious charge was prostitution in the first degree, a Class A misdemeanor. Unless, of course, Tanya had murdered David W. Barth.

Tanya knew getting arrested came with the territory of her profession. It was a minor inconvenience most times, unless the girl had an outstanding warrant or several arrests in a short period of time. Martinez was counting on the fact that because this was

Jackson's third arrest this year, she would be willing to cooperate to avoid jail time—unless, of course, she had committed the Barth homicide. Martinez already thought it unlikely that Tanya was the murderer, and now, seeing how small Tanya was, she shifted her attention to the dude in the car as the possible doer.

Once she had Tanya in custody, she radioed Franks and Beans to grab the driver. "Bring him to the office, and keep an eye on him until I get there."

"Do you want us to start an interview?" asked Nathan.

"No, just keep him on ice. I'll be there soon."

Nathan and Bush approached the town car from both sides, and Nathan tapped on the driver-side window, badge in hand and weapon by his side. His knock startled the driver from a nap.

"Open the door now, and keep your hands visible," commanded Nathan.

The driver looked back and forth between the two men and knew they were cops. He raised his hands and then opened the door. "I ain't doing nothing officers. What you wanna hassle me for?"

"Shut up, get out, and put your hands on the car. Spread your legs. You know the drill."

Yes, he did. After the detectives patted him down, they rear handcuffed him and told him to sit on the ground by his vehicle. His driver's license showed his name as Deshaun Gillings. He told Franks and Beans he was picking up a friend at the airport and was just getting a nap before his friend arrived.

"Oh yeah?" said Bush. "What airline? What flight number?"

Gillings stammered and then replied, "He's gonna text me when he gets here, I promise."

"Yeah. And what about the young lady you dropped off a few minutes ago?"

"I don't know what you mean."

While Nathan continued to interview him, Bush searched the town car. "Hey, Jerry," he said, holding up a Berretta 380 by the barrel. "Right under the front seat."

"What's this, Deshaun? You got a concealed-weapons permit?" Bush asked sarcastically, knowing he did not.

Nathan had Gillings stand. He patted him down a second time and sat him in the back on their unmarked car. He then requested dispatch to run the license, the vehicle, and his sheet for any priors or warrants.

Back the hotel room. Martinez began her interview of Tanya, who by now had put her skimpy attire back on. "OK, Tanya, I know your name is Thelma Jackson, date of birth one/seventeen/ninety-two. You've got three previous arrests for solicitation in the last nine months. I'm figuring the judge might want to send you away just for that. Not to mention you could get life for the murder you did last Saturday."

"What?" Jackson screamed. "You fucking nuts, lady? I ain't murdered nobody. This is crazy! What you talkin' 'bout?"

"Where were you last Saturday evening around—" Martinez stopped herself. "Actually, it was Sunday morning around one thirty."

Thoughts were swirling around Jackson's head. She had trouble remembering what she'd had for breakfast this morning, let alone what she was doing three or four days ago. Her life was simple: get up, get high, get a date, make money, get high again, and get another date. She figured she probably fucked or blew twenty to thirty-five johns a week. She worked alone but considered Deshaun her partner, so she shared whatever she made with him. He drove her to her dates, waited for her, and came to her rescue if he received their predetermined text signal (911 on his cell) if a john got out of hand or didn't want to pony up her fee.

"Look, Thelma," Martinez continued in her softer, good-cop voice, "I'm here to help you. But before I can do that, you need to tell me about Saturday night and Sunday morning. Think for a minute."

Then it started to dawn on Jackson: this ain't no routine Vice cop. "Look, lady, I don't know nothing about Saturday or Sunday."

"I'm going to ask you one more time. Then I'm going to take you down to central booking and charge you and your boyfriend outside"—she looked at her pad for the name Nathan had given her—"Deshaun with first-degree murder."

"He ain't my boyfriend, and we didn't kill nobody."

"Then tell me about Saturday night."

By this time, Franks and Beans had Gillings in the interview room at the detective squad room at PBSO HQ. Gillings had no idea what was going on, but when he entered the squad room, he saw what was written on the door: Homicide. What the fuck did that bitch get me into now? he thought.

At the hotel, Jackson was now in tears but still refusing to tell Martinez anything about Saturday or Sunday morning. Then it dawned on her. "Detective, do you mean the no-show? I swear I didn't do anything." She cried and seemed to lose control of herself. To Martinez she appeared to be really frightened.

"Look, Thelma, just tell me about Saturday night's no-show."

"Well," she sniffled, as Martinez handed her a tissue, "I get a call for a date around one thirty. I was already home relaxin' when my phone rings, and I see it's this client that I've done before, so I answer. He tells me he had a big night at the casino, and he wants me to come over and party with him. I tell him it's late, and I'm gonna need three hundred dollars to get dressed and stuff. He says no problem. He says, 'Make it two a.m.; I'll be home by then.' So I wake up Deshaun, and we go over to the address he gave me."

"Do you have the address still, Thelma?" Martinez asked.

"No, I don't keep no records. Once I get there, I toss that shit. But I know the place 'cause I been there before. It's a condo place in the Gardens about two streets east of Ninety-Five off PGA."

That part Martinez knew she had right. "OK, go on."

"Well, I get there around two a.m., maybe two-oh-five. I recognize the place, but I can't recall the client. I figured he'd be OK, though, because if he weren't, I would remember, know what I'm sayin'?"

"Yes, go on."

"Well, anyway, I ring, I knock, and I wait, and nothing, so I call the number that he called me on. It goes to voice mail."

"OK, Thelma, go on."

"I waited awhile. I kept ringing and knocking, but then I figured fuck it, and I called Deshaun to pick me up. He be waiting in the car for me, you know what I'm sayin'?"

"Yeah, I know," said Martinez. "Tell me, Thelma, did you see anybody else or notice anything out of the ordinary?"

"No, I was just pissed that this motherfucker got my ass out of bed, and then I got nothing for it. Good thing he's dead or I might kill his ass myself." Jackson looked at Martinez and said, "I didn't mean that, Officer."

Martinez patted her leg. "I know you didn't. Let's go." She handed Jackson over to Jerry Wilson, who would take her to central booking for processing on the solicitation charge.

"I thought you was gonna give me a break for talking to you!"

"I am. You're being charged with solicitation and attempted prostitution, not homicide. Isn't that a break?"

"Fuck you, you lying dyke bitch!" shouted Thelma Jackson as Wilson led her out of the room.

Why do people always call me a dyke when I lock them up? she chuckled to herself. I only kissed a girl once.

Then she called the office and told Nathan that he and/or Bush could start the interview with Gillings. When Martinez got back to the office, she and Nathan compared notes. It appeared that Jackson and Gillings were both telling the same story. Martinez decided neither of them had been involved with the Barth homicide. Then she told Nathan to book Gillings on the gun charge.

OK, so what's my next move? Martinez asked herself. She decided that she would go back to AAA in the morning, and she sat down in her cubicle to do some paperwork. She finished updating the Barth homicide file, including information about the arrest of

Thelma Jackson and Deshaun Gillings. On her way home to her house in Juno Beach, Martinez dialed the number Dio Bosso had given her. She didn't know why she called him and was relieved when her call went to voice mail. She did not leave a message. About a minute later, her phone rang, and she saw it was Bosso.

"Hello, Detective Martinez, this is Dio Bosso. I see you called me?"

For a second she thought to tell him it was a "butt call," but she knew she would have to explain to him what a butt call was, so she just said, "Yes, I did. I want to update you on the limo-driver homicide."

"I'm listening," replied Bosso.

"Well, I am going to visit AAA Limo in the morning, and I thought you might want to come along."

"Well, I was planning on interviewing the security staff tomorrow, but tell you what. How about we meet for coffee around nine a.m., and you can fill me in then?"

Bosso really did not think the Barth homicide was related to his case—just coincidence—but he did want to see Lydia Martinez again.

When the called ended, they both looked at their respective phones and smiled.

Bosso got up around six thirty, made a pot of coffee in his hotel room, and then put a call into Joe P. Joe was not a late sleeper either, and his phone rang as he was coming back from his daily early-morning run.

"Hey, boss. Good morning. What's up?"

"Listen, Joe, I'm going to meet Detective Martinez from PBSO at nine. I told John Pettway at Old Trail Village Security that I would be coming by to interview all of the security personnel who were on duty last Saturday. Why don't you start, and I'll meet you there, OK?"

"Sure, boss," said Joe. "So where are you meeting Martinez? Do you think her homicide has anything to do with our case, or is there another reason you're meeting her?" He chuckled. Since Celia died, Joe P. had been trying to get Dio hooked up with someone. He'd tried unsuccessfully to have Dio meet one of his wife's cousins or widows from her book club and gardening club. Each time Dio's response was the same: "I'm not ready" or "I'm too busy."

Dio hung up and thought about Martinez. Could she be interested in me? he wondered. Nah, she's probably got a boyfriend, or for all I know, she could be married. Just because I didn't see a ring doesn't mean anything. But we both know that her homicide and my burglary are not related other than by coincidence.

On Wednesday morning, four days after the heist, Dio arrived at the Loggerhead Café on US-1. Martinez was there already, even though Dio was ten minutes early. She was reading from a large manila folder and just smiled at Dio when he approached and sat down.

Why is this guy wearing a shirt and tie? she wondered. It's eighty-five degrees already.

"Good morning, Martinez. How's the coffee here?"

With that the waitress came over. "Coffee, sir?" She handed each of them a menu.

Martinez waited until the waitress was out of earshot and then began. "We locked up the hooker and her pimp last night. But not for the homicide"

Bosso was caught off guard, but only for a second. "The one your vic called the night of?"

"Both her story and her pimp/boyfriend checked out with what we know. I checked her phones, viewed tapes from the casino, spoke to his boss and coworkers, and it all fits—or should I say does *not* fit. Now I think he might have been singled out at the casino and followed home, and the doer somehow got in and robbed and killed poor Mr. Barth. The preliminary from the ME indicates that Barth was stabbed several times with a large-bladed knife, like a hunting knife or bayonet, smooth on both sides. He probably bled out in less than ten minutes."

"So why, may I ask, are you going back to AAA?"

"Don't really know, but I feel I may have missed something there. I never asked the owner if Barth had any problems with other drivers or customers. Want to come along?"

The waitress returned and asked if they were ready to order. Dio ordered two eggs over easy, bacon, rye toast, hash browns, and more coffee. Martinez ordered an egg-white omelet, gluten-free rye toast with no butter, and a green tea. She looked at Bosso, and he felt like, OK, so what?

"I see you eat healthy," he said to make small talk.

"I see you don't," she said with a smile. "You can't be too careful. A woman of my age has to be mindful of what she puts into her body." She gave him that sheepish grin, and again she looked at him with her piercing brown eyes. He felt a bit uncomfortable, and a warm feeling arose inside of him. He decided to change the subject.

"So, tell me, Martinez, what made you become a cop?"

Although she had been asked this question by every guy she'd dated, every guy she'd worked with, she just smiled and said, "I'll tell you if you tell me."

They both chuckled. The waitress brought their food, and they started to eat.

CHAPTER TWENTY-SIX

D etective Redstone got to his office later than usual on Tuesday
morning. He had been working pretty much around the
clock since he'd caught the Route 60 homicide, as it was now being
referred to. Tequesta PD reported back that the search of Penny's
house (with a warrant, of course) had come up empty, as had a
check with his neighbors. They had not yet talked to his employer,
whom they confirmed to be Old Trail Village Security. Det. Gabe
Manna, who was making this report to Redstone, said that OTV hu-
man resources had told him Penny was a senior security officer and
systems specialist. Manna had not told HR that Penny was dead.

"What's Old Trail Village, and what is a systems specialist?"
Redstone asked.

"You never heard of Old Trail Village?"

"No, Gabe, I live and work in the fucking sticks here."

"Yeah, OK, sorry. OTV is one of the wealthiest developments
in Florida. Most residents are worth fifty mil and up. HR told me
systems specialist is a fancy way of saying alarm-system installer
and repairman."

"Anything else?" asked Redstone.

"Yeah. Penny's personnel folder lists a brother, Kevin Penny, who lives in Jacksonville, as next of kin. I'll e-mail you all I got when I get back to my office."

Redstone thanked him and asked for the number he had for Old Trail Village and the security chief's name. "One other thing, Gabe. What did you tell the employer about why you were inquiring about Penny?"

"They didn't ask, so I didn't say."

Redstone figured he would probably have to take a trip over to Florida's east coast on this and thought he could milk it into an overnighter. His girlfriend, Florence Mayrose, had been bugging him of late to take her somewhere, as she was getting tired of him coming over to her place and giving her a quick fuck while he was on duty. He kept telling her that he was gonna leave his wife once the kids were grown. He'd been saying it for ten years

CHAPTER TWENTY-SEVEN

During breakfast Dio and Martinez traded life stories. Dio told of his career with the NYPD and how he'd risen through the ranks. Of course, he left out the Alison and DeAngelo homicides that had cost him his career. He did tell her about Celia and his son, David, who lived in Seattle and whom he rarely saw anymore. She seemed interested.

Martinez, for her part, was trying to figure out how much older Dio was than her forty-two years. From his story line, she figured him to be in his late fifties or early sixties. Tall, six one or six two, thin, looked fit. He reminded her, in some way she could not put a finger on, of Abraham Lincoln. Maybe it was the deep-set eyes and high cheekbones.

While she told her life story, he was trying to figure out how much younger she was than he. He pegged her at early to mid-forties. They were both right. After all, they were both very good detectives.

Dio took the check, and Martinez wanted to leave the tip. Dio liked that but said, "Listen, I get two hundred dollars a day for food from my employer, so I'm way ahead here. Please let me buy you breakfast."

"OK." She smiled. He followed her to AAA and just hung around the outside parking area while she went inside to speak to Thompson. Dio meandered around and found himself in a garage that had two bays and a mechanic working on a black town car. Dio went over to him and started to make small talk.

The mechanic, whose name tag on his dirty uniform shirt indicated his name was Lou, looked at Dio and said, "You a cop?"

"No, no, I'm a private investigator. My name is Bosso, Lou. How you doing?"

Lou was surprised Dio knew his name but then looked at his name tag. "I'm good."

"So, Lou, did you know Mr. Barth?"

"Yeah, sure. Billy B. was good people. As a matter of fact, this is his car—number twenty-six. Well, not his, but it's the one that was assigned to him."

Dio walked a little closer to the black town car, and as he was looking at it, Lou said, "Yep, two hundred forty thousand miles and she still runs great. That's on me. I keep telling Mal he should pay me more. I keep all his cars running like tops, and I could make much more if I worked for a dealership or had my own place..."

Dio tuned him out, just smiled as he walked toward the open rear trunk. Something in the trunk caught his eye. As he looked closer, he could see it was a Band-Aid with what appeared to be a drop or two of dried blood on the pad.

"You cut yourself, Lou?" Dio asked.

Lou, who was bent over the engine, looked up and said, "No, why?"

Dio didn't answer, just went back to his car and got a plastic baggie and tweezers. Back at twenty-six, he removed the Band-Aid with the tweezers and looked at Lou. "You sure this ain't yours?"

"No, sir," said Lou. "Where did you find that?"

Dio pointed to the trunk as he dropped the Band-Aid into the baggie. He started to walk toward his car as Martinez came out of the office with Mal. She did not bother to make an introduction, but Mal and Dio nodded to each other.

"Well, I'm done here," she said. She thanked Mal Thomas for his help.

Nodding, he said, "Billy was like family to us. We are all pretty close here. Did his family in Pittsburgh mention to you about a funeral or whatever?"

"We notified his next of kin—his sister, I believe," Martinez said. "We are waiting for them to claim the body and come here to ship it back. But that's all I have. How about I call you when I know more?"

"Thanks," Mal said.

She started to walk toward her car but stopped when Dio said, "Mr. Thomas, do your drivers keep a first-aid kit in the cars?" Martinez stopped and looked at Dio as if to say, Why are you questioning my witness?

"No, they're not required to," Thomas said. "Why do you ask?"

"Oh, no reason. I was just wondering. Thanks again."

"Sure thing," said Thomas as he waddled back to his office.

Dio stopped him again. "Er, Mr. Thomas, I noticed Mr. Barth's assigned vehicle in the bay over there." He pointed toward Lou. "Has anyone else used that car since Saturday?"

"Ted Glenn drove it over here from Billy's condo but no one else. Like I said, we had it scheduled for maintenance since Billy was gonna be away."

"What was that all about, Dio?" asked Martinez, calling him by his first name for the first time.

"Oh, nothing. I found this in the trunk of your vic's limo and thought it kind of odd." He held up the baggy with the used Band-Aid in it.

"Do you want me to have it analyzed? Maybe Barth cut his finger. I can check with the ME for any cuts and have the blood on that checked for a match."

"Would you mind?" he said.

"Sure. I hate loose ends too." She smiled at him.

He handed the baggie to her. She thanked him for breakfast and walked back to her car. He thought about asking her to dinner but decided, No, I'd better not.

CHAPTER TWENTY-EIGHT

When Rocco got back to the condo on Sunday night, he put Billy's $10K in the hidey-hole with the rest of the stash. While it was not like him to feel bad about someone dying, he could not shake the feeling that something was not kosher with Billy B. getting clipped. He thought about it for a bit and then said to himself, Well, whatever happened to the poor bastard, I'm $10K to the good. He ate a sandwich and fries that he'd had one of Kris Keefer's kitchen staff make for him to take home, and then his thoughts switched to Darla. Maybe he should have had her come over.

He turned on the TV but could not find anything he wanted to watch for more than thirty seconds. He just kept changing the channels. Finally he said out loud, "Fuck it," and then took out his cell phone and called the club.

Darla arrived at the condo about an hour later. She sat with Rocco on the sofa and had a glass of wine. Rocco was sullen; she expected it had to do with Billy B. Finally she said to him, "Come on, Rocco, let's go to bed." She grabbed him by the hand and led him to his bedroom.

Rocco was restless and could not sleep very well. He had a lot on his mind. Billy B.'s murder. Darla lying next to him, sleeping, with a smile on her face. Tommy wanting to sell the Inferno and the condo. Once again thoughts of what he would do and where he would go haunted his sleep. But having all that cash eased his mind, and he drifted back to sleep.

He woke up around eight o'clock to the smell of fresh coffee, and as he started to get out of bed, Darla came into the bedroom. "Don't you move," she said in a playful manner. She was wearing his shirt from the night before. Slipping it off, she got back into bed, and they made love again. In all his fifty-five years, Rocco had never made love twice within twelve hours. He was starting to feel better about things.

Rocco and Darla spent the rest of the day just hanging around the condo. Rocco thought about calling Tommy and telling him about Billy B., but he knew Tommy wouldn't give a shit, so why bother? Mondays were the only days that Darla did not go to the club, but she still spent a few hours on the phone with both Kris Keefer and Janelle, setting up schedules, making food and beverage orders, and completing payroll.

Darla asked Rocco if it was true that Tommy planned to sell Inferno. Rocco lied, saying he didn't know. Darla seemed more concerned for Janelle should Inferno close, as both she and Kris would have no problem finding work. "Plus," Darla joked, "I have you, Rocco."

Rocco just looked at her and smiled. He wanted to say, "Yes, you do," but he did not.

CHAPTER TWENTY-NINE

On Wednesday morning Chief Pettway was in his office when he received a call from Detective Redstone of the PCSO.

"Chief, Tom Redstone here. I'm a detective with the Polk County Sheriff's Office."

"How can I help you, Detective?" answered Pettway.

"Well, I got a homicide victim over here named Norman J. Penny. I believe he worked for you there; is that correct?"

"Holy shit. Homicide?" Pettway replied.

"Yeah, looks like he got ambushed on the side of the road on Route Sixty a few miles west of Bartow. Not sure if it was a robbery or just some psycho." Redstone did not want to go into too many details with Pettway, not at this point in the investigation, anyway.

"Oh my God, I can't believe this." Pettway sounded genuinely shocked.

"Tell me what you know about Penny, Chief. I will be driving over there in the morning. I have a warrant to search his house." He didn't tell Pettway that the house had been searched already by Tequesta's detective Gabe Manna. "And I want to interview you and some of his coworkers." Redstone then asked the usual questions: Did Penny have any enemies that Pettway knew of? Who were his friends? What were his work habits?

Pettway seemed too shocked and/or distracted and answered only yes or no. However, he did say, "Penny's been on vacation since last Friday and won't be back until—" Pettway stopped himself. "I mean, he wasn't scheduled to be back until next Friday."

Redstone could tell that Pettway was a little too shaken up by this news to be much help, so he figured maybe he would wait to continue the interview until he got over to the east coast. "Look, Chief, I'll be over there tomorrow. Give me your address, and let's set up a meeting for, say, one p.m.?"

"Er, yeah, sure. That works," said Pettway, still sounding dumbfounded.

"One more thing, Chief," said Redstone. "Let's keep this between you and me for the time being, OK?"

"Yeah, sure," replied Pettway.

Just as John Pettway was ending his call with Redstone, his phone rang again. This time it was Dio Bosso. *What does he want now?* thought Pettway, who just wanted to close his door and not talk to anyone. Yes, he felt real bad about Penny, but between the heat he was getting about the Stockwell burglary from the HOA (his employer) and from the Stockwells themselves, a dead employee, not to mention a murder, was the last thing he needed. It was all too much for him, and now this pain in the ass Bosso was calling him.

"Yes, Mr. Bosso, how can I help you?"

Dio could sense something in Pettway's tone that seemed off. He wasn't as willing to be helpful as he had been in past conversations. *Maybe it's all the flak he's getting from the burglary,* thought Dio. "Chief, either I or my partner, Joe Pollicino"—he never referred to Joe P. as his assistant, always his partner, even though the former term was correct—"have interviewed most of the folks that we believe might have noticed anything Saturday evening." Dio did not mention anything about the Barth homicide. "Can you think of anyone else we might want to speak to?"

"No, not off the top of my head," said Pettway, not mentioning the call from Detective Redstone about Penny.

Dio did not tell Pettway that he'd discovered how the burglar had entered the Stockwells' home. He'd also asked Daniels to keep that to himself, as he did not completely rule out someone on Pettway's staff being complicit in this crime.

CHAPTER THIRTY

By Wednesday afternoon Detective Redstone had secured the necessary paperwork and vouchers to make his way over to West Palm Beach. He had his girlfriend, Flo, meet him in Destin, about an hour from Bartow. She would leave her car there, and they would ride the rest of the way to the coast together. Flo was happy they were going to have a few days together, but Redstone didn't want to burst her bubble and tell her they would be gone two nights at the most. She was also not happy that they were booked into a Best Western.

"That's the best you can do for me, Tommy?" she carped.

"That's where the department tells me to stay," he lied. In fact, he could choose any hotel he wanted as long as he paid any cost over his $150 per diem. That was not going to happen.

Flo pretty much bitched during the whole two-hour drive, so much so that Redstone was ready to throw her out of the cruiser. Finally, he told her to shut the fuck up and enjoy their time together, which she did. They arrived at the hotel around eleven, and after checking in, they immediately had sex. Redstone then told her he had a meeting at one and left her in the hotel. He set out to meet with Detective Manna at the Tequesta PD. Then they drove to Penny's Norfolk Drive home.

Redstone liked Manna right away. He was knowledgeable, affable, and let Redstone run the search of the residence. Redstone told Manna that his partner back in Polk County, Mike Danton, had notified Penny's brother in Jacksonville. Danton had told him the brother did not seem overly distraught and reluctantly said he would drive down to Bartow, make the positive ID, and claim the body.

"I guess he knew his brother didn't have much, because, according to Danton, he never asked about any estate."

Redstone and Manna did a thorough search of Penny's house, but other than a large-screen Samsung TV, there was not much of value. No family photos, no paintings on the walls, very little food in the fridge or cupboard. One bedroom was obviously where Penny slept; it was neat in that the bed was made and the blinds were drawn. The other bedroom contained a single bed and a lot of tech equipment. The one-car garage was pretty empty save for a push lawn mower and some gardening tools. It was obvious to both detectives that Norman J. Penny had lived the simple life of a confirmed bachelor.

Twice during the search of Penny's house, Flo called Redstone, asking when he was coming home. Annoyed, he told her around six and said he would take her out for a steak dinner. That seemed to pacify her for the time being. Redstone was starting to wonder why the fuck he'd brought her along.

CHAPTER THIRTY-ONE

Pettway was hoping that the detective from Polk County—he'd forgotten his name and hadn't written it down—would get there before Bosso. Just as he thought that, he saw Bosso and his partner—Joe something, right?—get out of their car and approach the command center. Pettway's second-floor office had a view of both the front and back of the command center, and the four separate screens on his computer gave him the same view. He did not relish the thought of having to tell Bosso about Penny being a murder victim.

As Bosso and Joe P. walked toward the command center, Pettway could see the marked Tequesta PD vehicle approach the main gate. Oh, thank God, they were here. Maybe they could deal with Bosso and his questions. Pettway was starting to melt down under all of this negative shit happening at one time. His relatively easy gig here at Old Trail Village was becoming more complicated than he'd ever expected or was capable of handling.

He went downstairs to greet Dio and Joe and asked them if they would go up to his office, saying he had to attend to some business with these two gentlemen as he pointed toward Manna and Redstone. Although they were both in civvies and Dio did not see the marked car, he made them for cops, as did Joe P. They both just nodded and walked into the command center, Bosso thinking that Pettway probably had some other business to attend to with these two.

Pettway walked up to Manna and Redstone, right hand extended. "John Pettway, director of security here at Old Trail Village."

"Gabe Manna, Tequesta PD."

"Tom Redstone, PCSO."

"You guys hungry? I was just about to get some lunch. Why don't we hop in my car and go over to the clubhouse?"

Manna and Redstone both found the suggestion strange, as it was close to one o'clock. But what the hell, Redstone thought. Free food, I'm in. Manna thought the same thing, but neither one said anything.

Bosso saw the three men get into a marked Old Trail Village SUV and just said, "What the fuck?" He called Pettway on his cell. "John, Dio Bosso." (Dio never seemed to remember that his name and number came up on calls nowadays.) "I thought we had a meeting here."

"Sorry, but some urgent police business came up. I'll be tied up for at least an hour or two. Why don't you guys grab some lunch and check back with me later?"

Pettway's showing some balls, Dio thought, but he didn't like this any better. "Yeah, sure, we'll do that. Do me a favor, Chief. How about you call me when you're free? I've got some things to do also, so maybe we can get together later in the day, OK?"

"Sure, I'll call you later." Pettway hung up.

Dio looked at the phone and said to no one in particular, "Something's not right here."

On the way to the clubhouse, Pettway gave Redstone and Manna the ten-dollar tour, pointing out the homes of important people—CEOs, hedge fund managers, the top 1 percent, he chirped. Manna gave Redstone a look as if to say, Who gives a fuck? But they just listened. Thankfully the clubhouse was only about three miles from the command center, just off the ocean.

Pettway pulled up just past the valet and parked the security vehicle. Both Manna and Redstone were very impressed at the size of the clubhouse. It was easily twenty thousand square feet and very well constructed and decorated. Pettway was greeted as if he was a member, and he told the hostess they would eat on the patio. Pettway, who was wearing a coat and tie, did not want to tell the detectives they would need a jacket to eat in the dining room. Both had khakis and collared shirts, thank God, or they would have been turned away, and he would have been further embarrassed.

They sat on the patio, and right away Redstone started asking about Penny. "He was one of my best guys," Pettway said. "I hired him seven years ago as a security officer when we upgraded our access control and CCTV systems. I saw that he had some skills in that area, so I enrolled him in a couple of training programs. He did well, and we have upgraded our systems twice more since then. It seems every two years they come out with better technology." Pettway had pulled Penny's personnel folder and reviewed most of what he was telling Manna and Redstone. One thing you could say about Pettway was that he knew his job and knew his people. As far as dealing with a crisis, well, that was another story.

Pettway did most of the talking. In between stories he would move close to the two detectives and whisper, "See that guy over there? That's so-and-so. He was the chairman of this or the president of that."

Neither Redstone nor Manna gave a rat's ass and just nodded. Pettway ordered a burger and fries, and Manna and Redstone ordered the same. Pettway started to talk about the golf course and how he "took care" of the local cops with tee times on off days. It was Redstone who stopped him, knowing Flo was back in the room steaming about being left alone.

"Listen, Chief, tell me, did Penny get along with his coworkers? I noticed some of your guards are armed, but Penny did not have a G license, right?" A G license allowed a security guard to carry a firearm on the job in Florida.

"Well, yes, Penny got along well with everyone, and the reason he did not have a G license is that he had a misdemeanor arrest as a teen, and that would have been a problem for him had he applied. Anyway, the work he did for me with the access control and alarm system required a different license, which he had."

"What about his social life?" asked Redstone "Girlfriend, hobbies? Did he play golf or fish?"

"I think he had a girlfriend over on the western coast somewhere. At least that's what he told me. Said he was taking a vacation to go see her and go to the casino in Tampa. You know the ones the Indians own."

"The Hard Rock?" said Redstone.

"Yeah, that's the one."

This confirmed what Rachel Smith at 7-Eleven had told Danton, and it explained why he'd been on Route 60.

"So no hobbies."

"Nah. I know he liked the casinos, as I mentioned, and a couple of times, he invited me to go with him to that strip club here in the Gardens."

"Where?" asked Redstone.

"That's what the locals call Palm Beach Gardens."

"Which club?" asked Manna, who had been quiet up till now, but he knew Redstone would not know one club from the next.

"I forget the name," Pettway said. "The one on Congress and Military Trail. Got a name like 'heating' or 'boiling.'"

"You mean Inferno?" said Manna.

"Yeah, that's the one," said Pettway.

Manna now talked to Redstone. "High-end strip club with a three-star steak house and sports bar."

Redstone just nodded. Pettway picked up the conversation. "I think he played in a high-stakes card game in one of their private rooms. They say the place is run by the New York mob, and from what my contacts in the PBSO tell me, I would agree."

"How do they figure that?" asked Redstone.

"Easy," replied Pettway. "Never any problems. No fights, no girls getting locked up. Some of these places, you can't believe the amount of crime, shootings, fights, hookers—the works."

"Yeah, we know how it is," answered Redstone.

Their lunch came, and as they ate, Pettway made some more small talk and then said, "So what do you think happened to Penny? I mean, getting shot like that…"

"We don't know," Redstone said. "I was hoping you could shed some light on this for us."

They finished their lunch, and the waitress brought over a check for Pettway to sign. Of course, his lunch was free as part of his compensation, as long as he did not overdo it. He would have to fill out a voucher back at his office and submit it to the club's general manager, Rose O'Malley. Rose worked directly for the board of the HOA. She and her staff of two oversaw all of Old Trail Village's expenditures. Although the golf club was a separate entity, the golf professionals, the clubhouse manager, and even Pettway himself reported to Rose O'Malley in some way. Pettway tried to avoid her as much as possible, but she had already called him several times on the Stockwell "robbery."

Back at the command center, Dio and Joe P. kept themselves busy by reviewing the tapes from last Saturday once again. They observed nothing new. Pettway had left his office in such a hurry that he'd neglected to lock his desk and files. Norm Penny's personnel file was on Pettway's desk, and Dio read through it, more to pass the time than anything else. Joe P. went through the previous month's incident reports, which consisted mostly of calls from residents for medical assistance or suspicious persons (usually landscapers or tradesman authorized to be on premises). Joe P. commented on how well written they were and noted the use of standard police-style reporting.

Just as Dio was looking at his watch and seeing it was getting close to three o'clock, he noticed a nervous Pettway pull up with the two cops. Not wanting to get blown off again, Dio walked outside to meet them. Acting dumb, he said, "Well, Chief, I think we are done here for now." Before Pettway could answer, he stuck out his right hand at Redstone. "Hi, Officer. Dio Bosso, Lloyd's of London."

Redstone shook his hand. As Dio shook Manna's hand, Manna said, "Gabe Manna, Tequesta PD."

Dio looked at Redstone as if to get some acknowledgment, but Redstone just nodded. Pettway was fidgeting and trying to move Redstone and Manna back to his office when Dio continued, "I'm here investigating a serious theft of property. I'm sure the chief here told you about it."

"As a matter of fact, he didn't," said Redstone, showing his dislike for Bosso and his manner.

Pettway then nervously jumped into the conversation. "These detectives are here on another matter, Mr. Bosso, so if you'll excuse us, we have some work to do."

"Oh, sure," said Dio. "Let me get out of your way here." Looking back over at Joe P., he continued, "Let's go, Joe, and leave these gentlemen to their work."

As they walked away from each other, Dio stopped. Turning around, he said to Pettway, "So, Chief, when did you say your alarm guy—what's his name, Norm Penny?—when did you say he was coming back from vacation?"

Dio did not expect the response he got. All three of them stopped in their tracks, turned, and looked directly at Bosso and then at one another. By the looks on their faces, Bosso saw he'd hit on something. He just did not know what.

"Chief?" he said.

Pettway looked at Redstone as if to get approval.

"You'd better step inside, Mr. Bosso," Redstone said.

Once inside, Pettway reintroduced the four detectives to one another. Redstone, mishearing Dio's name, thought, What the fuck kinda Yankee greaseball name is Diobosco?

"Why don't we let Detective Redstone bring us all up to date here?" said Pettway.

Redstone nodded and told Dio and Joe P. about the Penny homicide—how it was discovered, where it occurred, approximate time and cause. He purposely omitted the fact that two different nine-millimeters had been used, indicating the possibility of two shooters. "No motive that we have established yet. Also, we did not recover Mr. Penny's cell phone. Chief Pettway here supplied us with his cell number, but calls we attempted went directly to voice mail."

"So your patrol deputy ID'd Mr. Penny from his driver's license?"

Redstone had forgotten to mention that Penny's ID and vehicle paperwork were also missing. He was impressed. "No, the perps apparently took his ID and the vehicle paperwork with them."

"Them?" said Dio. "You think there was more than one perp?"

Fuck, thought Redstone. "Yeah, we believe there was more than one perp."

"Based on?" Dio continued.

Redstone was starting to get pissed at this Yankee's line of questioning. Before he could think of how he wanted to respond, Bosso said, "Did your forensic people determine that Penny was shot with two different weapons?"

Redstone felt like he was on the witness stand, being badgered by some defense counsel, but he realized that this guy knew his shit.

Dio had made his point. He knew that Detective Redneck, as he would now refer to Redstone, was caught trying to hold things back from him.

"At the moment I don't see any connection to your case, Mr. Diobosco," said Redstone, "other than the fact that Norm Penny worked security here, as did several security officers."

"It's Bosso. B-O-S-S-O." Dio suspected Redstone was purposely mispronouncing his name, but he ignored it. "Yes, that's true. But Mr. Penny not only installed the updated alarm system in my victims' home, he also made a service call there last week."

Redstone just nodded. "Well, we've got to get going," he said, looking at Manna. "Why not give me your card, and I'll give you a call if I find anything out that might pertain to your burglary." Redstone got up to leave.

"Good idea," said Bosso, "and I'll take one of yours."

They all shook hands, exchanged cards, and then Redstone and Manna left. Dio did not mention the Barth homicide to Redstone, Manna, or Pettway. He could see Pettway was upset, and he didn't want to press him for more info about Penny. He told Pettway he would talk to him tomorrow, and he and Joe P. left the command center.

Pettway now had to report to Rose O'Malley on Penny's murder. This place is gonna be buzzing about all this shit for weeks to come, he thought.

When Redstone looked at Dio's card, he realized that Dio Bosso was two names.

As he drove out of Old Trail Village, Joe P. looked over Dio, who was deep in thought. "So you think there's a connection, boss, or just coincidence?"

"I don't know, Joe, but hopefully we will find out soon enough if these two homicides are connected to one another and to our investigation."

Joe had seen Dio like this. Going over every detail, every bit of information, trying to put his finger on how all of this had gone down.

They had an early dinner in the hotel restaurant. Afterward, Dio told Joe to get a good night's sleep, because tomorrow was going to be a busy day. Joe knew this was Dio's way of wanting to be alone; it was only seven thirty. But Joe said good night. He wanted to get back to his room anyway to call his wife, Margaret, and check on his grandkids.

As soon as Dio got back to the room, he called Martinez. She picked up on the second ring.

"Hey, Dio, how are you?" she said cheerfully.

"So, what do you think of this?" he said, without saying hello. "The security guard who installed the alarm system in my victims' house turned up dead in some backwater town called Bartow." Dio waited a few seconds for an answer, but Martinez said nothing. "Guy named Norm Penny. Worked here at Old Trail and got popped about ten hours after your guy."

"How?" she asked.

"Head shot, nine-millimeter. I spoke to the detective from"—he stopped to check his notes—"Polk County. You know where that is?"

"Yeah, I have an idea. I know it's northwest of here."

"Well, the detective handling the case came over here today. A guy named"—Dio looked at the card—"Det. Thomas Redstone, Polk County Sheriff's Office. You know him?"

"Florida is a big state, Dio," she answered.

"Yeah, well, anyway," he said, "there were two shooters, or at least two different nines. The kill shot under the right eye and then two make-sures in the chest."

Wow, thought Martinez. "This guy got a sheet?"

"One old misdemeanor for marijuana when he was younger, but no, nothing recently."

"You think there is a connection between this and my case? Or this and your case maybe?"

"I don't know, Martinez, I don't know. But it seems strange to me that both these victims came into contact with the Stockwells right before being murdered. It would not be a stretch to think there is a connection."

Martinez again was quiet. He was hoping she would say something. He didn't like the silence on her part. "I was wondering if you would do me a favor," he said. Again, she waited for him to continue, so he went on. "Do you think you could call this Detective Redstone? You know, compare notes, see if your vics had something in common. Did they know one another? They were the same age, both lived alone…"

"Where did your guy live?"

"He's not my guy," Dio said.

"Yeah, right, OK, sorry. Where did he live?"

Again, Dio had to check his notes. "Tequesta. Where's that?" he asked.

"Just north of you in Martin County. Listen, tell you what I'll do. Text me the guy's number, and I'll call him in the morning and see what I can find out. You have dinner already?" she said, as if they were old friends.

"Yes, I did." And as soon as he'd said it, he was sorry he had.

"How about meeting me for a drink, then? I'll drive up if you don't want to drive."

"Oh, I don't mind driving. I hear the bar in the Breakers on Palm Beach is a real nice place, and I'd like to see it."

"You have your company credit card? Because that's out of my league," she joked. It went over his head.

"I'm old school, Martinez. I think the man should always pay."

"Well, Mr. Old School," she said, "how about you call me Lydia? That's my first name." She smiled, even though she knew Dio could not see her.

"OK, I'll meet you there in an hour," he said, and they hung up.

CHAPTER THIRTY-TWO

When Redstone got back to his room at the Best Western, Flo was already dressed up and raring to go. She had the addresses of several steak houses within ten miles of the hotel and told Redstone she was famished. Redstone wanted to tell her he'd had a big lunch and wasn't that hungry, but he knew that would never fly. So he showered and put a call in to his wife, Peggy, to keep her happy, telling her he was going to dinner with some local cops and would probably stop for a few beers afterward. "I'll talk to you in the morning," he said. "Good night, hon."

Flo was throwing daggers with her eyes. "You know, Tommy, you told me you were gonna leave that bitch ten years ago. I don't know why I didn't leave you then. All you ever done is lie to me about us."

Redstone stopped her and raised his voice a bit. "Listen, Flo, I got enough on my plate with this fucking murder case. You want to stop busting my balls? I'm tired, and if you want to go to dinner, let's do it and try to enjoy the night."

"OK." Flo got ahold of herself. She could see Tommy was stressed. "Sure, Tommy, I'm sorry. It's just I've been waiting so long in this room for you to get back, and I was lonely for you." She went over to him, pressed her breasts into his chest, and started to kiss him passionately.

"I got to take a shower," he said.

"Too bad I got my makeup on or I'd join you," she purred.

Redstone was naked now. Before getting into the shower, he pulled her in to him again and gently pushed her head down his chest until she was able to reach his dick with her mouth. As she sucked him, he thought, This is why I put up with her shit.

Dio got to the Breakers in less than an hour. He hoped he had beaten Martinez there; he wanted to walk around the Breakers hotel, as he'd heard so much about it over the years. Again, it was hard to impress Dio, as he had been to some of the finest homes, castles, and estates in Europe since he'd started working for Lloyd's. Maybe he just wanted some time alone to think about Martinez. Was this attraction he was feeling for her real, and if it was, what would he do about it? What *could* he do about it? He reminded himself of the age gap between them.

He walked into the Ocean Bar and sat at a small table. An attractive young waitress came over, and he ordered vodka on the rocks with a splash of cranberry juice. When he saw Martinez enter the bar, he was stunned. Lydia was not in her usual jeans, with her hair pulled back and no makeup. She was wearing a black skirt, just above the knee, and a white satin blouse, and her dark, curly hair fell freely about her shoulders. He also noticed she was wearing makeup. Wow, he thought, she's even prettier than I thought.

He stood up as she approached his table. She was not carrying a purse, and he wondered where her gun was.

"Hi, Dio." She gave him a kiss on his cheek and handed him something. "Could you hold this for me?" He looked at it. "Lipstick. I hate carrying a purse when I'm not working."

"Oh, OK, sure," he said, looking at the tube. He held her chair as she sat. He thought she was beautiful, and as he placed the lipstick in his jacket pocket, he sat down. "So, I assume you're not carrying?"

"Why, no. I have you to protect me," she chuckled. Dio was flustered. "Just joking, Dio, relax. What's that you're drinking?"

He told her, and she ordered the same. During the next hour or so, their conversation went from their respective cases to their personal lives. They covered everything. Dio had never been so comfortable with anyone before, with the exception of Celia. Martinez had a pretty good sense of humor, and she was not afraid to tease Dio about his old-school way of thinking and talking. She also commented on the fact that he was wearing a sport jacket and tie—again.

After their second drink, Martinez said, "So after your wife died, did you meet anybody right away?"

"No. A lot of friends tried to fix me up after a year or so, but I had no interest. Plus, when this job started, I spent six months in London."

She asked about his son in Seattle, and she could tell it was a sore spot with him. He told her that David had married an older woman who had two kids of her own, and she came from a different background. Martinez, ever the sly detective, said, "Different how?"

Not wanting to sound prejudiced, Dio answered, "My wife and I were not religious, but Laura is a Buddhist, and she raised her kids in what we considered a very liberal lifestyle. We knew David smoked some pot in college, but they both became frequent users, smoking at home in front of her kids. She even put some pot in the food the first time she made dinner for Celia and me. It was just too much for us."

"Did they have any children of their own?"

"No, but we've had no contact since Celia died, so I don't know."

"How sad," she said.

"Yeah. Anyway, it is what it is. What about you? Any regrets not having any kids?"

Dio immediately wanted to bite his tongue, but before he could apologize, Martinez said, "So you think I'm too old to have kids, do you?"

"Er, no, that's not what I meant, it's just—"

She put a hand to stop him and said with a smile, "It's OK, Dio, I'm not offended. I'm over forty, so even if I wanted kids, I'm probably past that age. But to tell you the truth, my biological clock never ticked. Even as a kid, I knew what I wanted. I used to think that I should have been a boy. I loved sports, joined the ROTC, and served in the army. Then I went right into law enforcement. Plus, I always saw guys my own age as either silly or overly macho. So I just kept my distance and focused on my job and career."

"So maybe that's why you like me. I'm like a father figure."

"Who said I like you?" she said, once again catching him off guard. She waited for the effect then laughed. "Got you again."

Yes, Dio was smitten by this clever, funny, and attractive woman—plus she was one hell of a cop.

The next morning Martinez called Redstone on the cell number Dio had given her. He seemed reluctant to talk to her, but when she explained her homicide to him and said she thought there might be a connection between the two cases, he became a bit more cooperative.

Redstone was getting ready to leave for Bartow and wanted to get Flo back to her car and out of his hair. She'd been happy at dinner, but after they finished, she'd wanted to go out dancing.

"Are you fucking nuts, Flo? Dancing?" he'd asked.

"OK, OK," she said. "But how about we stop for a nightcap somewhere, maybe hear some music? I Googled a country-western place not too far from the hotel called the Square Grouper. What do you say, Tommy? Please?"

"Sure, babe, why not."

So they'd gone, and in spite of himself, Tommy had had a good time. But now he had to get back to business, and this female detective from Palm Beach SO was asking a lot of questions about his case.

"Did that old guy from New York put you on to me?" he asked.

"Old guy?" she said, trying not to sound pissed off. "I checked him out, and if I had the investigative chops he does, I would run for sheriff."

"Yeah, whatever. Anyway, what makes you think our cases are connected?"

"Well, the old guy, as you called him, is investigating the burglary of a seven-million-dollar Marc Chagall painting at Old Trail Village."

"Marc who?" said Redstone.

"Chagall, a famous Russian painter. Bosso is investigating the theft for his employer, and my victim, Barth, was their limo driver last Saturday, the night of the burglary. Your victim installed and maintained their alarm system. So he suspects there might be a connection."

Redstone did not like Bosso, but he admitted to himself that this guy knew his shit. "Well, the preliminary from our ME indicates Penny was shot with two different nines."

"What about a cell phone?"

"No, we did not recover a cell phone either."

"Your victim, Barth, was he shot too"

"No stabbed with some sort of bayonet or hunting knife. The ME has indicated that it appears the wounds were caused by some sort of military type weapon."

"OK, so let's keep in touch and see what develops," Redstone said before hanging up.

CHAPTER THIRTY-THREE

By Tuesday morning Linda Meeks was starting to worry about Norm. When they'd last spoken on Sunday, he'd said he would be in Tampa by Monday night, and she could meet him at the Tampa Hard Rock early Tuesday. He was not answering her texts, and her calls went directly to his voice mail. She called the hotel and confirmed that Norm had made a reservation for Sunday through Friday, but he had not checked in as of yet. Not sure what to do next, she decided to call the only other number she had for Norm, which was his work number at Old Trail Village.

The phone was answered by a security officer named Barger.

"Hi, is Norm Penny there?" Linda said.

Barger was taken aback and initially hesitated to answer. "May I ask who's calling?"

"Yes, my name is Linda Meeks, and I'm a friend of Norm's. We were supposed to meet in Tampa, but I haven't heard from him since Sunday, and he's not answering his cell."

"Yeah, well, can you hold on a sec? I'll check," said Barger. Without waiting for an answer, he placed her on hold and called

John Pettway. "Chief, I got a lady on the phone looking for Norm. What do I tell her?"

Shit, Pettway thought, more fucking problems. "Put her through to me." Pettway was getting overwhelmed by all of this. Robberies, murders…this was so different from the plushy job he'd always had here at Old Trail Village.

"Hello, ma'am, this is John Pettway, director of security at Old Trail Village," Pettway said when Barger put him through. "Can I help you?"

"Yes, I'm looking for Norm—"

"Yes, my officer told me." Not wanting to be the bearer of bad news, Pettway told her Norm had been in an accident and that she should call Det. Tom Redstone at the Polk County Sheriff's Office.

"An accident? Is he OK?"

"Just call this number, ma'am. That's all I can say." He hung up without saying good-bye.

Linda suspected something was wrong. If Norm had had an accident, wouldn't he have called her? She called the number Pettway had given her for Detective Redstone at the Polk County Sheriff's Office. A receptionist answered and told her that Detective Redstone was not available, and she asked the reason Linda was calling. Linda explained that she was supposed to meet her boyfriend in Tampa, and when he did not show for two days, she'd started making calls. She further explained that her calls to Norm went directly to voice mail, and it was very unlike him to not call back.

The receptionist asked her to hold on a minute and then transferred the call to the Detective Squad, where Mike Danton picked up the call.

"Polk County Sheriff's Office, Detective Danton. Can I help you?"

"Yes, Detective, my name is Linda Meeks, and I'm looking for my boyfriend, Norm Penny. I told the receptionist—"

"Miss Meeks, I have some bad news for you. There is no other way for me to tell you this, but Mr. Penny was the victim of a crime early Sunday."

"Is he OK?" cried Linda.

"I'm afraid he is not. He was shot dead on Route Sixty just west of Bartow."

"Oh my God!" Linda shouted into the phone. "How could this happen? Who would want to hurt Norm?" She was now sobbing, and Danton tried to calm her down.

"Miss Meeks, I would like for you to come over here to our office and speak with me or Detective Redstone, who is the lead investigator. Do you think you can do that? Maybe have a friend accompany you."

Linda was in shock and just said yes. Without asking anything else, she hung up.

CHAPTER THIRTY-FOUR

By Tuesday morning Rocco was feeling a little better. Yes, he was still concerned about Billy B.'s murder, but he figured shit happened. Now he had to focus on himself and what he was going to do if Tommy decided to sell the club. Rocco had no interest in buying it and was not sure if he wanted to stay and buy Vinny's condo as Tommy had suggested. He knew he wanted to stay in Florida, or at least someplace warm, maybe continue his relationship with Darla, but he was not sure about that either. He wondered if the cops might come around asking about Billy. It was no secret that Billy had been a regular at Inferno, but he'd also been a regular at several casinos and was probably at one of them prior to getting whacked. Rocco just felt uneasy when he thought about cops.

CHAPTER THIRTY-FIVE

By Saturday morning Dio was trying to figure out if there was a connection between the Barth and Penny homicides and the theft of the Chagall painting. The fact that Barth and Penny had both been at or near the Stockwells' residence before the crime gave him some reason to suspect that there was a chance of involvement. He had Joe P. go over Penny's personnel file, talk to Pettway and his staff again, and follow up with the detective from Polk County, whom both Dio and Martinez were now referring to as Detective "Redneck." Dio would follow up with Martinez, who was handling Barth's homicide. He was starting to like being around her, and he enjoyed her way of goofing on him.

Joe P. had finished all of the follow-up work Dio had given him by three o'clock, and he called Dio to say he thought they should meet and review what they had.

"Good idea, Joe."

Dio had left a message for Martinez but hadn't heard back from her. He was disappointed. He felt more and more that all three cases might be connected.

When Dio and Joe P. met and put their notes and heads together, they knew they had to find a common thread between the two homicides and their theft. Dio was sure Martinez would cooperate and go along with his theory; however, he was not so sure about Detective Redneck.

"What if we get both of them together to meet with us?" Joe P. suggested.

"I don't know if we can pull that off," said Dio. "Shit, the distance between the two homicides is a couple of hundred miles. Just because both vics were in the vicinity of our theft prior to their demise..." Dio didn't finish the thought. He was starting to doubt his own theory. He needed to find that thread before he could try to tie all three cases together. He felt that he had the answer, but he could not put his finger on it.

Back at the PBSO Homicide office, Martinez was reviewing her notes when Det. Jerry Wilson called her and told her that Thelma (Tanya) Jackson had pleaded out at arraignment and gotten sixty days. Deshaun Gillings had an outstanding warrant for assault and battery and had been remanded into the county jail. He then told Martinez that Tanya had mentioned to him that she'd first met Billy B. when she worked as a dancer at Club Inferno in West Palm, and he thought it might be a good idea to pay the club a visit.

Wilson was a strait-laced married man with a couple of kids, so Martinez knew he was not looking to go see some titties on the company dime. He also told her that as part of his job in Vice, he was required to visit these strip clubs from time to time and report any wrongdoing to his superiors as well as to the state licensing agency. He asked if Martinez might be willing to make the visit with him.

"Sure, Jerry," she said. "I like seeing some naked ladies from time to time. Just give me some time to go to the bank and get some singles to stick in their G-strings." Martinez chuckled. She liked to keep her colleagues guessing about her sexual leanings.

Wilson picked her up, and they drove up to Club Inferno, about a fifteen-minute drive from her office. On the way Martinez told Wilson about the Penny homicide, the burglary of the Chagall painting at Old Trail Village, and the possibility of all three cases being connected. She also told Wilson about Dio Bosso and how he was the one who believed all three cases were somehow connected. Wilson was not really interested but listened politely.

When they arrived at the club, it was around noon, and both Martinez and Wilson were surprised to see that the bar in the main room was almost full. Two ladies were pole dancing nude on the stage behind the bar. As Martinez and Wilson stepped inside, they were greeted by a thin blond lady with an accent.

Darla knew that these guests were probably coppers, but she acted as coy as ever. "Would you like a seat in the sports lounge or a booth here? Are you having lunch or just drinks?"

Wilson showed Darla his badge. She acted surprised, although she was not. "How can I help you?"

"We'd like to speak to the manager. We have a few questions we need to ask."

"Well, the manager is not here, but I'm the assistant manager, Darla Cummings." She extended her hand to the detectives.

"Is there some place we can talk in private?" Wilson asked.

"Sure. Follow me, please."

She led them into the sports lounge, which was fairly empty, and they sat in a booth in the back.

"I don't want to waste any of your time, ma'am," said Wilson, "so we'll get right to it."

Darla thought they might have gotten a complaint from a disgruntled customer, but once seated, Martinez spoke for the first time. "You said you are the assistant manager. Who is the manager? Or better yet, when can we speak to the owner?"

"Well," replied Darla, "the owner is, or was, Vincent Ruggerio, but he was killed in a car crash a few months ago. Sad, so sad. Such a nice young man. And the driver of the other car was an illegal from Mexico, with no license to boot. Can you imagine that?"

"I notice you have an accent, Ms. Cummings. Are you English?"

"No, Australian, but I've been here over thirty years, and I'm a citizen now."

"So, you run the club now since the owner died?" asked Martinez.

"No, not exactly. Janelle—Janelle Fishman, that is—she is the bookkeeper, does the payroll, and supervises the dancers. Kris Keefer and I, we run the kitchen, order the supplies, that sort of thing."

"Wow," said Martinez. "Three women running a place like this? You should get an award from NOW."

Darla didn't understand but let it go.

Martinez went on. "So, are there any management personnel who are male?"

"Well, only Rocco, but he's not here now, and he only helps out since Vincent was killed."

"Does Rocco have a last name?"

"Yez, I think it's DeAngelis or something like that." Darla had hoped to keep Rocco out of the conversation, but she could see the coppers were not going to believe three women ran a strip club without any male involvement. Plus, she still thought they were here about some complaint. Maybe one of the girls had gotten stupid and robbed a customer. Darla decided to go on the offensive. "May I ask why you officers are here? Did one of the girls do something illegal?"

Martinez didn't answer her question. "Do you know a customer name David Barth, known as Billy B.?"

"Oh, dear me, is that why you're here? Poor Billy. He was such a sweet man."

"So the answer is yes," said Martinez.

"Yez, he was a regular here. We heard about what happened to him. Do you think it had something to do with the club?"

Again, Martinez did not answer her question. "When was the last time Mr. Barth was here at the club?"

"I'm not sure when that was. I generally stay in the back by the office, and I try to get out of here before eight. I'm here mostly in the daytime."

"I see," said Martinez. "Tell me this, Darlene."

"It's Darla, no '-lene,'" she said.

"Sorry," said Martinez. "When was the last time you saw Mr. Barth here? Can you recall?"

"Well, I'm not sure. Like I said, I stay mostly in the back of the house." In fact, Darla remembered seeing Billy B. the Thursday before he was killed, but she felt she did not need to volunteer that information. "Is there anything else, detectives? I have to get back to the kitchen. I have a delivery coming in soon." She looked at her watch.

Martinez ignored her plea. "Tell me, did Mr. Barth have any friends here at the club? You know, like other regulars?"

Again, Darla could have named three or four of the regulars in the card game, but she felt she'd already said too much by giving them Rocco's name. She knew that Rocco had a criminal past, but she thought it was only gambling, maybe some loan-sharking. She also knew that Tommy and his father were racketeers, as she called them, and she was starting to get uncomfortable talking to the coppers.

Martinez could sense that Darla was holding something back but felt this was not the time to push her. "OK," she said, "we'll let you get back to your work." She handed Darla one of her business cards with the usual "if you can think of anything else…"

"Yez, of course."

Martinez then said something out of the blue just to see Darla's reaction. "One last thing, Darla. Do you know a man named Norm

Penny? I believe he was a friend of Mr. Barth's and frequented this club also."

Martinez saw the puzzled look on Darla's face as she replied, "No, I don't think so." Martinez knew she was lying.

As soon as Martinez and Wilson left, Darla went into the office and called Rocco. She told him about the visit from the two detectives and did her best to answer his questions about their conversation. They both knew the cops were there because of Billy B.'s murder. Only Rocco was concerned about any connection to the heist of the Chagall painting.

"OK," he said, "I wouldn't pay it too much mind. They are probably just following up on information they got from other people."

When Darla mentioned that she'd given them his name as the manager, she could feel him tense up.

"Why did you do that, Darla?"

"Well, I told them that me and Janelle and Kris run the club, but they didn't believe that three women ran this type of business. Plus, when I mentioned Vinny's accident—"

"OK, don't worry. Probably just routine follow-up on their part." Rocco still thought Billy had been killed by some hooker and pimp or some gang banger that had followed him home from the casino. "Anything else, Darla?" he asked.

"No, that's all. Except..." She hesitated.

"Except what?" Rocco asked.

"Well, they asked me if I knew Norm Penny too."

When Rocco heard that, he had to take a deep breath. How could they possibly have put those two together? He decided that he would call Penny when he got back to the club, where he kept one of the burner phones from the heist. When he got to the club later, he tried Norm's phone several times, but the call went directly to voice mail. He then thought about calling Tommy in New York, but as soon as he thought it, he figured he'd better not. For the first time since the heist last Saturday, he was starting to worry. But as he went over things in his head, he figured, What do I have to worry about?

When Martinez got back to her office, she decided to give Dio a call. She was not sure why; maybe she was hoping he would ask her out to dinner. They made small talk about each other's cases, and Dio did not mention anything about dinner. He did say that Joe P. was heading back to New York tomorrow and that he, Dio, would probably do the same in a day or two. Martinez thought he was waiting for a reaction from her, but none came. She changed the subject.

"I went to a strip club today," she said, hoping to get a reaction, but once again Dio did not bite.

"Oh, really? You don't seem to be that type," he said, laughing.

"No, just business. My vic, Barth, was a regular there, and I think Penny was too—you know, Detective Redneck's vic. He also hung out there. I guess a lot of guys do, but I find it interesting that two murder victims killed within hours of each other both hung out in the same place and probably knew one another."

"You think there's a connection?" Bosso asked.

"Not sure. How are things going on your case?"

"Slow. I got nothing, and Daniels is no help. However, I do find it interesting that both Barth and Penny had some contact with the Stockwells just before the theft. So maybe all three cases are connected."

"How do we prove that?"

"I don't know, but it's all I got right now. Anything else, Martinez?"

"Yeah. How about you buying me dinner on your company credit card tonight?"

Boy, she is something, Dio thought. Not shy at all. "Well, I had planned on catching up on some paperwork tonight, but if you promise to look as good as you did at the Breakers, then you're on."

237

They were both acting like a couple of teenagers, and they both knew it. "Great," Martinez said. "I can do that."

"How about seven thirty at Ruth's Chris on US One? I feel like a steak."

"Sounds good. I'll see you there." She hung up.

Rocco was still trying to reach Penny when Janelle Fishman came into the office.

"Hi, Rocco, you got a minute?"

"Yeah, sure. Whaddya need, Janelle?"

"Well, Darla told me about the cops being here today about Billy B.'s murder, so I thought I would call a friend of mine who works as a civilian crime analysist at the sheriff's office. She told me that as far as she knew, the visit here was routine, and they still think Billy was killed by a hooker or someone who followed him home from the casino. Apparently, he had a good night there and was seen flashing large amounts of cash."

"Yeah. So why you telling me this, Janelle?"

"Well, Darla said you seemed worried, and I—"

"Listen, I don't like cops, plain and simple. Never did, never will. So if they are coming around here asking questions, I don't like it, that's all. OK?"

It was the first time Janelle had heard Rocco raise his voice, and it made her feel uneasy.

"Anything else?"

"No," she said.

"Then get back to your office, and leave me the fuck alone."

Janelle, who by now was welling up with tears, just turned and went.

Back at her house, Martinez was getting ready when she decided to give Detective Redneck (she liked the nickname Dio had given him) a call. His cell went to voice mail, and she did not leave a message. Instead she called the Polk County SO detective office number and got his partner, Detective Danton. Danton knew who she was, as Redstone had filled him in on his trip to Palm Beach Gardens, so it saved her having to go over all the basics of their cases and how they might be connected. She told Danton that they might want to look into the Club Inferno connection, as both her victim and theirs were regulars at the club, and the club was owned by members of the Ruggerio crew from New York.

Danton didn't say much or ask any questions, just thanked her and said he would pass the info along to Redstone. Danton didn't know or care who the Ruggerios from New York were, and as far as he knew, neither did Redstone. They would cover all the basics of this case, but being that Penny was not local, they would get no pressure for results, and in a week or two, it would go cold. End of story.

Once again Martinez beat Dio to the restaurant. Shit, he thought, is she ever fashionably late? I guess not, but boy, she looks good. "Hi, Martinez. You're looking nice this evening."

She just smiled and said, "I thought you were going to call me by my first name." Without waiting for an answer, she continued. "I spoke to the maître d'. He said we can sit whenever we want, so if you want, have a drink at the bar first."

Dio looked around. The place was half empty. "Good, you must have pull here," he said, trying to one up her.

She gave him a punch in the arm. "Very funny, mister, very funny."

They both laughed, and Dio said, "Let's sit. I'm hungry."

For the next hour or so, their conversation went back and forth from small talk to their respective cases. Dio ordered a bottle of an expensive Italian super Tuscan to go with their porterhouse for two. They both liked their steak medium rare. More stuff in common, Dio thought. As their dinner was cleared from the table, Dio turned the conversation back to police work.

"So, tell me, how was your visit to the strip club?"

"Well, two things. First, both my victim and Detective Redneck's victim were regulars at Club Inferno. I passed that info along to Redneck's partner, but he seemed to blow it off. Anyway, my Vice detective, Jerry Wilson, told me the place is high end, food is top shelf, and there have been very few complaints filed against it, as opposed to other strip clubs in Palm Beach County. Wilson explained to me that the club is owned by the New York mob, so that would explain the lack of problems, but it's run by three local ladies. Now how's that for a contradiction?

"My victim Barth, was, according to the manager, an easygoing, simple sort of guy. Liked to gamble and bet on games, not much into the ladies."

Dio waited until she finished and then said, "Do you know the name of the New York mob that runs the place?"

"Yes. Wilson told me the licensing is under the name of Vincent Ruggerio, but he was killed in an accident several months ago. Are you familiar with that name?"

Dio nodded. "Yeah. The Ruggerios were part of the Columbo crime family but split off and joined the Gambinos about fifteen years ago. The old man, Big Pete, died here in Florida, and his son Tommy now runs the crew."

Martinez was impressed by this but didn't want to show it. She continued. "After this Vincent Ruggerio guy died, another New Yorker sort of became the de facto manager of the club, but he was not there when I spoke to the manager."

"Did you get a name?"

"Yeah, I wrote it down but can't recall it off the top of my head."

Dio just nodded. Then Martinez said, "Rocco something or other."

Dio almost chocked on the piece of porterhouse he had just put into his mouth "What? Did you say Rocco?" He was almost shouting. "Was it DeAngelis?"

"Yeah, maybe. What's wrong, Dio?"

He didn't answer. He got up without excusing himself, went outside the restaurant, and called Joe P. on his cell phone. Joe picked up on the second ring.

"Hi, boss, what's doing?"

"Listen, find out when Rocco DeAngelis was released from prison. I want to know everything he's done, every place he's been to since he got out."

"Sure, boss. You got something?"

"Just go and do it."

As he was walking back into the restaurant, Martinez was coming out to meet him. "Dio, are you OK? Is something wrong?"

"No, no, not at all. Let's go back to our table. I'll explain."

CHAPTER THIRTY-SIX

Rocco was starting to feel very uneasy. Not only were the cops coming around, he still had not been able to get in touch with Penny. He decided to take a shot and call Tommy in New York. He used the burner phone he still had from the heist, which was not yet a week old.

"Tommy, I need to talk to you. Can you call me on this number from a pay phone?"

"Rocco, this is 2015. There are no more pay phones. You can talk on this line. It's clean." Tommy could tell Rocco was upset; he was speaking fast and not making much sense. Tommy knew why, of course, but did not let on.

"One of the guys I used turned up dead, and the other is missing. What the fuck is going on?" Rocco was shouting into the phone—very unlike him, Tommy thought.

"Roc, calm down a second, will you, and tell me what's your problem."

"Like I said—"

"Roc, I don't want you to worry about yourself. You're not in any danger."

"Not in any fucking danger? What are you talking about, Tommy? You told me there would be no bad shit after the job. Did that fucking Rudukas have those two goons take my guys out? Is that what you're telling me, Tommy? That's fucking bullshit, Tommy, fucking bullshit."

"Rocco, just fucking relax." Tommy was now raising his voice, and Rocco got ahold of himself. "Those two guys didn't matter, and we could not take a chance with them. They were civilians. Listen, Rocco, the Duke wanted you clipped too. I had all I could do to keep that from happening, so just calm the fuck down and move on from this."

"So you're saying I owe you? Fuck that, Tommy, fuck that!"

"You getting any heat from the cops?"

Rocco took a deep breath and said more calmly, "No, not really. They came to Inferno asking about the one guy—the limo driver, Barth—but they think he was done by a hooker or someone who followed him home from the casino. Nothing on the other guy."

"Listen to me, Roc. Just calm down and go about your business. I'll be coming down in a few days. The club has been sold, so I have to come down and sign over the papers."

"Who did you sell to, Tommy?"

"Rudukas," he said, and then he hung up.

Back at the steakhouse, Dio was telling Martinez the story of Rocco DeAngelis and the Drake hotel robbery back in 1993. She had never seen him this animated or excited in the brief time she'd known him, but she could see he felt confident that he had the answer to a lot of questions about his case and maybe about hers too.

"The theft of the Chagall and the way it was done are right up this guy's alley," Dio said. "Before I put him away back in 1994, he was reputed to be one of the best when it came to big heists." He went on to tell Martinez how Rocco DeAngelis had been unknown to anyone in the NYPD's organized crime bureau. "Even the top organized-crime investigators had never heard of him. It was like he didn't exist. When we cracked the case, the guy we flipped said he'd never heard of the guy until the Drake hotel job. Very professional, and believe me, I don't think we would have broken that one had it not been for one of the guys in the crew starting to date a girl who was held hostage during the crime."

"So why are you so sure this DeAngelis guy is involved here?"

"I just am. But of course, mere suspicion is not proof, and that's we need to get."

"So you think DeAngelis killed Barth after the job and Penny too?"

"Well, that's the thing. In all of his past jobs, DeAngelis never used violence. Sure, he might tie people up or cuff them, like in the Drake job, and it was rumored he made his bones by taking out a Columbo capo named Eddie 'Veal' Marsala back in the 1970s, but that's about it." He told her about what an oddball DeAngelis was, how he'd never said a word when Dio finally brought him in. "Even after I promised him a reduced sentence if he would give me some info on the Ruggerios, not a fucking word—oops, sorry, Martinez."

"It's OK. I've heard that before."

"Yeah, this guy acted like a prisoner of war—gave his name, which we knew, asked for a lawyer, and took the Fifth. As a result the judge gave him the max—twenty years in Danamora."

"Well, how did you break the case if this guy went mum?"

"Like I said, we got a tip on one guy in the crew from a young lady he was dating. She was held hostage during the robbery, and one of the guys in the crew—John Cappolino, as I recall—started to date her. When she found out who he was, she came forward and gave him up. I had just assigned a twenty-four-seven surveillance on him when I got word to back off. The NYPD Narcotics Division and the feds had him on a major cocaine sale to an undercover.

"At that time I was the executive officer of the Major Case Squad. We were told to back off Cappolino. When the feds and the NYPD narcs finally arrested him, he was facing life without any chance of parole. Plus, the Ruggerios put out a contract on him. He had one option: flip and maybe get into witness protection, which he did. In addition to helping the feds in their case, he gave us information on the Drake. Several other members of the Drake crew were involved in Cappolino's cocaine business and were killed by the Ruggerios. Cappolino had no solid information on either Big Pete Ruggerio or his son Tommy, but he gave us Rocco. At the time no one—not the NYPD, the FBI, or the New York State Police— had even heard of Rocco DeAngelis. He had no Social Security number, had never applied for a driver's license or signed up for the draft, yet he had been a made member of the Ruggerio crew for over twenty years and had been pulling off very large heists for most of that time. DeAngelis was the only one convicted of the Drake hotel robbery. Of the other eight members, five were killed by the Ruggerios, one died of natural causes, and two disappeared to Sicily. Cappolino was put into witness protection, and I have no idea where he is or if he is still alive. As for Rocco DeAngelis, well, for some reason I was fascinated by him. I even visited him a couple of times in prison, trying to get him to talk to me. During the investigation I learned that we were born on the same day in the same hospital. That fascinated me too: two kids born the same day to Italian immigrant parents, born just a few hours apart. One becomes a cop and the other a criminal. Weird no?"

Martinez did not answer but just looked at Dio. She could see how excited he was, as he felt he was close to solving his case.

"I kind of forgot about Rocco DeAngelis over the years," Dio went on. "Never gave him much thought after the last time I visited him in prison and tried to establish some kind of dialogue. I have Joe P. checking with state corrections in New York to get us updated. I have a strong feeling that if Rocco DeAngelis is here in Palm Beach Gardens, then he is a prime suspect in the heist of the Chagall painting from the Stockwells' home."

"So you don't think he killed Barth and Penny?" Martinez asked.

"Not directly, but if they're involved, then their murders are connected. Do me a favor. Call Detective Redneck and have him check Penny's corpse for a small abrasion, like a paper cut, on his hands. Then have him send you a DNA swab and Penny's blood type. I want you to compare it to the Band-Aid I found in Barth's town car."

Back in New York, Joe P. checked with state parole and learned that Rocco had been paroled after serving nineteen and a half years of the twenty-year sentence handed down to him by Judge Matthew Damico in March of 1994. Through the efforts of his attorney, Lyman Solniker, DeAngelis's parole had been transferred to Florida. Joe P. contacted his parole officer, Desiree Witherspoon, of Florida State Parole. She informed Joe that yes, DeAngelis was her client, and he reported to her every two weeks, had a paying job, and passed his drug test each time she administered one. She commented that she wished all of her clients were as clean as he was—"Although," she added, "he's a strange little man."

Yeah, that's DeAngelis, Joe thought. Joe verified that DeAngelis had shown Witherspoon pay stubs from his employer, given as "1441 Military Trail Realty Corp.," a.k.a. Club Inferno. The stubs indicated Rocco was being paid $550 per week as an assistant manager.

PART SIX

Rocco And Dio Meet Again

CHAPTER ONE

Joe P. called Dio and related what he'd learned from Rocco's parole officer. He told Dio that he'd gotten a call from an old police colleague of his named Carlton B. Crawford, who was the head of security for Christie's Auction House. Christie's was the auction house where the Stockwells had purchased their Chagall painting. Crawford had worked with Joe P. when he was in the Narcotics Division but had taken a disability pension after getting shot in a drug operation. Joe P. had contacted Crawford when he first got to Florida and asked him to see if he could get him a copy of all the people who'd submitted bids (in person, online, or through a proxy) on the stolen Chagall painting. Crawford had explained that there were some privacy issues involved, but he would see what he could do.

"Look, Joe," Crawford had said, "I'm going out on a limb here," the point being he wanted Joe and Dio to know he might call in a favor one day, which, as Joe knew, was fine. It was the way things worked in their profession. Sort of one hand washing the other. Crawford had called back the next day.

"Whaddya got, Carl?" Joe had asked.

"Well, you wanted me to find out who else besides your client bid on Marc Chagall's *The Green Violinist.*" He went on with the same story about privacy. Joe wanted to tell him to cut to the chase, but he knew Carl was again trying to tell him they owed him one, so he let him finish. "Well, anyway, I can't give you all the bidders, as even I don't know who some of them are, but I did find one thing you might find interesting."

Joe thought, Please just give me what you've got and stop with all of the other bullshit. But he listened.

"Well, I found out that one of the proxy bidders was none other than David Berkowitz."

"What, the Son of Sam?"

"No, no, Joe, the mob lawyer. You would think the guy would change his name."

Joe laughed. "You had me there for a second, Carl. Go on."

"Berkowitz is the lawyer for the Russian mob, and Sergei Rudukas has purchased other works of art by Russian artists. Berkowitz stopped bidding at two million, and, as you know, your client paid seven-point-two plus tax, and ten percent for the house."

"Interesting," Joe P. said. "I'll pass it along to Dio."

Crawford had been hoping for a little more in the way of thanks from Joe P. Joe knew it but did not want to give him the satisfaction. He thanked him for the tip and hung up.

When Joe P. reached Dio in Florida, he was still in his hotel room getting ready to meet with Sam Daniels again. Daniels claimed to have some new info he wanted to share about "their case." Meanwhile it was now ten days since the Chagall had been stolen, and all Dio had was a method of entry into the house and the fact that Rocco DeAngelis, master thief, was more than likely involved. What bothered Dio were the two homicides. In all the years Rocco was pulling jobs in New York, there was no history of violence. Dio was sure Rocco had been the shooter in the Marsala and Paladino hits that got him made, but even then, whacking a couple of no-bodies was not his style, or at least it hadn't been twenty or so years ago.

Maybe Daniels really has something, Dio thought, but then he figured not. He called Martinez, and without getting into pleasant-ries, he asked her if her lab people had come back with the blood type on the Band-Aid found in Barth's town car and if they'd iden-tified the odor on his mouth and lips.

"Yes to both. You're two for two, Dio. Good police work," she said in that teasing voice Dio had come to like but was in no mood for now. He said nothing, just waited. "Yeah, well, the blood type on the Band-Aid was O positive, and Barth was AB positive. The odor was chloroform, which suggests that Barth's doer used it to render him unconscious before he or she stabbed him to death. Also, the ME indicated the weapon used was a military type, prob-ably a dagger or straight-edged bayonet. Not like the 007 gravity knife we found in Tanya's purse."

"That's great. Listen, Martinez, can you do me a favor?"

"Yeah, sure, Dio. What do you need?"

"Call Detective Redneck over there in…" He paused, trying to recall the county.

"Polk," she chimed in. "Like the president."

"What? Oh, yeah, whatever. Anyway, ask him to check Penny's blood type and, if the body hasn't been released yet, to look for a small abrasion, like a paper cut, on one of his fingers."

"You already asked me to do that, Dio."

"Oh, yeah, I forgot. Thanks." He told her he had to go and then hung up.

Wow, Martinez thought, what a change in his tone. Did I do or say something to piss him off? She shrugged. Men. Who could figure them out?

When Dio hung up, he realized that he might have been a little curt with her. Maybe I should call back and apologize, he thought. No. I got no time for this. I've got work to do.

He decided to call Sam Daniels and see what he had. Daniels said that his sources told him that Club Inferno was being sold to some Russian guy from New York. Dio thanked him and hung up.

Martinez was reviewing her notes on the Barth homicide when she got a call from Detective Redstone. He told her he had received her message and was sending over all the pedigree information on Penny, including his blood type, which was O positive. He also told her that he'd checked the body for small abrasions and noticed that the right index finger had a quarter-inch cut right below the fingernail.

Martinez was kind of surprised at how friendly and cooperative Detective Redneck was. Maybe he wasn't such a redneck after all.

"So, Martinez, you think our cases are related? Can you share why you wanted the info I gave you on Penny?"

"Well, it's not so much me as Bosso. He seems to think that there may be a connection between the theft of the Chagall painting and our murders." Martinez was not sure if she should give him any more than that, in spite of the fact he'd given her the information she'd requested.

"What is Bosso basing this assumption on? Does he have something else?"

Martinez hesitated but continued. "Well, I discovered that both our victims hung out at the same topless joint here in the Gardens, a club that is managed by a guy Bosso put away over twenty years ago. I think he is making the connection based on that."

"Seems like a stretch to me, but if it will help me solve my case, I'm all in. By the way, Martinez, what do you think of Bosso?"

Martinez was not sure if he was fishing, looking to see if maybe they had something going on. "He seems knowledgeable, smart, and OK to work with." That was all she said.

"OK, then, I'll send the info. Keep me posted."

"Sure, Detective, take care." She hung up and went over to the large printer / fax machine to await the transmission from Redstone.

Martinez called Dio and told him what she'd gotten from Detective Redneck. She referred to him by that name out of deference to Dio, even though her last conversation with Redstone had proven him to be more helpful and professional than either she or Dio had given him credit for.

"How about we meet in my hotel lobby bar to discuss what we've got?"

"OK, I'll be there in a half hour."

When Martinez shared the information about Penny's blood type and the cut on his finger, Dio just shook his head. She had expected more of a reaction and a show of gratitude, something in the way of "great, good job," but he just nodded as if deep in thought.

"So, what's our next move?" she asked.

"Don't know. I'm still waiting for some more information from Joe P. up in New York."

"Well, do you have a theory that you'd like to share?" Martinez was somewhat offended that all of a sudden, this man with whom she'd shared drinks, dinner, and life stories, this man for whom she was starting to feel an attraction, was now acting like a kid who didn't want to share his toys. She decided to confront him. "Dio, what's up? You're acting like I did something wrong. All I've done so far is try to help you, to help us solve our cases. But ever since you learned about this Rocco guy being here in Florida, you're acting so different."

Dio was taken aback by her frankness. Before he answered her, he had to think a minute. He realized that she was right. He had acted the same way to Celia over the years, and it made him sad. He waited a minute and said, "You're right, Martinez. I'm sorry, I really am. It's just that when I get this close to solving a case, I sometimes get overly worked up in trying to figure out the last piece. Please forgive me."

He looked like he was going to cry, and she started to regret bringing it up. But then something unexpected happened. Dio reached over the table and, taking her hands in his, stood, pulled her up, embraced her, and held her close. She was almost ready to push him away but then just relaxed and let him hold her.

"You and I have to figure out a way to put all our facts together and confront DeAngelis," he said. "But unless he has changed in the last twenty years, he will probably not say boo. This guy won't say shit with a mouthful."

CHAPTER TWO

Rocco had Darla drive him to the private airport in West Palm to meet Tommy and his lawyer, Harold Gould. Tommy had come down to sign and file the paperwork giving ownership of Club Inferno to Sergei "the Duke" Rudukas, who would be flying down the next day with his lawyer, Berkowitz, and his muscle, Blatnikov and Smolinski.

As usual, Rocco didn't say much, and he seemed more sullen than usual. When they were alone in the office, Rocco went over to Tommy and whispered to him, "So how much time do I have?"

Tommy looked at him, wide-eyed. "What? What the fuck you talking about? Nothing is gonna happen to you."

"No, I mean how much time before I have to leave the club?"

"Oh," Tommy said. "I thought...Never mind. I asked Rudukas to guarantee the jobs of any of my people—including you, Janelle, Darla, Kris, the dancers, and the bar and floor staff—anyone who wants to stay. He had no problem with that. But I think over time he'll bring his own girls, and his goons will start smacking people around just for fun, and they will fuck this thing up. Poor Vinny will be rolling over in his grave." Tommy didn't tell Rocco that he was only selling the business and the licenses but would be retaining ownership of the building, so if Rudukas lost the business, he could always take it back or sell the building to someone else.

"I don't know what I'm gonna do, Tommy. The cops have been sniffing around about that…other thing, ya know."

Tommy just nodded, knowing it was no problem for him. "Listen, Rocco, you got that money still, right?" Knowing Rocco, he probably had every dime of it. "So you want to buy Vinny's condo? I'll sell it to you for what I owe on it plus fees."

"I'm not sure, Tommy. I'm not gonna work for the Duke, that's for sure."

"Well, whatever you decide, I gotta know soon. I got a meeting with a Realtor to look at Vinny's place tomorrow."

Tommy asked Darla to drive him and Gould to the Marriott, where he'd booked two rooms for himself and Gould, not wanting to stay at Vinny's condo while Rocco was there. As he walked into the hotel, they decided to stop at the bar for a drink. Gould then went to his room to review some of the legal documents for the closing. While sipping his scotch on the rocks, Tommy happened to glance in the mirror. He almost dropped his drink when he thought he recognized a familiar face sitting at a table with an attractive female companion. Tommy could not believe his eyes. Can that be him? he thought. What the fuck is he doing here? Dio fucking Bosso.

Tommy finished his drink and left the bar, trying to avoid being seen by Bosso. Meanwhile, at the table, Martinez and Bosso were going over the info they had received and trying to figure out how the theft of *The Green Violinist* had gone down.

"So here is what I think," said Dio. "DeAngelis is working at or hanging around Club Inferno and meets Barth and Penny. We've already established that both deceased were regulars there, and we know that Penny played in a high-stakes poker game. Chances are Barth did too, and we can verify that by speaking to one of the women you said manage the place. This may be a stretch, but listen to my theory. When the Stockwells purchased *The Green Violinist*, it made the papers, correct?"

"Yes, you showed me the story from the *Palm Beach Post*."

"OK, let's say that Penny mentions it at the card game and tells the other players that he did the installation of the motion detectors at the Stockwells', as well as the updated access control system."

"OK, go on," she said.

"Well, what if Barth adds to the story by telling the group that he is the driver of choice for the Stockwells? DeAngelis hears this and puts a plan together to steal the Chagall."

"That is a stretch, Dio. How do we know that DeAngelis was able to convince those two to get involved in something that could put them both in jail or worse?"

"Not sure. Maybe they owed money to the club or to Rocco for gambling debts. Maybe it was greed. They were both degenerate gamblers, were they not?" The more Dio verbalized his theory, the more plausible it sounded, both to him and to Martinez. "Suppose DeAngelis convinced Barth to get him access to Old Trail Village by hiding in the trunk of his town car. I viewed the security tapes, and according to Pettway, security never inspects the trunks of private vehicles. We found the Band-Aid with Penny's blood type on it, which could place him inside the trunk. When I initially inspected the crime scene, I discovered that entry was gained by cutting out a glass panel in the rear patio door, parallel to the alarm keypad. And Penny not only installed the system in the Stockwells' home; he also made an unannounced service call there a day or two before the theft."

"So, you think DeAngelis came up with the plan, recruited Barth and Penny, and then murdered them both after the crime went down?"

"That's the part I can't figure out. DeAngelis is not, or at least *was* not, a violent guy, and as I recall, he always had a 'buyer' for whatever it was he stole prior to the job."

Just as Dio finished, his cell phone range. It was Joe P.

"Hey, boss, how you doing?"

"I'm good, Joe. Whaddya got?"

"Well, after Crawford gave me the info on Rudukas's attempts to buy the Chagall, I put a call in to Jed Donohue. You remember Jed, Dio?"

"Yes. He was a young detective in Auto Crime I wanted to bring into Major Case, before the shit hit the fan." He looked at Martinez when he said that to see if she'd picked up on anything.

"Well, he's now a sergeant who runs the Russian-mob task force in OCCB. He told me that the Duke and Tommy Ruggerio are buddy buddy, and his sources tell him the Duke is buying a strip club in Florida from Ruggerio."

Dio slapped his hand down on the table so hard that Martinez jumped, and people at another table looked over in surprise. "That's great news, Joe, good work. It ties into my theory."

"Which is what?" asked Joe P.

"Can't go into that just yet, but I'll talk to you later."

Joe knew that was code for "I'm not alone and can't talk," so he hung up.

Dio looked back at Martinez and just smiled. "We got 'em."

Back at the Inferno, word had spread that Tommy was in town and was going to close the deal on the club with some Russians. Janelle was in the office when Rocco came in.

"So, is it true Tommy is selling?" she asked.

"Yeah, but you don't have to worry. All of your jobs—you, Darla, Kris, the staff—are secure."

"What about you? Is your job secure?"

Rocco just looked at her and didn't say anything.

"Well, I've been thinking about moving. Last year my daughter and I bought a little three-bedroom cottage on a lake in Gallatin, Tennessee, about a half hour from Nashville and about twelve hours from here in the Gardens. My grandson will be starting school next year, and when we looked at the schools there, they seemed OK. She's a single mom, and I help her out when I can—you know, babysitting, a few bucks here and there." Rocco just nodded. "They still have three or four homes for sale, and Darla has been thinking about it too. She drove up with me a few months ago and really liked it. It's not as hot as Florida in the summer. It does get cold in the winter, but it's still a real nice quiet place to live."

Darla never mentioned it to me, Rocco thought, but then he realized that their conversations were usually one sided and about the club. "Well, whatever you decide is up to you," he said. "You can stay or go. I'm sure Rudukas won't care."

"Who?" Janelle asked.

"The guy buying the club. That's his name, Rudukas."

Dio and Martinez finished their drinks and bade each other good night. Dio's next move was to figure out a way to approach Rocco without raising him up. He wanted to surprise him, catch him off guard. The next morning he called Desiree Witherspoon, Rocco's parole officer. After introducing himself, he briefed her on what he had.

Witherspoon was reluctant to get overly involved, as Rocco DeAngelis was doing what was required of his parole—working, staying clean, and not getting into trouble. She told Dio that she only wished half her clients were as good as Rocco. Dio explained further that he just wanted an opportunity to speak to Rocco one on one in a neutral setting.

"Look, I have him scheduled to come on Friday, the day after tomorrow, at one p.m.," Witherspoon said. "If you want, you can come in, and I'll give you an interview room."

"Great. I really appreciate your cooperation."

CHAPTER THREE

O n Friday morning, almost three weeks after the Chagall heist, Dio woke up at six, showered, shaved, and put on a fresh shirt and tie. Martinez was picking him up at seven thirty for breakfast, and they were going to the Florida Department of Parole to meet with Desiree Witherspoon and hopefully Rocco DeAngelis. Martinez could tell Dio was excited about meeting and interviewing Rocco after all these years. During the ride and all through breakfast, Rocco was all Dio would talk about. Martinez thought Dio seemed almost star struck or at least fascinated by this Rocco DeAngelis. Well, maybe that was an exaggeration, but Dio certainly seemed very excited about seeing him again. He was like a kid waiting in line to see Santa in a department store.

Rocco had almost forgotten about his ten o'clock appointment with his parole officer. His phone rang at eight; it was Witherspoon, reminding him to come in. He thought it was unusual, as she hadn't given him a reminder call since his first two appointments, but he didn't think much of it and was glad she'd reminded him. With Tommy in town, the Duke coming in today, and the pending sale of the club, he was up to his ass in alligators. Plus, he actually felt bad about Billy B. getting clipped. He wasn't that upset about Norm Penny, as he thought Penny was a fat fucking know-it-all.

Rocco got ready. He wanted to call Darla and have her drive him to West Palm, but then he decided he would call Uber. This way he didn't have to talk about the sale of the club, which was all she, Janelle, and everyone else had on their collective mind.

When he arrived at the parole office, Witherspoon greeted him in her usual curt manner.

"Hello, DeAngelis." She handed him a plastic cup and pointed him toward the men's room. Usually she accompanied her parolees to the bathroom to make sure they peed in the cup themselves, but she knew Rocco was drug-free. The one time he saw her after having taken a hit on Darla's blunt, he told Witherspoon about it, and she gave him a pass.

After he returned from the men's room, Witherspoon put him in an interview room and told him to have a seat, as she had something else pending and would be a few minutes. Rocco thought this was odd—usually he was in and out—but he really didn't care. He had nowhere to go except back to condo or the club, and both places were losing their appeal to him.

Rocco had been sitting in the interview room for about fifteen minutes when the door opened. He expected Witherspoon with the results of his drug test and the usual keep-up-the-good-work bullshit. What he saw instead almost caused him to gasp.

"Hello, Rocco. It's been a while," said Dio. "I can't say it's nice to see you."

Most times Rocco's silence was deliberate. However, seeing Dio Bosso after all these years and here in Florida threw him for a loop, and he was truly stunned.

Dio sat down without offering Rocco his hand. He recalled that the last time he'd done that, Rocco had just looked at him and belched on the sandwich Dio had brought him. They sat across from each other in complete silence for about three minutes. Rocco stared straight ahead, seemingly looking right through Dio. Dio, on the other hand, busied himself removing a file and a legal pad from his weather-beaten attaché.

"So, Rocco, I guess you're wondering why I'm here."

Rocco got up and went to the door. He grabbed the handle, but the door was locked.

"Am I under arrest, Witherspoon?" he called. "Did I violate my parole? You can't hold me here. I want to call my lawyer."

"Gee, Rocco, that's the most I've ever heard you say at one time," Dio said. "Just sit down and hear me out."

Rocco gave him a look and said, "Fuck you" but sat back down.

"I want to ask you one question, Rocco." He paused for effect. "How do you see yourself spending the next twenty years of your life? Do you want to spend it back in Danamora? Or maybe in some prison here in Florida, where no one will know you're a made guy or give a rat's ass about you? You'll just be some little old man spending his remaining days in some shithole prison in middle-of-nowhere Florida. Think about that, Rocco. I got to take a leak." Dio got up and, using a key Witherspoon had given him, left the interview room.

In an adjacent room with a two-way mirror, Witherspoon and Martinez waited. Martinez briefed Witherspoon on everything they had, including their theory on the Barth and Penny homicides, to keep her from letting Rocco go. Both Martinez and Dio knew Witherspoon could not hold Rocco against his will, but she did have the failed drug test of a few weeks ago to fall back on if she had to.

Rocco knew he was being watched, but it didn't matter. He could sit there all day doing nothing, not moving, not giving the fucking cops any tell that he was nervous or scared. What he thought about was different this time, though. He did not want to go back to prison. At sixty years old, he would certainly die there. He thought about Tommy and how he knew that Rudukas had had his goons, Ivan and Yuri, kill poor Billy B. and Norm Penny. Tommy had taken the money from Rudukas and turned his back on Janelle, Darla, Kris, and everyone else Vinny had considered his Florida family. Tommy claimed he'd stopped Rudukas from taking Rocco out along with Billy B. and Norm, but Rocco knew that was bullshit. He was a made guy, and although Tommy might have OK'd his hit, the rest of the Gambino leadership, especially Lino Trentino, would not have. Rocco felt he owed Tommy nothing at this point.

Martinez continued watching Rocco through the two-way mirror. What a strange little man he is, she thought.

After about fifteen minutes, Dio reentered the interview room carrying a can of Diet Coke. He placed it in front of Rocco and sat down.

"Before I let you leave, Rocco, I want you to hear me out. Hear what I have to say, and then you can leave, maybe."

Rocco said nothing. Surprise, surprise, thought Dio. "First of all, Rocco, you should understand that I am no longer a police officer. I am employed by Lloyd's of London, which is the insurer of a painting called *The Green Violinist*, by Marc Chagall." Normally Dio looked for a tell when he spoke to a suspect, but he knew he would get no such reaction from Rocco, no matter what facts he threw at him. "I suspect you committed the theft, along with two others who are now deceased, both the victims of brutal homicides. I suspect that you somehow convinced David W. Barth, known as Billy B., and Norman J. Penny to aid and abet you in this crime. I know both of these individuals were frequent customers of the Club Inferno, where you were employed as an assistant manager. How am I doing so far, Rocco?"

Rocco just continued staring through Dio.

"I believe that on the night of Saturday, September 17 you and Mr. Penny hid in the trunk of Mr. Barth's town car to facilitate entry into the gated community of Old Trail Village, located in Palm Beach Gardens, Florida. After Ambassador and Mrs. Stockwell, the rightful owners of the painting, departed their residence in Mr. Barth's town car, you and Penny gained access to the home and removed the painting, replacing it with an imitation. Entry was gained by cutting a hole in the glass in the rear patio door. Penny disabled the alarm.

"Now, Rocco, I know that read like a report, and I did in fact leave several of the usual investigative whos, whats, and whys out. But I can assure you that when I go before a grand jury, along with the detectives investigating the Barth and Penny homicides, we will have no problem getting an indictment against you for grand theft, burglary, and two counts of first-degree murder, which, here in the Sunshine State, carries the death penalty. But here's the good news, Rocco. The average time to carry out the death penalty, considering appeals and so on, is thirteen years, and at seventy-three, if you're still alive, it's unlikely they will give you the needle. They'll just let you live out your life in prison."

Again, Rocco looked straight ahead, showing no emotion, but on the inside he was thinking. Thinking about his options, thinking about Darla and thinking about a cottage on a lake in Gallatin, Tennessee.

After laying out his theory on the heist to Rocco, Dio stood up. Rocco was not overly surprised that this cop had figured it out. Well, he wasn't a cop anymore, but to him, once a cop, always a cop. Once a thief, always a thief.

After about ten minutes, Dio came back into the interview room, this time accompanied by Martinez. "Rocco, this is Detective Lydia Martinez from the Palm Beach County Sheriff's Office. She is the lead investigator on the David W. Barth homicide."

"Hello, Mr. DeAngelis," she said. Rocco just looked at her.

"Detective Martinez and I, along with other detectives from the Palm Beach Gardens PD and Polk County, are working together on this. I am going to make you an offer, which I want you to consider before you give me your usual 'go fuck yourself.' Here's the deal. We are all in agreement that we can get a conviction on the crimes I mentioned without any problem. Juries here in Florida are sometimes biased against what they consider New York mobsters coming into their house and killing people. We know you stole the Chagall painting, but we don't think you have it hanging on a wall somewhere so that you can admire the artist's fine work. I know you well enough to suspect you had a buyer before you pulled off the job. We also suspect that killing your accomplices was not your idea, but knowing the people you have been involved with, it should not be a surprise to you. Finally, we suspect you were paid a handsome fee for 'acquiring' the painting. How am I doing so far, Rocco?"

Not expecting a response, Dio went on. "OK, so what I need is to get the painting back. What Detective Martinez and her colleague in Polk County need are the name or names of the people who murdered the victims. You give us that, and we talk to the detective and state attorney assigned to the painting heist. We are confident they will appreciate your cooperation in recovering the stolen painting. Also, you get to keep the money you were paid for the heist. We don't care about how much it is. And finally, you may be required to testify. Think about it, Rocco. We will be outside for a bit. Oh, and by the way, should you decide to tell me to go fuck myself, Detective Martinez will place you under arrest for the murder of David W. Barth. Another detective from the Palm Beach Gardens PD is presently going before a judge to obtain a search warrant for the condo owned by the late Vincent Ruggerio, the condo where you are currently living. That detective will then place you under arrest for the burglary and other related crimes committed at Old Trail Village. After you are booked and processed for those crimes, a detective from Polk County will transport you to that location, where you will be charged with the murder of Norman J. Penny. I doubt you will be given bail, so you have to assume that unless you cooperate with me and Detective Martinez here, your Uber ride here today was your last taste of freedom. Hopefully it was a pleasant ride and the driver gave you a five-star rating. It might be the last ride you take without being handcuffed."

Dio and Martinez got up and left the room.

When they went outside, Witherspoon looked at Bosso and said, "That little guy did all that shit?"

"Yes, ma'am."

"Well, I'll be dammed. I knew he was mobbed up, but I never suspected he was much of a badass. He looks like—" She stopped, as if she couldn't find the right words. Then she said, "What a strange little man."

While Dio was interviewing Rocco, Martinez put in a call to Daniels to bring him up to speed on their progress. Dio had told her he realized he should have included Daniels in this part of the investigation and had him join them. Daniels had told Dio he had some new information on the case. Now, when Martinez asked him about it, he said that he'd heard from his sources that Club Inferno was being sold.

Martinez wanted to say, "No shit, Sherlock," but all she said was, "Wow, that's interesting. Listen, Sam, I'm at the Division of Parole in West Palm with Bosso, and I think we may have a suspect in your burglary. Bosso is talking to him now, so maybe you can meet us here, and we can fill you in."

Daniels hesitated and then said, "Well, I can be there is fifteen minutes."

"OK, good. We are in PO Witherspoon's office, room 407. Also, Sam, could you also have someone from your office write up a request for a search warrant for Vincent Ruggerio's condo at the Heron Club?"

"Sure. Is there a connection?"

"Yes. I'll fill you in when you get here."

Dio figured he might have a difficult time convincing Daniels to go along with his offer to Rocco, should Rocco decide to take him up on it. He didn't think Rocco had much choice, but then again, he knew this guy was a hard-ass when it came to cooperating with the police. Would he really want to spend the rest of his life in jail rather than cooperate? Well, if you had to pick one person who would do that, it would be Rocco DeAngelis. But first he had to work on Daniels.

While he was waiting, he placed a call to Jeremiah Clifford in London. Clifford was at home, and Dio explained the situation without going into all of the details. He needed Clifford to contact the Stockwells' attorney, John Powers, and have Powers convince them not to press charges against Rocco DeAngelis for the burglary if the painting was returned unharmed.

Clifford was impressed at Dio's results. I knew I hired the right guy, he thought. And I'll be saving the company several million dollars in an insurance claim.

Dio was fairly confident the Stockwells would be satisfied with getting the painting back. They wouldn't want to deal with the legal system and the media circus that would accompany a trial. Daniels would be a different story. To get Daniels to back off, Dio also told Clifford to be prepared to have Powers contact Chief Pellitiere of the Palm Beach Gardens Police Department once the Stockwells agreed not to press charges.

CHAPTER FOUR

B ack in New York, Joe P. was working with Jed Donohue of the OCCB Russian desk to get support for his investigation. Jed had six detectives working exclusively on Rudukas and his crew. They had a court-ordered wiretap in the office of the Brighton Beach night club, Bely Mishka, owned by the Duke. This was his head-quarters, but the information coming out of it was of no legal use so far. Jed did confirm that the Duke was flying down to West Palm Beach with his lawyer, David Berkowitz, to close on the Inferno. Jed also told Joe that they had an informant, Dmitri Levishenko, a member of the Duke's crew, who flipped after getting busted for selling three kilos of cocaine to an undercover NYPD officer. Jed's detectives and members of the Narcotics Squad were sharing the information they'd gotten from Levishenko.

CHAPTER FIVE

D io and Martinez waited about an hour for Daniels to arrive.
When he got there, he walked into Witherspoon's office carrying a Starbucks coffee and a half-eaten donut.

"I'm starving. Haven't had lunch yet," he said.

Dio just gave him a look and said, "Sam, step in here." He
pointed to the viewing room.

Daniels walked in and immediately went to the two-way glass
and looked at Rocco. "Who the fuck is that strange-looking little
guy?"

"That, my friend, is the guy who planned and executed the
theft of *The Green Violinist*," said Dio, as if he were introducing the
guy who'd cured cancer. Even Daniels picked up on it. Dio laid
out for Daniels how the theft had gone down, including the homicides of Barth and Penny. He left out any mention of the Russian
involvement.

"So where is the painting now?" Daniels asked. "And can I arrest this guy based on your theory?"

"Well, Sam, we are working on that." Dio then related to Daniels exactly who Rocco DeAngelis was and their mutual history. Dio went on to tell Daniels about the offer he'd made to Rocco. He wanted to gauge Daniels's reaction to giving Rocco a pass on the burglary, or at least talking to the state attorney, if he cooperated fully. Dio knew that if Clifford and Powers asked the Stockwells not to press charges if the painting was returned undamaged, Daniels would have no choice, but Dio wanted to make Daniels believe that he was part of the decision-making process. He felt he owed him that.

"I don't know, Dio," Daniels said. "This is a pretty big case here in the Gardens, and even if I wanted to help you, I'm not sure my bosses would go along with it."

Dio knew Daniels's bosses would go along if Ambassador Stockwell told them to, but he just said, "Well, think about it."

Dio want back into the interview room, this time with Daniels. "Rocco," Dio said, "this is Detective Sam Daniels of the Palm Beach Garden PD."

"Stand up," said Daniels. "Rocco DeAngelis, I am placing you under arrest for burglary in the first degree and related charges." He spun Rocco around and rear cuffed him. "You have the right to remain silent. Anything you say may be held against you in a court of law."

As Daniels continued to Mirandize Rocco, Rocco just stared at Dio. Dio thought he saw fear in Rocco's eyes. As Daniels started to lead Rocco out, Rocco leaned toward Dio, and Daniels relaxed his hold. Rocco put his mouth to Dio's ear and whispered one word.

"Rudukas."

Dio looked at him and nodded as Daniels led Rocco away.

Dio called Joe P. in New York to bring him up to speed on what had transpired in Witherspoon's office. "I think Rocco is going to cooperate, Joe. Can you believe that?"

Joe could sense the excitement in Dio's voice and was feeling that rush himself. He in turn told Dio about the great cooperation he was getting from Jed Donohue. "You were right, boss, when you spotted his talent when he was a young detective. He's assembled an outstanding team of detectives working the Russian desk. They had a confidential informant on the inside and a detective who was fluent in Russian to translate and transcribe all of their wiretaps. The CI, whose name was Dmitri Levishenko, also told them that Ivan Blatnikov and Yuri Smolinski were the go-to guys for contract hits not only for Rudukas but also for the Ruggerio crew."

After speaking with Dio, Joe told Donohue that Blatnikov and Smolinski looked good for the two homicides in Palm Beach Gardens. Donohue was all in. He assigned two of his detectives, Adam Gregory and Colleen O'Brien, to maintain surveillance on Blatnikov. Detective Marty Stacy and Detective Dino Borisovitch, who had been born in Russia and was fluent in his native tongue, were assigned to Smolinski. The remaining two detectives in the squad, Rich Nicholson and Dave Price, were assigned to support the other teams. Donohue knew he could pick up a couple of extra bodies from another squad, or call in a favor from one of his buddies in patrol, and get a couple of uniforms to work surveillance in plain clothes with his detectives.

Joe told him that he would get back to him with more info as soon as he had it. Dio had told Joe that Daniels had verified that Blatnikov and Smolinski were in the Gardens by viewing tapes from the hotel check-in desks. "He hit pay dirt at the Marriott. I had Ann send me their mug shots, and he found them checking in to the Gardens Marriott at the same time we were there. Imagine that. He also got them renting a car, a black Ford Explorer SUV. The rental car was returned in New York, so I want you to go to the Avis at JFK and see what you can find out. We are waiting for Detective Redneck to get back to Martinez with his follow-up at the

7-Eleven on Route Sixty to see if they can match the car of one of the Russians to the time of the Penny homicide."

"OK, Dio, I'm on it."

When Joe P. got back to Donohue and told him what Dio had discovered in Florida, he too became excited. Joe told him that he would get back to him with more info as it came in. He asked Jed to see if he could start the process of getting search warrants prepared should they want to move on the Duke and his crew.

"Joe, this is New York, not Florida. We've got to have solid probable cause here to get a judge to move on a search warrant. You should know that."

Joe didn't answer, just waited, a trick he'd learned from Dio.

"Let me see what I can do, Joe," said Jed finally.

"Thanks, Jed," Joe said, and hung up.

Things were moving fast, both in New York and in Florida. Dio believed all the pieces were falling into place. He realized his primary concern was to recover *The Green Violinist* and return it to its rightful owners, the Stockwells. The cop in him, however, wanted to see justice for Barth and Penny, and he wanted to see the local detectives he was working with solve their respective cases. Especially Martinez.

On the ride back from Witherspoon's office, he kept talking about the various aspects of the Barth homicide. Finally, Martinez spoke. "Barth is my case, not yours, Dio. Your case was solved when Daniels arrested DeAngelis. What you should be focused on is getting the painting back to the Stockwells, not the next steps in my investigation."

Dio was taken aback by her sudden rebuke. He wanted to respond but didn't know how.

"You know, Dio, I was beginning to think that you and I had something going on between us. But I guess I was wrong."

Dio paused for a moment and then said, "I don't think you were wrong. I started to have feelings for you too, but when things started to heat up in our cases, I guess I got a bit carried away. I'm sorry, Lyd."

The conversation ended there, as they reached the Palm Beach Gardens PD office.

Before Daniels booked Rocco on the burglary charge, he notified his superior, Captain Jack Harkness. Harkness in turn called Chief Pellitiere. Both arrived at headquarters within thirty minutes. Daniels was disappointed that both Harkness and the chief were more concerned about the whereabouts of *The Green Violinist* than about information on the perpetrator of the crime.

When Dio and Martinez heard this, Dio understood. Clifford had gotten to Powers, and Powers had gotten to the Stockwells. Dio asked Daniels if he could speak to Rocco, who was in a holding cell.

"Sure, be my guest. I'm still waiting to get an ASA to write this up so I can get him before a judge."

Dio entered the holding room where Rocco was sitting, handcuffed to the table. "Want a soda or coffee, Rocco?"

Rocco just shook his head. Dio pulled up a chair and sat next to Rocco rather than across from him.

"Rudukas. Does he have the painting?"

Rocco looked at Dio for about ten seconds and then said, "Rudukas hired me to get him the painting. He was pissed that he tried to buy it at auction and lost out to the Stockwells, but I don't think he would have paid seven million for it anyway. I think he just wanted his proxy to find out who'd bought it and then steal it. I heard he has a collection of Russian works of art—some bought, some stolen—in a building he owns in Brooklyn. Only goes there alone, just to admire the art. Supposedly nobody else in his crew is allowed to go there or knows where it is. I would guess that's where the painting is."

"What about the actual burglary and the murders of Barth and Penny?"

Again, he said, "Rudukas. He had his goons, Blatnikov and Smolinski, take them out is my guess."

"Was Tommy involved?"

Rocco hesitated. "Tommy set it up, but I won't testify against him; you know that."

"You may not have to testify against anybody if this works out the way I hope it will."

Dio got up and left the interview room. When he walked out, Martinez came up to him.

"Get anything out of him?"

"Yes. A couple of Russians killed Barth and Penny."

Dio called Joe P. in New York and had Jed Donohue join in on a three-way call. "Jed, see if your CI knows of a house the Duke owns, a place that only he goes to. I think that's where we will find *The Green Violinist* and other stolen works of art he's been collecting."

"Sure thing, Dio. We have him holed up in a safe house, and I have my Russian detective Borisovitch doing the debriefing."

"You got anything, Joe?"

"Yeah, boss. I went to the Avis car rental at JFK, and guess what? In the SUV Smolinski and Blatnikov rented, the cleaning crew found a blue canvas duffel bag with a cell phone in it. The phone was dead. They tried the number on the rental agreement, but that was probably a burner phone anyway. So they put the phone and the duffel bag in their lost and found. I got them both, and Jed sent the phone to TARU—the technical assistance and resource unit—to see what they can come up with. I also had Jed send the duffel bag to the lab to see if they can get some DNA off of it."

"Good work, Joe and Jed. Thanks for all your help. Jed, when I get back to New York, I'm taking you and your team to Peter Lugar's for dinner."

"What about me, boss? Can I come too?" Joe joked.

Dio just chuckled. "OK. I'll talk to you both later."

CHAPTER SIX

No one missed Rocco at the Inferno. Tommy and Gould were waiting for Rudukas and his attorney. They planned to close on the sale in one of the private rooms and then have lunch.

Rudukas flew down with Berkowitz, Blatnikov, and Smolinski on NextJets on Tommy's dime. Once the deal was sealed, he would leave the goons there until he could send down Olga Millanova, who ran Club Bely Mishka for him. She would relocate and manage Inferno, along with Janelle and Darla, if they chose to stay. Either way, Rudukas didn't care. He would use Inferno as another place to launder his illegal earnings just like Tommy did.

CHAPTER SEVEN

B ack in the PBSO office, Martinez briefed Lieutenant Pooley and Sergeant Dixon on the status of her case. She also put in a call to Redstone to bring him up on the latest. When she told him that her investigation had led her to believe that Russian mobsters had committed both their homicides and that those same mobsters were now in town, or would be soon, he thanked her and told her he would be there in three or four hours.

Martinez knew that the players in all three cases, Barth's and Penny's homicides and Daniels's burglary, were now in the Gardens, and she started to put a tactical plan into place. All she needed was just a bit more information out of New York on the Russians. She thought about Dio and felt sad that she'd had feelings for him and thought he'd had them for her. But the way he acted as the investigation had picked up steam made her wonder. Did she act the same way? Was this why she was alone?

Her phone rang, and she saw it was Dio. Her first thought was to let it go to voice mail, but she picked up. "Hello, Dio."

"Hey, Martinez…" He stopped. "Listen, Lyd, I just want to say that I know I've been acting strange, but once we get this work behind us, maybe we can…" Again, he hesitated. "You know, sort of—"

"Listen, Dio, let's just solve one mystery at a time, OK?"

"Yeah, sure."

"Listen, Joe P. is getting some good intel on Rudukas from our NYPD friends. He's either on his way down or here already, and the two goons, Blatnikov and Smolinski, are with him. I'll bet they did both yours and Detective Redneck's victims."

"Yes, we know. Detective Redstone is on his way here, and I am in the process of drawing up a tactical plan. We are planning to take them down later today at the closing at Club Inferno."

Dio was taken aback by the fact that he'd not been invited to join the raid. But then he remembered he was no longer a cop. At least not in Martinez's eyes, not anymore. "Well, that's great. You will let me know how it works out, won't you?"

"Why? You don't want to be there? You're not still babysitting your old nemesis Rocco, are you?" she said in that teasing way of hers that he had come to love. His heart warmed up, and he felt a wave of emotion that he had not felt in a long time. He knew then he was falling in love with Lydia Martinez.

"No. I mean, yes, I'll be there, and no, Daniels has DeAngelis at the Gardens PD lockup."

Back in New York, things started to move fast. TARU confirmed that the cell phone found in the rental car returned by Blatnikov and Smolinski had belonged to Norm Penny. That was enough information for Sergeant Donohue to get a search warrant for both their residences. Sergeant Donohue and Detectives Gregory and O'Brien executed the warrant at Smolinski's Brighton Beach home, and Detectives Marty Stacy, Dave Price, and Rich Nicholson hit Blatnikov's apartment in Canarsie. Both teams were assisted by officers from the elite Emergency Services Unit (ESU), who tactically gained entry to each location ensured that the residences were secure before the search began.

Both teams hit pay dirt. In Smolinski's apartment the search team recovered several weapons, one of which was a Glock nine-millimeter. They also recovered large sums of cash, jewelry, and about a pound and a half of marijuana. When the ESU team took down the door of Blatnikov's house, his girlfriend was hiding in the bedroom and had to be restrained. Like in Smolinski's search, the team recovered guns, cash, and jewelry. In addition, Marty Stacy found a nine-inch military bayonet. On the hilt was Cyrillic writing; Marty assumed it was a military-type weapon. During the search Blatnikov's girlfriend, who told the detectives her name was Paulina Bilal, kept looking up at the ceiling as if she was waiting for something to happen.

Back at the safe house, Detective Dino Borisovitch was playing chess with Levishenko. There were also two uniformed police officers present for additional security. When Borisovitch got the word on the searches, he told Levishenko what had been recovered, and he wanted to know if there was anything else the teams should know.

"Did they check the apartment upstairs from Ivan?" he asked.

"Why?"

"That's where Rudukas goes when he wants to be alone. Paulina is not Ivan's—she belongs to Rudukas."

Dino told the two uniformed officers to keep an eye on Levishenko. "Hey, Officer, I gotta step out and make a call. Make sure our friend here doesn't move any of my chess men around, will ya?"

The cop just nodded and looked at Levishenko. Dino called Donohue and told him what the CI had just told him. Donohue knew they could not hit the upstairs apartment without getting a new search warrant or amending the one he had. He called Marty

Stacy and told him to stay there and keep Paulina under wraps. He was going to court to get an amended search warrant to include the upstairs apartment, but he needed the apartment number, which Stacy gave to him. Donohue then told Stacy to have Price, who'd written up the original warrant, meet him in court in twenty minutes. They were fortunate that Judge Jack Conlin was in his chambers. Conlin was a well-respected jurist among members of the NYPD. Once Conlin signed the amended warrant, they called Stacy back and told him to hit the upstairs apartment.

Joe P. arrived at the Canarsie apartment just as the ESU team was about to enter the second apartment in Blatnikov's building. The entry team had a difficult time getting in. In addition to having several traditional locks, the double door was about two feet thick and made of steel. Once inside, the team were stunned by what they saw. The walls were covered with works of art, tapestries, and painting of all sizes. None of the cops were fine-art majors, but they all knew this was fine art. The floors were covered with Oriental rugs, and there was only one queen-size bed in one of the two bedrooms. The apartment was also furnished with what appeared to be antique furniture. No one paid particular attention to a smaller painting hanging on the living room wall, a painting titled *The Green Violinist*, by Marc Chagall.

CHAPTER EIGHT

etective Redstone and his partner, Mike Danton, arrived at
Palm Beach Gardens PD. They joined Daniels and Martinez
and the rest of the team that would execute the search warrants
Daniels had obtained from Palm Beach County circuit judge
Leland Sulka. Unlike the judge in New York, Judge Sulka issued
the warrants to Daniels over the phone. All Daniels would have to
do was appear before the judge after the warrants were executed
and record the results.

Joining the team were PBSO Homicide lieutenant Pooley,
Sergeants Bobby Dixon and Chris Clarkson, and Detectives Nathan
and Bush (Franks and Beans). Gardens PD captain Jack Harkness
would be in charge of the operation. Dio remained in the background as Daniels and Martinez laid out the tactical plan and each
participant's assignment.

"Captain Harkness, Detective Daniels, Sergeant Dixon, and
I will hit the club," said Martinez. "Lieutenant Pooley, Sergeant
Clarkson, and you two"—she pointed to Franks and Beans—"will
hit the condo at the Heron Club. Each team will be accompanied

by two uniformed officers from the Gardens PD." Looking directly at Dio, she continued. "Mr. Bosso will be joining us but will travel in his own vehicle and stay in the background."

Dio nodded in agreement. Before departing the police station for Club Inferno, Dio asked Daniels if he could speak to DeAngelis one more time.

"Sure. We're going to be leaving here in about ten minutes or so."

Dio went into the holding pen where Rocco was sitting. "They are going to hit the club and Vinny Ruggerio's condo at the Heron Club," Dio said. "They have search and arrest warrants, and I suspect you are going to have company here shortly."

Rocco just looked at Dio, thinking, Shit, they find the money, I'm really fucked.

Just then Dio handed Rocco his cell phone and said, "I gotta hit the head. I'll be back in five minutes."

Rocco didn't know what to do. Was this a setup? Was the phone bugged? Was the room bugged? But he knew he had no choice. He dialed Darla's cell phone, and she answered on the second ring.

"Hello?"

"Darla, it's Rocco."

"Rocco, where are—"

"Just listen. Where are you?"

"At the club. Where are you?"

"Listen to me. Get Janelle, and get out of there now." He told her to go to Vinny's condo and get the money out of the hidey-hole in the bedroom closet. "I have no time to explain. Just do it. Take the satchel, put it in your house, and don't go back to the club, at least not today."

Darla asked again where he was. She wanted to tell him that she and Janelle were getting one of the private rooms ready for a luncheon that would follow the closing, but he did not give her time. He hung up just as Dio reentered the holding room. Rocco gave Dio the phone and nodded to him as if to say thanks.

Just as Tommy and Rudukas finished signing the documents transferring ownership of Club Inferno to a new corporation Berkowitz had set up for the Duke, the raiding party entered the club, weapons at the ready. The two uniformed officers from the Gardens PD were armed with shotguns and racked the slides upon entry through the unlocked front door. Initially Blatnikov and Smolinski went for their weapons, but in the face of overwhelming odds, they thought better of it. Martinez and the team from PBSO searched the two goons and placed them under arrest for the murder of David W. Barth. Redstone informed them that after they were arraigned in Palm Beach County, they would be transported to Polk County and charged with the murder of Norman J. Penny. Daniels arrested Tommy and Rudukas for conspiracy to commit burglary and transportation of stolen property. Both lawyers, Berkowitz and Goldstein, protested the actions, but Captain Harkness told them to pipe down as he handed them the warrants signed by Judge Sulka.

Darla found Janelle as soon as Rocco hung up. "Janelle, let's go," said Darla as she grabbed Janelle by her arm.

"What are you doing? What is going on?" a shocked Janelle asked Darla.

"I'll explain in the car. Let's go, *now*."

During the ride to the Heron Club, Darla told Janelle about Rocco's phone call. They arrived at Vinny's condo, and Darla used the key Rocco had given her after they became lovers. Rocco had told her exactly where the money was stashed, and she wasted no time finding it and getting out of the house. As they pulled out of the gate, they saw the police vehicles with Sergeant Clarkson and his team, who were entering the Heron Club to execute the search warrant in Vinny's condo.

Tommy and Rudukas were given bail, and upon returning to New York, the Duke was met by Sergeant Donohue and Detectives Stacy and Borisovitch and placed under arrest for possession of stolen property. An inventory of the artwork, most of it stolen, in the Canarsie apartment was valued in excess of $30 million. All of the items were catalogued and placed into evidence by Detectives Price and Nicholson, with the exception of *The Green Violinist*. That painting was handed over to Joe P., who had it professionally packed and then left with it for West Palm Beach Airport. As Rudukas was led off to jail, detectives from the Cold-Case Squad were debriefing Levishenko on other crimes committed by Rudukas, Smolinski, and Blatnikov, including the murders of Danny Carbone and Bobby Bruno after the Drake hotel heist.

The evidence collected by Joe P. from the Avis car rental at JFK was vouchered and a report sent to Detective Redstone to add weight to his homicide prosecution of the two Russian goons for the murder of Norm Penny. The lab found DNA matching not only Penny but also the two Russian goons. The district attorney in New York was agreeable to letting Polk County, Florida, prosecute Smolinski and Blatnikov first, as Florida had the death penalty for first-degree homicide. After that they would be tried in Palm Beach County for the murder of David W. Barth.

After Redstone and Danton's interrogation, Smolinski and Blatnikov both agreed to plead guilty to all of the charges against them, including the Barth homicide, if the death penalty was taken off the table. In addition, they would cooperate with the New York County district attorney in the prosecution of Sergei "the Duke" Rudukas.

Back at the Gardens PD headquarters, Chief Pellitiere and Palm Beach County sheriff Rick Romaine held a joint press conference. All of the South Florida newspapers and television stations had their prime-time anchors and crime reporters present. On the law-enforcement side, Detective Martinez, Lieutenant Pooley, and Sergeant Dixon represented PBSO, and Captain Harkness and

Detective Daniels represented the Gardens PD. Chief Pettway was there on behalf of the Stockwells and Old Trail Village.

Pellitiere spoke first and congratulated all of the officers involved in rapidly solving "these heinous crimes committed against our citizens." When Sheriff Romaine spoke, he gave credit to Detectives Redstone and Danton from the PCSO, who'd assisted in the investigation, and thanked their counterparts in the NYPD for their assistance in the investigation. Kudos were also handed out to Old Trail Village Security chief Pettway, whose security team had been instrumental in the investigation. No one mentioned that the case had actually been broken by Dio Bosso.

Dio met Joe P. at the private section of Palm Beach International Airport. Clifford had OK'd Dio's request to have Joe fly the Chagall down on a private plane so he could keep the package in sight the entire trip. Upon his arrival Dio and Joe drove directly to the Stockwells' home in Old Trail Village and handed the painting over to Ambassador and Mrs. Stockwell. Dio was not expecting a lot of praise from the Stockwells, but a simple thank-you would have sufficed. Instead they acted as if he and Joe had just delivered a takeout pizza. No offer of congratulations or thanks was forthcoming. Joe was more pissed than Dio, who just shrugged it off.

After the exchange Dio drove Joe back to the airport. He was in a hurry, as one of his grandsons was playing in a high school basketball championship, and he wanted to be there to see the game. Dio understood, but he felt a bit sad and jealous of Joe's closeness to his children and grandchildren. It was these times when he missed Celia the most and felt the hurt of his own situation with his son.

Just as they got to the airport, Dio's phone rang. It was Martinez. "Hold on, Lyd. I'm dropping Joe off at the airport."

Joe got out. "Thanks, boss. I'll talk to you tomorrow."

"OK, Joe. And by the way, good work."

"Thanks, boss."

They both nodded, and Joe walked to the waiting private jet.

Dio returned to his phone. "Hi, Martinez, what's going on?"

"Well, my head is aching over all of the paperwork I still have to do, plus after the press conference, the sheriff and the chief took us all over to the Marriott bar for drinks. I'm still here if you want to grab a nightcap."

"Sure, I could use a drink about now. I'll be there in twenty minutes."

CHAPTER NINE

In the aftermath of the raid at Club Inferno and the arrests of Tommy Ruggerio and Sergei Rudukas, the state liquor authority issued a temporary suspension of the club's operating license. The Stockwells agreed not to press charges against any of the parties involved in the theft of *The Green Violinist*. They seemed pleased to have it returned but did not express any thanks to any of those involved in its return, and they refused through their lawyer, John Powers, to speak to the media.

Sam Daniels and John Pettway received most of the praise for quickly solving the theft and murders that had occurred in the Gardens. As a result of the Stockwells' decision not to prosecute, Judge Sulka had no choice but to release Tommy and Rudukas. Upon his return to New York, the Duke was arrested by Sgt. Jed Donohue and Detectives Gregory and O'Brien for possession of stolen property. More charges would follow once Blatnikov and Smolinski, who were now cooperating with the police, were fully debriefed. In addition to the cell phone found in the rental, weapons seized from Smolinski and Blatnikov were matched through ballistics as the weapons used in the Penny homicide.

No charges were filed against Rocco DeAngelis, and he, Darla, and Janelle left Palm Beach Gardens the day after he was released. They drove to Gallatin and stayed in Janelle's cottage on the lake. Rocco gave Janelle $250K and asked her to find a small business to buy so they could wash the balance of his money. She purchased a small tavern called the Mine Shaft just off the lake, which catered to the locals as well as the influx of vacationers in the summer months. She renamed the place Jan & Dee's, and Darla, who was her partner, planned to upgrade the decor and the quality of the food.

Rocco, as usual, kept a low profile. He and Darla planned to buy a place of their own once Janelle's daughter and grandson moved up from Florida. For the first time in his life, Rocco did not think about pulling a job—not that there was much to steal in Gallatin. And for the first time, Rocco started to exercise. He purchased a kayak and enjoyed paddling on the lake each morning.

Dio returned to New York a few days after the painting was returned to the Stockwells. The night before he left Florida, he and Martinez had dinner.

"So, Dio, will this be the last time I get to enjoy a meal on your company's dime?"

"Er, well..." She laughed in that way that made him want to reach out and give her a hug and kiss. "Not if you come to visit me in New York. They got some great restaurants there. Actually, I have a better idea. I'll be going to the home office in London in about two weeks. Why not join me there?"

"Umm, will we have to share a hotel room?"

Once again, she'd caught him off guard. When he hesitated, she laughed again.

"You know, Martinez," he said, "you're something else."

The End.

ACKNOWLEDGEMENTS

Thanks to Chris Persico and Janet Stoakley and the team from Create Space for helping me complete this project.

ABOUT THE AUTHOR

Like his character Dio, Robert Trotta is a retired detective of the New York City Police Department. After his career in law enforcement, he cofounded T&M Protection Resources, an international security consulting and investigations firm.

Trotta and his wife Pam are now enjoying retired life in beautiful Jupiter, Florida.

Made in the USA
Lexington, KY
23 February 2018